GUILTY

AS

SIN

INSPIRED BY TRUE EVENTS

KEN WILSON

This book is dedicated to the thousands of children who die each year in the United States from parental or guardian neglect, abuse, negligence, and murder. This is a tragedy that must be reversed, and I pray this book in some way helps.

ACKNOWLEDGMENTS

First, my many thanks go to my very special wife, family, friends, and editor, who have literally been at my side throughout this writing process. I would also be remiss if I didn't thank the many fellow authors who helped me tremendously, with advice and words of encouragement.

I would also like to recognize all first responders for the work they do and for their dedication, especially in aiding children in distress and danger.

DISCLAIMER:

All names, characters, events, incidents, and places used in this book are the product of the author's imagination or are used fictionally. Any resemblance to actual persons, living or dead, businesses, companies, events, or locales is entirely coincidental. References to the States of Montana and Texas were used because of the author's personal familiarity with both locations and in no event should be construed as a negative reflection on any governmental agencies of either state.

INTRODUCTION

Although it is true that many children die of accidents, many of those accidents are preventable. There are also children who die each year as a result of suicide. Many of these deaths, but certainly not all, could have been preventable. These children, who had tragic and brief existences, often did not have a voice to speak for them. Many came from broken families and were in foster care, managed by state agencies required to protect vulnerable young people.

Yet, in many cases, the state fails miserably. It fails when its employees neglect to follow the due diligence required of them, or because state legislatures fail to provide funding or write laws specific enough to enable those agencies to do their jobs.

Politics sometimes gets in the way of children's welfare and safety. Being a retired state employee, I understand all too well the excuses offered by these governmental agencies. Short of staff and legislative funding, and overwhelmed by the bureaucracy of government, they are unable to protect the young children placed in their care. Yes, bad things do happen to good people, but when it comes to our children, that should never be an excuse.

This book is a fictional account of one such child who died under questionable circumstances before he reached the age of eleven. I formed this character as a representation of the fate of thousands of foster children across the United States. This boy could have lived in any state, been of any ethnicity, or from any culture. The first nine years of his short life occur in East Texas. There, he had a brother three years older than himself. During the last eighteen months of his life, he lived in Livingston, Montana. Sadly, his circumstances are mirrored in an all too often broken system. His case reflects betrayal and abuse at the hands of those who should have loved him.

You'll see numerous points of view appear in the book, from the victim to the perpetrators to law enforcement to insurance fraud investigators to court officials. Detective Russ Wyatt is a lead character and the *only* character who actually narrates the action. Yet, he is a small part of a much larger puzzle. I have him weighing in at the beginning of the story and picking up again about halfway through, and his participation is always preceded by an opening under the chapter title.

Although fictionalized, this treatment and story arc gives readers an idea of how actual cases are tracked, solved, and prosecuted.

1.

FILICIDE

"I can't murder a kid, Lora," Leroy Riker said.

"If you do exactly as I say, we'll be rich," Lora Riker replied.

"But what if we get caught? Do you have any idea what the life expectancy is for a correctional officer in prison, especially one who kills a kid?" Leroy argued.

The lids of Lora's hazel eyes closed like a garage door, trapping her soul and conscience inside. Leroy knew the look. When her heavily eyeshadowed lids flew open, it was as if he was staring into the eyes of the devil. Or, an Eve, handing him an apple wrapped in thousand-dollar bills. *God, I love her. But she's terrifying,* Leroy thought.

"I have everything planned out to the last detail," Lora insisted, tapping her temple with a fingernail in desperate need of a manicure, "so there is no way either of us will get caught. The insurance companies will have to pay us."

Sweat trickled down Leroy's face as a sick feeling in his guts roiled. "But a child, Lora? Does it have to be a child?" he pleaded, while subconsciously wiping his brow and face. It was then that Leroy could smell the fear and apprehension in his perspiration.

It was no use.

"Look, Leroy. The kid is going to be ours in name only," Lora said in her most soothing tone as her husband paced the floor. "These foster kids are already lost in the bureaucracy. What real future do they have anyway? We might even be doing him a favor."

"I just don't think I can—"

"If you can't do this for me, for us, then what do you think will happen?"

Leroy saw her raised eyebrow and the "gotcha" she mouthed before blowing him a kiss, accompanied by a goodbye wave.

"Lora…no!" came the plaintive reaction. "I love you!"

"Well, stupid is as stupid does, Leroy." And with that, Lora scooched her broad derrière out of the living room recliner and sashayed into the kitchen, leaving her husband with his mouth wide open.

It sucks to love Lora, thought Leroy, as his wife brought him a beer. *And it sucks to be blackmailed.* He shook his head and could feel his sideburns turn a more vivid shade of gray. *I'm screwed if I do, and I'm screwed if I don't.*

2.

NOTHING SHOOK ME, EXCEPT...

Notes

Detective Russ Wyatt on the Case

When a young boy, not yet eleven years old, dies during a fishing trip, it's a tragedy. But when he dies in the presence of his newly adoptive father, whose wife had recently taken out two life insurance policies, it raises suspicions. If you ask me, it smelled to high heavens.

My role in all of this? As the lead detective for the Park County, Montana Sheriff's Department, I, Russ Wyatt, was very well-versed in criminal investigations and had a nose for dubious financial transactions. Following the money has always led to the truth, but not necessarily justice. In this case, I knew in my gut that a child had been fostered, adopted, and killed for the life insurance payout. Filicide—parents murdering their own children—was nothing new, yet still rare. But proving it? That was another matter altogether.

After investigating a full spectrum of crimes for over two decades, nothing shook me. Except this. The autopsy photos. Something about the boy and his awful demise struck a nerve.

"Are you okay, Russ? You're looking pale," said my partner Steven Judd. He, not me, was usually the queasy one, so he sounded a bit surprised.

"Yeah," I answered. "It's just that the kid was a redhead. And adopted. Like me."

I gently touched the edge of one of the images and couldn't tell where the bloody head wounds stopped, and the tussle of red hair began. The fact that I now had a grandson the age of the victim made the death of this innocent child hit home even harder. It took me to a long-ago memory, one that included my own fresh start and normalcy. I wondered what this small victim felt when he was finally adopted and eager to settle into his new "forever family."

3.

THE IRISH

Notes

Detective Russ Wyatt on the Case

"We've named you Russ Wyatt," announced my dad in family court on the day of my adoption so many years ago. "Russ means 'little red,' and our family name, Wyatt, means 'brave in war.' And son, we couldn't be prouder to officially welcome you to the family."

I recall the explosion of applause from the judge, the witnesses, and my new siblings. I recall the aroma of Irish apple cake that awaited at home, the presents, and grandparents who rushed in to hug me. I was just nine years old and fit right in with this big-hearted clan of Celts. I liked my new moniker—Russ Wyatt—and didn't miss my original name, John Smith, at all. It was bland and nondescript and seemed to bury me in even more anonymity. It was bad enough being lost in the foster care system, let alone with an unmemorable name.

I was one of the fortunates who was rescued from the revolving door of foster care by loving parents who never once referred to me as adopted. I was then and remain today, Russ Wyatt, their son, period. There is no way to describe the feeling of inclusion and acceptance, and I cried tears of happiness in my very own room for weeks after my adoption because I was finally loved and wanted. It still makes my eyes well to think about that feeling.

But not so for little Michael Riker. No fresh start for him. No normalcy. Snapping back to the photos before me in Michael's file, I couldn't help but think, *This little guy didn't stand a chance. Not with the two dirtbags who adopted him for all the wrong reasons.* It made me angry—me, a man slow to anger. Me, a detective who knew better and had been trained against becoming too personally involved. Emotional clutter was always detrimental to nailing a case.

"Hey, Russ," said Judd, interrupting my trip down memory lane. "Whatcha thinking?"

"I'm thinking we have a murder to solve."

❉ ❉ ❉

Cracking white-collar crimes like financial malfeasance and insurance scams isn't as dry as it sounds. Sometimes, it segues with the most grisly, stomach-churning, and depraved of crimes — drug and human trafficking, murder for hire, and now, the slaughter of an elementary-aged boy for insurance payouts.

Uncharacteristically, I had to remind myself, once again, to stay calm, cool and collected. In the case of Michael Riker, it would be all about finding and following the money trail, establishing a sequential event timeline of this unspeakable horror, and ensuring the monsters would be held accountable and never allowed to do this again. An ounce of deterrence to others was also a desired objective.

Determined, I set about collecting all the pieces to the puzzle and began to assemble them into a coherent picture.

I rose from my desk and began pacing the worn linoleum floor in my office, something I did when needing to think. It wasn't long before I could feel the steam building under my shirt collar. Initially, I assumed this would be a slam dunk case, not knowing then what I know now. I could not have been more wrong. Totally and completely wrong.

I was soon to learn that even coming close to proving a case against the Rikers would involve more than just tiring footwork and long hours. Nothing about it would be like I imagined, despite my extensive years in the profession. Later, I would come to the realization that the Rikers were diabolically psychopathic, and our legislative, judicial, and foster care systems were lacking.

I asked God time and again, "Why do you allow bad things to happen to good people?"

What follows is an account, told through many voices, of how and why an innocent child, Michael Riker, was used, abused, and murdered for profit.

4.

MEET THE RIKERS

Leroy Riker, otherwise known as Correctional Officer Riker, Badge Number 40, was employed by the Montana State Department of Corrections at the men's high-security prison in Deer Lodge, a community approximately 147 miles northwest of Livingston. Leroy was short and stocky. His five-foot, eight-inch frame supported 220 pounds of mostly muscle, except around his waist. His dark brown eyes and his military-style short brown hair, with some premature graying on the sides, gave him the appearance of someone with either a military or law enforcement background. Neither of which was true.

At age 44, he'd been with the prison system for twenty years. Working around career felons for that many years made it necessary for him to be in control, or at least give the appearance of being in control; it would be perceived by inmates as a sign of weakness otherwise.

Leroy heard about and witnessed gruesome scenes, such as inmate stabbings, murders, and sodomy. These events, inside the walls of the prison, along with his knowledge of the crimes for which the inmates were incarcerated, hardened and desensitized him. He never outwardly took his work home with him—home where he, ironically, wasn't in control at all. It didn't matter that he had a reputation for excessive use of force with the inmates. When it came to Lora, he was the beta to her alpha. He idolized the woman without really understanding why. A therapist would have told him he was drawn to Lora because she was crueler and more vicious than he was. She was the version of him he could only hope to be.

Lora, an avid opportunist in every way, saw Leroy as a useful tool. Someone to be used over and over again until he was no longer needed. They had been together for about fifteen years. Financial and marital difficulties plagued them, including Lora being arrested for domestic violence. On that occasion, both had been drinking heavily and got into an argument. Lora was holding a large kitchen knife and cut Leroy's arm. Leroy called the police and Lora was arrested. The next day, after Leroy sobered up, he withdrew his complaint by saying it was just an accident. He said Lora had been working in the kitchen and he had surprised her when he walked up behind her and lovingly grabbed her around the waist.

Lora would never let him live it down. How dare Leroy have her arrested! To punish him, she allowed her obsessive-compulsive spending to run wild. She shopped at the mall, but more so online, and gambled frequently at the various casinos near Livingston. Leroy was beside himself, trying to keep up with the payments and insufficient fund fees. Finally, Lora was arrested on two occasions for writing bad checks. Neither occasion resulted in criminal prosecution, but it was a wake-up call. She had to get her hands on money, a substantial amount, and then she could spend as she saw fit. She would no longer be beholden to Leroy's scrawny state paycheck and his constant badgering about overspending.

Thus, Lora concocted a side hustle. Leroy provided her the inside intelligence of other dirty correctional officers who could be bought or blackmailed and where particular vulnerabilities existed within the prison for smuggling. Her role was to broker deals and accept bribes from people on the outside who wanted drugs or other contraband smuggled into or out of prison or to have someone beaten up or killed. This service came at a price that was paid to her directly and kept Leroy somewhat protected. Leroy didn't want to be tied to this shady activity and get his hands dirty. Yet, he usually followed through because she threatened to withhold sex from him, or worse, threatened to report him to law enforcement.

"Cross me, Leroy, and we both go down," she threatened. "I'll do much better in prison than you. You'll be killed, and I won't, so don't be stupid."

Leroy once nearly regretted following Lora's orders. She told him about a contract against two inmates who were prepared to testify against someone else. The person behind the contract didn't want the inmates killed, but rather a message delivered to strongly discourage the inmates from testifying. On that one occasion, both inmates were sent to the infirmary with injuries Leroy inflicted. When he argued self-defense and said both inmates attacked him, his superiors let the incident slide — proof it would take the word of more than two inmates to go up against the word of one correctional officer.

For that, Leroy was hated, feared, and despised by a lot of inmates, except for the lifers, as well as by some fellow correctional officers. Some of the inmates, co-workers, and the administration saw him in the same light as Lora, as just a useful idiot. But Riker was revered by others for his seemingly Teflon ability to avoid culpability.

Basically, he was a dirty correctional officer with few boundaries…other than he had never killed a child, and he never expected to. Yet, his bleached-blonde queen bee had other plans. Being hopelessly in love with all five-foot, two-inches of her, not to mention her girth which almost matched his at 205 pounds, Leroy accepted his fate. If she wanted to adopt a boy and kill him for profit, then that's what would happen.

5.

A SEED PLANTED

Lora Riker had worked as a custodial supervisor at the all-women's high-security prison in Billings, Montana. The prison was in the opposite direction from where Leroy worked, about 115 miles east of Livingston. At the women's prison, Lora supervised a four-inmate janitorial crew. The work wasn't difficult, and the women, including Lora, had ample time during the day to sit around and chat in Lora's small office.

Judd and I would later discover that according to two of these women, Lora showed a keen interest in the crimes for which they had been convicted. The conversation turned to what they'd do differently to avoid getting caught.

"In other words," Judd said, "they'd sit around and discuss how to commit the perfect crime."

"Nothing like getting expert advice from someone stupid enough to get caught," I sarcastically responded.

One of the inmates, Emily Murkoski, was in prison for conspiracy to commit the murder of her husband. As told by Emily, she hired a "hit man" who subsequently told another inmate about his crime and who had hired him. That other inmate shared this info with the police in hopes of receiving a reduction in his sentence. The "hit man" eventually turned against Emily for the exact same reason. Emily said, "I should've killed that bastard husband of mine myself or I should've killed the "hit man" under some pretext like I caught him burglarizing my home or he was a suspected rapist who had broken into my house. That would've been justifiable homicide."

Lora chimed into the conversation. "I know a spouse can't testify against the other spouse, so maybe you should've married the "hit man.""

Another woman, Monica Handly, was in prison for insurance fraud, typically considered a "white collar" crime.

Monica told Lora, "The only reason I got caught was because I was careless and didn't take enough time to plan the fraud far enough in advance. I won't make that mistake again."

That prompted a longer discussion concerning the details of the insurance fraud for which Monica was convicted. Monica said she and her husband owned a house they had purchased for $800,000, when home values and mortgage interest rates were high. As a result, they didn't have any equity in the house, and it wasn't worth anywhere close to what they owed against it. Monica's husband came up with a plan to get out of the mortgage and recover more money than they'd invested. His scheme was to provide the insurance company with forged documents showing they owned $850,000 of valuable personal items such as art, collectibles, and high-end jewelry. He would then purchase a personal property rider for these valuables and warned Monica not to say anything about it. She had to act clueless. Then when the house burned down, which it would, the insurance company wouldn't be able to link either of them to the fire, even though both would be committing insurance fraud and arson. That cleared the way for an insurance claim for the loss of the house and its contents.

Sure enough, the insurance company could not initially prove Monica had any knowledge of the forged receipts. Additionally, the insurance company couldn't prove she had any personal knowledge of the property rider. And even better, she and her husband could not be forced to testify against the other.

Monica said it was difficult to be found guilty of an insurance fraud if you didn't know anything about an insurance policy in the first place. But then her husband's so-called iron-clad alibi fell apart. He said they were not in the state at the time of the arson fire, yet pings from the couple's mobile phones were picked up on cell towers within a mile of their house at the approximate time of the fire. Busted.

Also, Monica explained she'd attempted to use some of the forged documents to obtain a personal bank loan and the prosecutor obtained a copy of the bank loan application and supporting documents. Those supporting documents unequivocally proved she was aware of the forged paperwork. Ultimately, the prosecution established that she knew about the additional rider and proved she knew they didn't own any of the items listed on the rider.

"Live and learn," quipped Judd as we studied a transcript of Monica's interview with law enforcement.

"That's an understatement," I responded. "Lora Riker soaked up these lessons and built on them, it seems. But we'll bring her down. We have to for the sake of that poor boy."

The Rikers' codependency, greed, lack of conscience, and ability to pick the brains of other criminals would become the perfect ingredients in their murder plot. The lack of legislative funding for the state foster care system and the incompetence of administrators were the perfect ingredients to make the scheme possible.

But first, the Rikers had to find their perfect victim. It was time to go child shopping, and it turned out that a boy named Michael was ripe for the picking.

6.

MICHAEL

Near Tyler, Texas
Early spring

Michael Maddox lived the first nine years of his life with his mother, Martha, in East Texas, in an area known as the Piney Woods region, near the small community of Chapel Hill. Chapel Hill is one of the oldest communities in East Texas, located just eight miles southeast of Tyler. Michael never knew his father, Cecil, who died of a drug overdose not long after Michael was born. He barely remembered his older brother, Eric, who had been removed from their mother years earlier and became lost in the foster care system. Nor did he ever meet his maternal grandparents, who had distanced themselves from Michael's mother. He often wondered what his life would've been like if he too, had a living father. *What was he like? What did his hugs feel like? What did his voice sound like? What might they have done together?*

The boy loved every type of outdoor activity, such as hiking, camping, fishing, or just going on road trips to see different places. Unfortunately, his mother was unable to participate in these activities. That's where Douglas Rodriquez stepped in to fill the void left by the death of Michael's father. Douglas, a neighbor, took Michael under his wing, and they developed a close bond. Douglas paid for Michael to attend Camp Tyler just eight miles south of Chapel Hill. It was a place for kids just to have fun and be kids but doubled as an outdoor school where the little campers could learn different outdoor skills. Shelter-building, cooking over an open fire, bird watching, and aquatic studies were among Michael's favorite activities, but swimming lessons were a challenge. He had never learned to swim, most likely due to a terrifying experience at a public pool where an older boy held his head under water. As a result, Michael had nightmares about drowning and a phobia of deep water. The camp counselors had their work cut out coaxing the reluctant boy into the water.

Douglas did everything he could to shield Michael from the truth about his parents' drug addiction. He took Michael fishing as often as possible and taught the boy how to cast, find and bait his own hook, and carefully clean a fish. One of their favorite fishing places was Purtis Creek State Park, located just 52 miles west of Chapel Hill. The park had a fishing pier, and Texas State Parks didn't require a fishing license.

On one such fishing expedition, Michael reeled in a twenty-inch striped bass. His arms tired when reeling the feisty fish into the net, held by Douglas, and onto the dock that stretched out into the lake a good twenty feet. Michael was proud of doing all the hard work by himself. This was the first fish he had ever caught entirely by himself, and as Douglas was about to kill the fish with a club, Michael suddenly yelled, "NO!"

Douglas slowly lowered the fish club. He looked at Michael, with a confused look on his face, and asked, "No what?"

"Please don't kill it," Michael pleaded.

"Why not? Don't you want to take it home and show your mother? This would make a good meal."

"No. I don't want to take it home. I don't want to eat it. I especially don't want to kill it. Can't we just put it back in the water once we take out the hook?"

"If that's what you really want to do. You caught it, so the decision is all yours," Douglas said.

"I just don't like the idea of killing anything. I just like fishing."

Changing the subject, Douglas asked, "What do you want to be when you grow up, Michael?"

"Something really exciting," Michael replied.

"Like what?" Douglas asked.

"Maybe a fighter pilot, or Hollywood stuntman, or a firefighter, or a stunt pilot, or a construction worker on skyscrapers, or maybe even an astronaut."

"You'll need to study hard, go to college, save your money, and find a career where you can use your brains and not your brawn," Douglas replied.

7.

MAX TO THE RESCUE

Michael and his friends made a fort out of small, downed trees in the pine forest near his house. It wasn't really a fort but rather logs stacked about two feet high in the shape of a square. They made sure the logs were not too high to prevent stepping or jumping over, but high enough for them to hide behind in order to protect the fort against imaginary, attacking Indians. This log fortress was their Alamo, which they valiantly defended with their Daisy air rifles.

Whenever Michael played in the forest alone, he always took his trusty Daisy and his loyal, black cocker spaniel he named Max. The dog showed up one day at his home, and Michael convinced his mother to let it stay until its rightful owner was found.

Max developed a routine that kept everyone in the small community in stitches. Each afternoon, he walked the two blocks to meet the milk trucks as they returned from their daily milk deliveries. All the drivers would watch for the black cocker spaniel, with long floppy ears, and one of the drivers would invariably have a small, leftover carton of milk. The driver would place the carton into the dog's mouth, and Max would carefully carry it home before opening it. Max placed the milk on the ground and opened the carton by chewing a small hole into the side facing up. No one was fortunate enough to see Max going about the task of opening the milk carton. The empty carton with a hole in its side big enough for the dog's tongue was evidence enough. Regardless, everyone got a good laugh at the dog's antics.

Max and Michael were inseparable. Michael would talk to Max like his best friend and confide his deepest thoughts and fears to the dog. For his part, Max was a good and empathetic listener.

Michael's mother had given him a coonskin hat for his sixth birthday. He liked to imagine he was the old trapper who caught the raccoon and then made it into the hat he proudly wore. The problem, however, was that the label inside the hat read, "Made in China."

Oh well, I'll pretend it's from Texas, Michael thought.

Michael liked to make believe he was leading a group of settlers, or was an Army scout, or was hunting buffalo, cougar, or grizzly bear. His loyal tracking dog was always at his side. On one occasion, Michael and Max raced toward the fort, a race Max always won, but the dog stopped abruptly just before jumping the fort wall. Max started franticly barking and jumping up and down and back and forth at something just the other side of the log wall.

Michael approached the fort carefully because he had never seen Max behave this way before. As he peeked over the log, there was a large, angry snake ready to strike at any moment. Michael wasn't sure what kind of snake it was, but he knew there were poisonous snakes in East Texas. He patted Max on the head as a reward and decided they would play in the woods some other day. Michael wanted to tell his mother how brave Max had been that day, but feared his mother wouldn't allow him to play in the woods again if she thought there were poisonous snakes there.

8.

YOU MUST WANT TO CHANGE

Martha Maddox knew she had a drug problem and met periodically with her counselor. She was ashamed of the kind of mother she was to Michael. When he was about to turn ten years old, Martha's counselor told her, "You're running the risk of losing Michael, just like Eric, if you don't get yourself some real treatment and into a totally new environment." Those words hit home, for indeed, she had already lost her firstborn to the system. She had given up Eric because she knew she was unable to properly care for him due to her addiction. The last thing she wanted to happen was to lose Michael. She loved both her boys and welcomed the opportunity to do better with Michael.

Martha asked her counselor, "What do you recommend?"

The response was immediate. "First off, you must want to change, otherwise, nothing positive is ever going to happen. You need to move far away and put some distance between you and your drug sources. Regardless of what you decide and where you go, think what is best for Michael first and yourself second. You are still young and have a full and productive life ahead of you. But first and foremost, you must break your dependency on drugs."

Martha thought about the counselor's words and decided to have a talk with Michael; a real mother-to-son talk. Martha sat down with Michael for the first time he could remember.

This must be serious, Michael thought, so he listened intently while his mother spoke.

Martha started off by saying, "Michael, I've been thinking it would be good for both of us if we made a new start in a new state. I have a little money from your father's social security. If we were to move, where would you want to go?"

Michael enjoyed reading. During most every school recess, he could be found in the library rather than outside playing with other kids. When Michael was seven years old, he picked up a book about Montana. He loved everything about Montana. He knew it was called the "Big Sky Country" for a good reason. Where he lived in East Texas, there wasn't much to see; but in Montana, there were tall mountain ranges, and prairies with antelope, bear, deer, mountain goats, and sheep, and real buffalo. Michael learned about the Lewis and Clark Expedition in school and read more about it in library books. Montana included some of the places the Lewis and Clark Expedition had spent time exploring. Michael thought the history of the state was almost as interesting, if not better, than the history of Texas and the Alamo.

Without hesitation and with a great deal of enthusiasm, Michael loudly proclaimed, "Montana! They've got real cowboys, and Indians, and big, tall mountains, and lots of wildlife, and places to fish, and things like that. Montana also has sky that goes on forever. Did you know Montana is called The Big Sky Country? Can we really move to Montana, Mom? Can we?"

Martha was taken aback by Michael's response and enthusiasm. If she could find a small western town, with good schools, opportunities for her to find a real job for a change, and good medical infrastructure, maybe the counselor was right. It would be a good change for them both.

Martha told Michael, "Let's both sleep on the idea tonight, and if you still feel the same way in the morning, I'll start checking out the towns in Montana."

Michael went to bed full of excitement, more so than he could remember ever having. He was confident he wouldn't change his mind overnight and hoped his mother wouldn't either. The next morning over breakfast, they began their discussion again.

"So, Michael, now that you've had an opportunity to sleep on what we talked about last night, how do you feel about it this morning?"

"I still want to move to Montana, Mom.

"Okay then, that much is settled. Is there any part of Montana you are interested in?"

"I want to be close to fishing, and camping, and hunting, and mountains. I want there to be lots of wildlife and rodeos. Like, maybe close to a small town, but something bigger than Chapel Hill. I also want to have kids my own age to play with."

Martha laughed, but only to herself. She didn't want Michael to think she was laughing at him.

She decided to contact the Montana Visitor's Bureau that day.

"Hello, is this the Montana Visitor's Bureau?" Martha asked. "I'm thinking about relocating to western Montana with my ten-year-old son. Someplace with good schools and medical services, inexpensive housing, and opportunities for employment."

"The western region is broken up into four zones," the volunteer said. "I suggest the zones in and around Helena, the state's capitol, and around Bozeman and Missoula. Those are the larger cities in western Montana. I can send you maps and brochures of those regions and specific zones, as well as information concerning home buying and rental prices, schools, and infrastructure."

"Michael, I've just spoken to a nice lady in Montana, and she's mailing us some information. You and I will sit down and go over it together when it arrives."

Michael was excited. He realized this was the first time in his young memory that he had been included in any talks with his mother, let alone any of the decision-making. He felt much older than his years and was now the "man of the house." He wasn't sure what had changed in his mother, but he was pleased that something clearly had improved.

It took five days for the material from Montana to arrive. Martha was still doing well and staying away from drugs, but history had taught her she wasn't out of the woods yet. She needed to stay focused. They sat at the kitchen table and spread the brochures and maps out as she'd promised Michael. In northwestern Montana, there was the Glacier Country zone, then the Southwest Montana zone, and the Yellowstone Country zone. The brochures had beautiful pictures and information about each area, and from the state highway map, they were able to get a really good idea of where each zone was located.

Glacier Country zone was named after Glacier National Park. It was further north and bordered Canada. Martha and Michael agreed that would be like trading bordering Mexico in Texas to bordering

Canada in Montana. Martha told Michael he could expect extremely cold weather that far north. Michael decided to eliminate that part of the state. Next up was southwestern Montana. It had a lot of possibilities and was in consideration. Last but not least was Yellowstone Country. The biggest plus in Michael's mind was its proximity to Yellowstone National Park. In order to further limit their options, Martha suggested either they flip a coin or draw straws. Heads would mean southwest, and tails would mean Yellowstone.

Michael said, "Let's draw straws."

Martha said, "Okay, the shortest straw means we go to southwest Montana and the long straw means we go to Yellowstone Country. The straw you draw, Michael, will decide where we go."

"At the count of three, we each show our straws," Martha said. Michael revealed his straw and Martha the other.

"I won," Michael exclaimed, as he proudly displayed the long straw in his hand.

"Now," Martha said, "we need to select a specific county within Yellowstone Country. If we select a county with a major highway going through it, such as Interstate 90, getting places would be faster. Also, towns along an interstate highway have better infrastructure and amenities." That helped limit their choices down to Gallatin, Park, Sweet Grass, Stillwater, and Carbon Counties.

"I like the name Park County best because it has the shortest name and the easiest to remember. Plus, it borders Yellowstone National Park," Michael said.

"Now we're getting someplace," Martha said. "The best opportunities for finding a job will be in the county seat, which appears to be Livingston."

With that exercise completed, the next stage would be house and job hunting. Martha didn't want to travel all that way unless she knew there was at least a place they could afford to live that accepted pets. The Yellowstone Country brochure gave her specific information about apartment managers, real estate agents, and home rental managers.

But what about Max? Can he come too?" Michael asked.

"We can't very well leave him behind, now can we? He's part of our family now."

"Really?!" Michael exclaimed.

"Really. I've already checked with an apartment manager in Livingston. He told me as long as Max is well behaved and housebroken, the apartments are pet friendly. They even have a fenced in area behind the building for pets to use and to run in," Michael's mother said.

"Did you hear that, Max?" Michael said. "You're going to have a new home." Max wagged his short tail at hearing his name.

By June of that year, Michael's school recessed for summer break. Martha had given her landlord the required two-week notice, and they were on the road to Montana. Martha had found a pet-friendly, low-income, two-bedroom apartment in Livingston and sent the required deposit, including the first and last month's rent. She also arranged for a moving company to pack up their personal belongings and have them delivered to the apartment about the same time Martha hoped she and Michael would arrive.

"Michael, do you want to help me plan our route to Montana?" Martha asked. Sitting down with several state highway maps, they planned a route north that would be fun and interesting. They settled on driving through Tyler, continuing through Dallas, and across the Texas panhandle. From there, they would drive north to Denver and then turn northwest through the Wind River Indian Reservation. They would then enter the Grand Teton National Park at Moran, Wyoming, and continue north through Yellowstone National Park, entering the park at the south entrance, and then exit Yellowstone National Park at the park's north entrance near Gardiner, Montana. From there, it would be a straight shot north on Highway 89 to Livingston. The trip would cover 1650 miles, and Martha was allowing at least four nights and five days of travel time.

Martha's hope was to make this drive memorable for them both since neither had ever ventured outside of Texas. They periodically called the apartment manager from pay phones about their progress. To save money, Martha brought an old tent they both could sleep in, and two sleeping bags with air mattresses. For meals, she relied on traditional thick-cut Texas white bread, and peanut butter for lunch, cold cereal and milk for breakfast and a package of hotdogs and buns for dinner. Everything fit nicely into a small ice chest. Martha was confident she would be able to grill the hotdogs over an open fire at each of the campgrounds where she planned to stay.

The first night found them in a campground near Amarillo. Without much to see or places to visit along this route, they made good time. The following night, they made it to Laramie, Wyoming. The next day they were inside Grand Teton National Park. Everything was new and exciting. They pitched their small tent at the Colter Bay Village Campground, and during the day saw buffalo, elk, and antelope.

The following day was going to be a leisurely drive into Yellowstone National Park. Martha had made camping reservations near Old

Faithful. They had plenty of time to watch the reliable old geyser show its stuff, to the disappointment of no one. Michael had seen pictures, but the pictures didn't hold a candle to seeing the real thing.

During the night, Michael and his mother woke to the eerie sounds of wolves, howling, singing and yelping to each other. She said it was just coyotes, but Michael had heard coyotes before and knew the difference. Rather than being scared, Michael was mesmerized by the wolves' primordial wildness. Martha, not so much.

As they packed to leave their beautiful campground that last morning, Michael said, "Mom. Look, there's a bear with two cubs walking along the side on that hill."

"Good eyes, Michael. You're a natural at spotting wildlife."

Sure enough, Martha caught a glimpse of a grizzly and two cubs traversing a hillside a safe distance away. That was a thrill!

Michael relaxed during the remaining three-hour drive to Livingston with a happy heart. He dared to dream that his future in Montana would be a great adventure that was just beginning.

9.

SPYDER

Livingston, Montana
Midsummer

Now, the really stressful task of finding work and moving into their new apartment began. Martha also had to get Michael registered for elementary school before the next school year began. At least she had some money left over, as well as her deceased husband's social security income. The combination of those two, plus whatever food stamps for which she might qualify, would last at least six months before finances became desperate.

Job hunting was difficult. Martha had no job references from her assorted part-time Texas jobs, having been fired from all of them. Still, she was now qualified for SNAP (Supplemental Nutrition and Assistance Program) from Montana's Department of Public Health and Human Services.

Martha soon got to know other low-income tenants in her apartment building. The complex was also small enough for everyone to know each other, which had some advantages as well as disadvantages.

By September, Martha met Spyder. It turned out they resided on the same floor and had the same drug counselor. Soon, Spyder was making Martha offers for "merchandise."

"I have something you need," he said, temptingly.

"What makes you believe I need anything?"

"I just know these things."

"And what might that be?"

"Let's just call them ink cartridges."

"What colors do these ink cartridges come in?"

"Either black or white."

"Right now, I can't afford anything."

"Tell you what I'll do," Spyder said. "I'll give you one cartridge of each color, no strings attached, and you can just think about it."

"That would be okay, but I don't want my son anywhere near those ink cartridges."

"When do you want me to bring them over?"

"My son will be in school tomorrow, so any time after he leaves."

Martha thought she had sufficient willpower to resist using any drugs, but the financial strain weighed heavily on her. *What could it hurt just to have something around the apartment? The price is certainly right,* she thought.

Spyder came to her apartment the next morning after Michael left for school. He handed Martha a small white packet and an equal size black packet wrapped in cellophane, each inside a coin size baggie. Martha, from her vast experience, knew exactly what she was receiving and the approximate quantity of each product.

Spyder said, "Here you go, just as promised and no strings attached. If you want any more, just ask, and I'll deliver. But the rest won't be free. I have overhead costs, you know. We can always discuss a trade, if you get my drift."

"Oh, I get your drift all right, but only in your dreams, Spyder," Martha responded.

Martha took the two packets and closed the door. She looked around for a place to hide them and settled on the bathroom drawer holding her makeup. She had a special container into which both items fit nicely, and Michael would never have a reason to poke his nose there.

It wasn't long before Martha resorted to her old drug habit from Texas. She was now purchasing "black ink cartridges" from Spyder every other day. Michael noticed the change in his mother within the first week. She no longer made his lunch. She no longer woke him up in the morning, and she no longer did his laundry. Michael often went to school wearing the same clothes and underwear day after day. When lunch period came around, Michael would find a quiet place he could go to be alone. His teachers recognized there was something wrong and tried to talk to him and find out if there were any problems at home or if he was feeling okay.

Michael only shrugged off their concerns by saying his mother was sick or he wasn't hungry. He then started to have incontinence issues during the school day whenever he became anxious, stressed, or scared. He asked to be excused to go to the bathroom and always had a clean pair of white briefs in his backpack. He changed in the bathroom stall and stuffed his soiled underwear into a plastic bag. When he got home, he rinsed everything out in the bathroom sink and dried his newly cleaned briefs with a hair blower. His mother was never aware of what he was doing.

One day in the classroom, Michael took a textbook from his backpack, and the bag of clean underwear fell onto the floor. The kids around him laughed and made fun even when the teacher tried to restore order. She finally slammed a yardstick on her desk. The loud slapping sound had the intended result and the class settled down, but the noise startled Michael. He lost bladder control and then quickly picked up the underwear bag and tucked it in his backpack. Michael was very embarrassed and even more so when it was obvious to everyone in the classroom that the front of his pants were wet. He then asked to be excused to go to the bathroom, where he changed underwear.

While he was gone, the teacher had a word with her students about how inappropriate it was to make fun of someone. When Michael returned to the classroom, some of the kids were snickering, but they didn't laugh out loud. All the teacher had to say in a stern voice was, "Class!"

After school was over for the day, Michael's teacher spoke with the school nurse and asked for advice on what to do in the future, in the event there was a reoccurrence. The nurse suggested that Michael be sent to her office rather than escalating the matter to the principal at this early stage. If necessary, she'd make the decision to involve Michael's mother, or she'd leave that up to the principal. Within the same week, there was a second occurrence, and the school nurse had a conversation with Michael.

"Michael, are you having any problems at home?"

"I'm worried about my mother because she's sick all the time. She sleeps a lot, and she has problems waking up."

"Is this something new for your mother, or have you experienced anything like this before?"

"My mother was sick a lot before we moved from Texas, but she got better after we arrived here. Then she started feeling bad again like she did before we moved. She sometimes gives herself a shot to make herself feel better, but then she always goes to sleep right afterward."

"Where does your mother usually give herself a shot?"

"In front of her elbow. Sometimes it'll be lower down on her arm, between her elbow and her hand."

10.

SCHOOL INTERVENTION

The school nurse decided it was time to involve the principal and let her make the decision whether to contact Michael's mother, Child Protective Services, and/or the police. As "mandatory reporters," both the principal and the school nurse had a legal obligation to make a formal report whenever the health and welfare of a child became a concern. The principal hoped to resolve the issue first by some further investigation. Speaking to Michael's mother was the first step, and the next appropriate step might be to contact Child Protective Services or the police.

The principal first attempted to call Martha but received no answer. She didn't want to leave a phone message and decided to make an unannounced home visit. The principal and the school nurse arrived at Martha's apartment around 3:30 that afternoon. The nurse served as a witness and had the necessary medical knowledge and observation skills, which would prevent the principal from jumping to any conclusions. Both were very concerned about Michael's home life and how that might affect him at school.

When they arrived, Michael was playing in his bedroom, and it was obvious Martha had been asleep. When she answered the door, she appeared groggy, and her pupils were constricted. The nurse also noticed Martha had dark circles under her eyes, her skin was flushed, and she had a runny nose. Based on her nursing education, these were all symptoms of possible opioid use. As Michael's principal and the school nurse started talking to Martha, she became defensive and didn't understand what they were talking about. She wasn't aware of any incontinence issues concerning her son, and certainly, as his mother, she'd be the first to know such things. They asked Martha about Michael not always having a lunch or clean clothes, and Martha's response took them both by surprise.

"Michael's old enough to make his own lunch if he wants one and he knows how to wash his own clothes. I don't appreciate what you're suggesting. I'll have you know I'm a good mother. I want you both to leave now, and the school should butt out of my business!"

Abruptly, the conversation was over.

Once outside, the nurse asked, "Did you notice the miosis in her pupils?"

"What's miosis?"

"That's when someone's eyes are constricted, typically from opioid use. I also noticed Martha was exhibiting other symptoms of heroin use, such as the needle marks in her arm, her drowsiness, and her quick irrationality."

The principal responded, "We have a legal obligation to notify Child Protective Services within twenty-four hours once we become aware of something that might be child abuse, child neglect, child endangerment, or something potentially harmful to a child. I'll do that first thing tomorrow morning."

The following morning, the principal called Child Protective Services and explained her concerns about Michael's well-being. CPS told her they'd follow up as soon as possible.

✿ ✿ ✿

Several weeks passed, and Michael's issues got worse with each passing day. Not only did the incontinence become more frequent, but his clothes were never clean and he appeared unkempt. He was disruptive in class and was aloof from others.

Everything came to a head one day as Michael took something out of a side pocket of his backpack. A small pill bottle fell onto the floor and rolled under another student's desk. His teacher witnessed the incident, and just as he reached down to pick up the pill bottle, she said, "Give that to me!"

The school had a very strict policy that prohibited students from bringing medication to school unless it had been previously approved. When Michael's teacher looked at the bottle, which had no prescription label, she could tell the bottle contained something, but whatever it was, it obviously wasn't pills.

The teacher told her students, "Open your textbooks to page 45 and begin reading. I'll be right back."

With Michael and the pill bottle in tow, she took him directly to the principal's office.

"Michael, what is this? You know you can't have any medication in school without approval," said the principal.

"I don't know. I've never seen that before."

"How do you suppose it got into your backpack, then? You know we'll have to call your mother about this."

Michael began sobbing because he really had no knowledge of the pill bottle, and he didn't know what else to say. The principal took a closer look at the contents of the bottle and observed something black, wrapped in cellophane. She wasn't positive about what she had in her hand, so she punched the intercom and told the school nurse, "Please come to my office."

She handed the bottle to the nurse, who took it back to her office for examination. When she returned, she handed the principal a handwritten note which confirmed the suspicion that they were most likely looking at black tar heroin. How it came to be in Michael's backpack was a mystery.

"Well," the principal said, "Michael, you can go back to class."

"What's going to happen?" the boy asked, obviously distraught and anxious.

"We'll talk to your mother. Don't worry, Michael, I believe that you had nothing to do with the pill bottle. You are not in trouble."

Relieved yet shaken, the boy headed back to his classroom.

"This changes everything," said the principal to the nurse once Michael was out of earshot. "I'm going to contact the Livingston Police Department and have them here when Martha Maddox arrives, assuming I can reach her by phone. We can't question Michael further without his mother present. Let's have the police speak to her before we do anything else."

11.

KNOCK AND TALK

"Thanks for calling," officer Crawford told the school nurse and principal. "We've been seeing more black tar heroin on the street recently, and its high potency is reason for concern. An increased number of overdose patients are arriving at emergency rooms, and without quick medical intervention, many overdoses are fatal."

"So you think this might be heroin?" asked the school nurse.

"We'll have preliminary test results in just a few minutes," Crawford answered as he tested the substance. "Yep. Heroin. It will take additional testing in a lab to determine if it's identical to other black tar we're finding. Hold off from contacting the boy's mother, and I'll follow up with her myself."

"All right," agreed the principal. "Please keep us posted."

Crawford took possession of the pill bottle with its suspected contents. Back at the station, he submitted the black substance to the crime lab, who confirmed it was the exact composition as the black tar that was claiming so many lives in the Livingston area. What Crawford still didn't know was how the container of heroin got into Michael's backpack. He didn't suspect the young boy was selling or using it. However, there was the real possibility that Michael's mother was somehow involved, especially considering the statements from the school nurse and principal.

Crawford was a helpful type of cop who didn't want to see Martha Maddox lose custody of her son if drug treatment would be a benefit. After speaking with the two City of Livingston police detectives, Robert Conway and Keith French, he asked, "What do you think, detectives, if I do a knock and talk with Martha Maddox?"

"Go for it. That would save us time in the long run," detective French said.

"Great. I'll report back on her level of cooperation and my personal observations, and then you decide what to do next."

"Ms. Martha Maddox? I'm Officer Crawford with the Livingston Police Department. I would like to talk to you in private concerning your son Michael. May I come in, please?"

"What's this about? Is he in trouble?"

"He might be, but I'm hoping you can clear up some questions for me. Apparently, some drugs were found today in his possession."

"Michael didn't say anything to me when he got home."

"That's probably because no action was taken at school, and I wanted to follow up with you personally first."

"Yes, please come in. I'll tell Michael to stay in his bedroom while we talk."

Officer Crawford noticed the tell-tale signs of addiction right away — Martha's pupils, the dark circles, and her general jumpiness. Her body odor indicated she wasn't taking care of herself.

"First off, do you know how drugs might have gotten into Michael's possession?" Crawford asked.

"I have no idea. Michael's a good boy and a good student. His father died of a drug overdose when he was very young. He never knew his father. I struggled with addiction when we lived in Texas, but I've been clean since we moved to Montana."

"So, no controlled substances have been in your home since moving to Montana? Is it possible the drugs were inside of something when you moved, and you just forgot about them?"

"That's possible. What kind of drugs are we talking about, and what were they in?"

"Ms. Maddox, we found black tar heroin inside a pill container."

At that moment, a knock on the apartment door caused Martha to excuse herself. All Crawford heard her say was, "Not now, Spyder, the police are talking to me about Michael."

When she returned, Crawford asked, "Who's Spyder?"

"He's just a neighbor who lives down the hall."

"Does Spyder have a last name?"

"I really don't know his last name. Everyone just calls him Spyder."

Crawford recognized "Spyder" as a street name for a local drug dealer, but he didn't want to let on and continued their conversation.

"What kind of drugs did your husband overdose on, and what kind of drugs were you using in Texas?"

"He overdosed on heroin, and that's what I was using. That pill container likely came with us when we moved. I have no idea how it got in his backpack, but I'll be sure to ask him."

Crawford noticed Martha's lack of eye contact and general fidgetiness. "I'd like to speak to Michael while I'm here, and maybe he'll tell us the answer. Would you please ask Michael to step out here?"

"He's probably tired from a hard day at school…"

"Just ask him to step out."

"Michael, the police would like to speak with you," Martha hollered louder than necessary, probably out of nervousness.

"Hi, Michael. My name is Larry Crawford. I'm a police officer for the Livingston Police Department. You're not in any trouble. I just want to talk to you about what happened in school today and I could really use your help."

"Okay," said Michael," looking somewhat relieved.

"You see, I have a mystery I'm trying to solve, and I think maybe you can help me solve it. Would you like to help me?"

"Oh sure. I like solving mysteries and I'm very good at stuff like that."

"This mystery has to do with the pill bottle that fell out of your backpack. Do you remember that happening?"

"Yeah. I was trying to get an eraser from my backpack, and my hand must've pulled the pill bottle out. It rolled under Sam's desk. Ms. Moore got mad at me and took me to the principal. They said I brought drugs to school without permission. I told them I didn't, and I didn't know where they came from or how they got into my backpack. I don't think they believed me, but that's the honest truth, cross my heart and hope to die."

"That really helps me, Michael. Like I told you, regardless of how the pill bottle got into your backpack, you're not in any trouble. I just want to make sure you didn't just happen to find the pill bottle someplace and maybe put it into your backpack. If that's what happened, it's okay to tell me. The stuff that was inside the pill bottle is very dangerous. If you found it, I want to make sure there's not any more out there someplace that someone else might find."

"I've never seen that pill bottle before in my life, and I don't how it got into my backpack. And that's the truth."

"Thank you, Michael. You really helped me solve my mystery."

"You're welcome," the boy answered politely and headed back to his room.

"What happens next?" Martha asked.

"I'll prepare a report to our detectives. They might contact you directly if they have any further questions," Crawford explained.

❀ ❀ ❀

As Crawford drove back to the police station, he reflected on Martha's verbal and non-verbal responses to his questions. He had been trained to recognize the signs of heroin use, and Martha exhibited many of those same signs. He'd also noticed that when she was told Michael had drugs at school, her first question was not about what kind of drugs. It was as if she already knew it was heroin. The other thing that bothered him was Martha switching between the present and past tense use of the verbs "is" and "was" concerning what type of drug she was using in Texas. Lastly, Crawford had been careful not to reveal where the pill bottle in Michael's possession was found, yet Martha specifically asked about the pill bottle being in Michael's backpack. *How did she know to ask about the backpack?* he wondered.

12.
OVERDOSE

"911. What's your emergency?"

"It's my mother, I can't wake her up."

"Is your mother breathing?"

"I think so, but it's really hard to tell."

"Where's your mother now?"

"She's sitting on the floor in the corner of the bathroom, and she has a needle sticking out of her arm."

"Okay, emergency aid has been dispatched. I want you to not touch anything in the bathroom and open the apartment door when I tell you to. I'll stay on the phone with you until the Fire Department medics arrive. Do you understand?"

"Yes ma'am, but I'm really scared."

"You've been very brave, and you did the right thing calling 911. How old are you? Do you hear the sirens yet? They should be arriving just now at your apartment building and will be knocking on your door very soon."

"I hear the sirens."

"Good. Now do me a favor and walk over to your door and when you hear the knock, open the door and show the medics where your

"

mother is. Then you can hang up the phone and find a place out of the way of the medics. Do you understand all of that?"

"Yes ma'am. I'm nine. The firemen are here. Bye."

On the bathroom floor and counter, the medics found a spoon, a cigarette lighter, an elastic strap, and a black substance they recognized as possible heroin. There was also a black residue still on the spoon. They pulled the syringe from Martha's arm and injected her with a dose of Narcan to counteract the heroin. The fire department medics then asked dispatch to send the police to their location due to the presence of a suspected controlled substance, and also out of concern of possible child neglect and endangerment.

Martha was transported to the Livingston Hospital in critical condition. There was hope she'd make a full recovery, thanks to Michael's quick thinking, the medic's injection of Narcan, and the work of the emergency room staff.

Michael spent three days and two nights at a temporary foster home waiting for his mother to be discharged from the hospital. He didn't sleep any of those two nights. He was worried about his mother and whether he would ever see her again.

On the third day of Martha's hospital stay, the CPS caseworker took Michael to see his mother. She was discharged within the hour, so the caseworker drove them both to their apartment. Upon their arrival, Michael's mother realized she didn't have her purse or her apartment keys.

The caseworker explained, "Your purse is in the possession of the police department for safekeeping, along with your apartment keys, which is all standard police procedure. The police didn't know what your medical condition was, and they couldn't leave your apartment and personal belongings unsecured without assuming liability."

"Oh. Then what do we do?" Martha asked.

The caseworker told Martha, "I've made arrangements for someone from the police department to meet us here to return your purse and other personal items."

As Martha and the caseworker talked in front of the apartment door, a female officer walked up carrying Martha's purse in an evidence bag. Martha was a little surprised to see her purse labeled as evidence.

The officer told Martha, "Your purse was placed into the evidence bag the same night you overdosed. Apart from an inventory search of your purse's contents and using your apartment key to gain access to execute a search warrant, the purse has been under the custodial control of the police department."

Martha didn't pick up on the statement concerning her keys being used to gain access to her apartment in order to execute a search warrant, but she was about to. Martha, Michael, and the caseworker stepped inside the apartment. Martha quickly noticed a piece of paper on the kitchen counter she didn't recognize. When she looked at the paper it read, "Search Warrant." *How were the police able to search my apartment while I wasn't here, and how did the police gain entry?* she wondered. Her biggest concern was how it would impact her and Michael's future.

The state caseworker saw Martha looking at the search warrant and asked to see it. She then said, "Michael, I'd like to speak to your mother alone. Is that okay with you?"

"Sure," and off he went to his bedroom and closed the door.

"Martha, I'm sure you realize the difficult position we're in. You overdosed in your home and risked the health and safety of Michael. Child Protective Services will petition the court to have a greater role in Michael's well-being and you can expect to get a notice from Family Court requiring your attendance at a hearing. The court is likely to appoint a GAL, also called a Guardian Ad Litem, to intervene on Michael's behalf. CPS is also aware of the concerns Michael's elementary school expressed about Michael having heroin at school. Once the court has made specific provisions in the form of a court order, someone from my office and the GAL will be making regular house calls to check on you and Michael. If the police found anything during their search, you can expect to hear from them as well."

"What's going to happen? Will Michael still be able to live with me?"

"Unless I hear differently from the court or the police department, Michael will stay with you until the first family court hearing. After that, it's going to depend mostly on you and to some degree, the judge. You must attend every hearing ordered by the court, and you must follow every instruction from the court, the GAL, and CPS. Do you understand?"

"Yes, but what about the…the…"

"The drugs? There's still the separate criminal matter of you being in possession of a controlled substance. It's up to the police and the county prosecutor to decide how to proceed. If you're arrested, charged, prosecuted, and/or convicted, the family court judge will take all that into consideration. It's in your best interest to retain a family law attorney as soon as possible, or at least consult with one before the first family court hearing."

"But I can't afford an attorney!"

"If you are criminally charged, you'll probably qualify for a court-appointed attorney in criminal court."

Facing all of these challenges at one time, Martha voluntarily relinquished her custodial rights over Michael. Once again, she flashed back to what happened in Texas to eldest son Eric years earlier. Rinse and repeat. Her kids were tragically doomed to the foster care system because she was an addict. Sadly, this same scenario played out with hundreds of unfit parents and their unfortunate children all over the United States and beyond.

13.

FATE OF A FOSTER CHILD

Michael got settled into his new foster family and new routines. One condition the Rikers had to agree to before becoming foster parents was Michael and Max, the black cocker spaniel, were a package deal for the duration of the dog's life. The state recognized how critical the dog was to Michael's mental and emotional well-being and that it was important the boy and the dog not be separated. To sweeten the deal, the state offered to pay the Rikers an additional $200 per month, on top of the $1,700 in foster child support money.

Michael's new Livingston home was much like the one he left behind in Texas, except it had three bedrooms and not just two. The Rikers lived in a residential area of similar homes, but remote from downtown or anyplace fun.

Michael did enjoy having an older half-sister, as he considered her. Susie Riker was fun to be around, and to him, she was a cool 13-year-old in junior high. She introduced him to her friends, and some had brothers about his age.

Fortunately, Michael was able to attend the same school, East Side Elementary, that he had previously attended when living with his mother. The administration and teachers knew Michael was now a foster child living with a new family. All his elementary school teachers liked him, although they became concerned not long after the new year began. Once again, he wore the same, dirty clothes day after day. Some appeared to be hand-me-downs, and some shirts buttoned on the left instead of the right — meaning he was wearing girls' clothes.

Michael's behavioral issues continued in the classroom, much like the previous school year, such as low attentiveness and squirming at his desk. His incontinence continued to be very embarrassing for him. His teachers were concerned about his home life and asked for a parent-teacher conference. The meeting was scheduled for the following week at a time and day convenient for his foster parents. Mr. and Mrs. Riker arrived for the meeting on time, as they didn't want to give the impression of being disinterested.

"Welcome, Mr. and Mrs. Riker and Michael. I am Michael's teacher. On my right is our school nurse, and on my left is our principal. First and foremost, we want you and Michael to understand our purpose for having this meeting. It's not to criticize either of you as foster parents. We totally understand there are things in Michael's past for which neither of you are going to be aware. Our goal as educators is to work with parents to identify and address some of those issues in the best interest of Michael. That said, we want to discuss with you some concerns we have and possibly identify any areas where we might work together to see improvements. Does that sound good to you both?"

"Of course, and we totally agree with you. Michael has only been with us a few weeks now and we know little to nothing about his earlier life or education in Texas or after he first arrived in Montana," Leroy said.

"Great. As his teacher, I can tell you Michael is very smart, and he tries hard to make friends and fit in. There have been times when I've noticed he has difficulty sitting still and is not as attentive as other students. Between all of us, our biggest concern is that he continues to have some incontinence issues which could be medical or emotional. That causes a great deal of embarrassment for him and might be a contributing factor to his lack of attentiveness and his squirming in his desk. Is this an issue either of you are aware of?"

"No. This is the first time we've heard of this. Michael, why haven't you said anything to us? You know you can talk to either of us about anything," Lora said.

"Because I was embarrassed and didn't want to bother you."

"Michael," the school's nurse continued, "are you getting enough sleep at night?"

"Yeah, I think so."

"Is there anything worrying you?"

"I'm worried I won't be able to live here forever, and I'm worried about my first mother."

"That's understandable. You were having some of the same problems last year, weren't you, when you lived with your mother? Why do you think that was?"

"Yeah. I was worried about my mother then too. She was sick and slept a lot. And when we got to Montana, she got very sick once and she went to the hospital after giving herself a shot. Then I got put into a temporary foster home for a few days. Then she got into trouble and went to jail. That's when she gave me up because she couldn't take care of me from prison."

The Rikers immediately noticed the looks of empathy on the school staff's faces and adjusted their expressions to match.

"Michael, why do you think you sometimes wet your pants? Do you feel like you have to go to the bathroom and just can't hold it, or does it just happen when you don't expect it?" the school nurse asked.

"It just happens, like, you know, when I'm nervous, or something scares me. I don't do it on purpose."

"That's okay, Michael. No one believes you do it on purpose either. Mr. and Mrs. Riker, did you know Michael brings clean underwear to school with him in a plastic bag and changes out of his soiled underwear in the school's bathroom?"

"No, we didn't know about that either. I do all the laundry and I've never noticed anything like that," Lora said.

"Michael, what do you do with your wet underwear when you get home from school?" Leroy inquired.

"I wash them in the bathroom sink and then dry them with the hair dryer, just like I've always done. After they're dry, I put them back into a new plastic bag and throw away the old bag."

"Like you did when you lived with your mother?" the nurse asked.

"Yeah. My mother was either sleeping or gone someplace when I got home from school."

"Is that why you sometimes squirm at your desk?"

"Maybe. My bottom sometimes itches."

"Mr. and Mrs. Riker, I'm going to suggest Michael receive a doctor's exam to rule out any medical causes for his incontinence. If that turns out negative, encourage him to let you know whenever his underwear is wet."

"Will do," said Leroy.

"I think Michael just needs reassurance from you both that he has a new home and is safe and secure. Continue to give him lots of support and encouragement. His attentiveness should improve if he's no longer uncomfortable."

"Absolutely," said Lora, patting Michael gently on the back.

"And Michael, please let your teacher know whenever you need to be excused to go to the bathroom. Together, we can help you through those embarrassing moments."

"Yes, ma'am," said Michael.

"So, are we all on the same page?" the principal asked.

"We certainly are," said the Rikers.

"Michael, I want to make sure you get a good night's sleep each night and have a nutritious diet. School is very important, and we all want you to do your very best."

"As his foster parents, we also only want what's best for him," Lora interjected. "We intend to adopt Michael at the earliest opportunity, and that should make him feel more secure."

14.

THE ADOPTION

"Can you believe this crap?" Lora hissed at Leroy once they returned home. While Michael was outside playing, they discussed their session with the school staff. "And I do mean crap. What kid Michael's age poops his pants? It's disgusting."

"Still, you have to keep him clean and fed," said Leroy.

"Yeah, well, easy for you to say. '*My bottom always itches.*' Give me a break. He probably has lice or fleas from that damn dog."

"Lora, I mean it. You can't let on that he's just a payout to you. You have to keep up the pretenses and be a good mom, or people will notice."

"Yeah, well, you have a point. At least I won't be stuck cleaning his underwear for long. You're gonna put that kid out of his misery soon, and life will be a lot richer around here."

"Just remember, that damn dog is worth an additional $200 per month for the time being, and the dog goes when the boy goes," Leroy said. "And tell me again, just how do we get life insurance on a foster kid, Lora?"

"I swear, Leroy, you are missing a brain. What would you do without me? I have explained this to you before. We get the foster

59

kid first, and then in a couple months, we adopt the kid. Then, we buy the life insurance policy."

"How are we going to pay the premium? You keep bouncing so many checks now that we can't even pay the check fees," Leroy replied. "And how can we afford a foster kid? We can't afford the daughter we already have!"

"Simmer down," Lora said. "The state will pay us each month. Fostering is a bit of a moneymaker, but nothing compared to calling in a life insurance policy. If we select the foster child wisely, we might also get paid after the kid is adopted."

"I still don't know how this is supposed to all work out," Leroy replied.

"Stop thinking so much, Leroy. My job is to do the thinking. Like I told you, all you have to do is exactly what I tell you to do. Just think of all that money," Lora replied. "There will be more than enough to pay the insurance premiums and after we cash in on the insurance, we'll be debt free for the first time in our lives."

"Well, you're not the one killing a kid…"

"Oh, like killing ever bothered you before."

"Now, Lora, that was different."

"Not so much, Leroy. You got paid to look the other way when those inmates took out that snitch."

"That was different. He wasn't a kid."

"Oh, but he molested kids," shot back Lora with a smirk.

"Well, what's worse? Molesting them or killing them? Lora, you're putting me in a very dangerous position. If I get busted, they'll kill me too."

"Look, you're practically a pro at this. Besides, under my plan, there is no way the cops or the insurance companies can prove you knew anything about the life insurance policies. That means you don't have a motive for the killing. Do you understand? Without a motive, the authorities can't prove nothing," Lora said. "It will look like an accident, and kids have accidents every day of the week."

Once again, Leroy turned a shade paler. It still blew his mind that the boy in his house was nothing more than a sacrificial lamb, something to be fattened up and slaughtered for the insurance proceeds. Lora was certainly a monster without a conscious, and his conscious asked, *What does that make me?* Before he could shake the question from his mind, his conscious answered, *A monster too.*

Michael's formal adoption was finalized in early October. The court hearing was a family event, and his new big sister, Susie, gave him a hug. Michael was happier than he'd been in a long time. He still felt abandoned by his mother, but he hadn't forgotten the words of encouragement from the judge. Maybe, in time, he would be able to forgive her, but now he finally had a real family and a sibling, and a new name. Michael Riker. It sounded cool and gave him a feeling of belonging and safety. This new home, he decided, would be his forever home.

"Can I ask you both a question?" Michael asked.

"I think you meant to say, may I ask you both a question?" Leroy corrected.

"Yeah. May I?"

"Of course," Leroy responded.

"What should I call you both now? Do you want me to call you? Leroy and Lora, Mom and Dad, or Mother and Father?"

"Whatever you want, son," Leroy said.

"Absolutely, whatever you want," Lora said.

"Okay, Dad. Okay, Mom."

15.

LIFE INSURANCE

Six days after Michael's adoption was final, Lora told him, "I'm going to buy you some life insurance, just like we did for your sister Susie." Michael didn't know what life insurance was, but he thought it sounded like a family thing to do if Susie already had the same thing.

Lora took Michael to the Northwest Life Insurance Company to meet Ray Heath, the insurance agent. Michael sat quietly in his chair and listened intently while Lora and Mr. Heath talked about insurance stuff.

Lora told Mr. Heath, "I want the same whole life policy for Michael, like the one we purchased for Susie. It'll accumulate a cash reserve both kids can use for their college education or anything else they might need as they get older. Once they are over eighteen, they can decide for themselves if they want to keep the policies or cash them in. By taking out the life policies now they'll always be grandfathered in as being eligible for additional insurance if they want it."

Lora provided Mr. Heath a copy of Michael's adoption papers and the legal documents changing his name from Michael Maddox to Michael Riker. Lora answered a lot of questions, and Mr. Heath made notes of each response.

At the end of the meeting, Mr. Heath asked Michael, "Can you sign your name?"

Michael responded by saying, "Do you want me to print or sign my name in cursive?"

Mr. Heath turned to Lora and said, "What does he mean by "cursive?"

Her response was, "I think he means in long-hand."

As Michael signed his new name, Lora wrote a check for $75 covering the first month's premium for Michael's basic life insurance policy of $250,000, which also included an additional $150,000 in accidental death benefit.

Once they were home, Michael asked Susie, "How long have you had your life insurance?"

"Only a few weeks now. The same day my parents learned they could adopt you and you were coming to live with us permanently my mother took me to get my life insurance."

"Susie," Michael asked, "do you know how much your life is worth?"

"The same as yours," she replied. "$400,000."

"Dang! That's a lot of money!"

❉ ❉ ❉

Eight months after the first life insurance policy, Lora took Michael and Susie for another appointment, this time to the office of The Montana Life Insurance Company.

Lora said, "I want to purchase a life insurance policy for $250,000 for each child. Do you also offer accidental life coverage?"

"I'm sorry," the agent said, "my company doesn't offer accidental life for children, but the base amount of $250,000 is possible. Do you currently have any other life insurance policies in effect?"

"Each child has policies with Northwest Life Insurance," Lora replied. "I intend to cancel both of their policies just as soon as this new policy is effective. The other policies are too expensive."

The agent thought her explanation was curious because she initially wanted the exact same coverage for both children as what they already had. The only difference being his company didn't offer accidental life. The agent was also aware his company's insurance premiums were more expensive than the ones she intended to cancel, which were for $400,000 each.

"Do you have legal authority to act as Michael's guardian or anything from the court giving you that authority?" the agent asked before writing up a new policy for Michael.

As Lora provided him with a copy of the adoption papers, as well as the change of name documents, she told him, "I want to keep both policies a secret from Leroy. I want to surprise him with my initiative and how responsible I can be with such matters. I'll set up an automatic bank withdrawal for the premium payments."

"Just so you know, it is customary for Montana Life Insurance to provide written notice of the proposed change to Northwest Life Insurance. The total monthly cost of this new policy will be $90 for each child."

A few days later, the first insurance agent received the notice of the insurance change from Montana Life Insurance. He called and asked Lora, "Is it correct you intend to cancel the policies for both children and you plan to purchase a policy for lesser coverage, but with higher premiums?"

Lora's only response was, "How much money does Michael have in his cash reserve account?"

"There is only enough money in his account to pay for one more month's insurance premium."

"Okay, when the cash reserves are used up, I want to let Michael's policy lapse for non-payment, and it'll cancel on its own. Correct?"

"That's correct. The policy will automatically cancel after the premium payment has lapsed thirty days beyond the due date."

In the interim, there were two overlapping life insurance policies with a combined value of $650,000. The day before the first policy was scheduled to expire for non-payment of premiums, Lora went to see Michael's first insurance agent at his Northwest Life Insurance office.

"Please apply this $75 money order to Michael's policy to keep it in effect for one more month. After that, I'll let the policy lapse," she told the agent.

The following day, Lora picked up two fishing poles, a boy's bicycle and a child's tackle box she had on layaway at a sporting goods store in Livingston. The tackle box cost $5.95, the child's fishing pole and reel cost $8.99, the fishing pole and reel for Leroy cost $15.95, and the boy's bicycle cost $59.99. Some of these items were intended to be birthday gifts for Michael's upcoming eleventh birthday in three weeks.

While Lora was picking up the layaway items, Leroy took Michael for a "sports physical," even though Michael wasn't taking any sports-related activities requiring a physical. Once the physical was completed, Leroy told the elementary school nurse, "I want you to make sure the physical results get into Michael's official school file."

The nurse told Leroy, "There's really no need to put the results in his school record because we don't require a physical unless a child is going to participate in a sport."

Leroy responded, "I want to speak to the school principal."

The principal came to the nurse's office and told Leroy the exact same thing, but Leroy was still insistent. So rather than continue to argue with him, the medical results were placed into Michael's school file.

After Leroy left, the principal said, "I wonder what that was all about?"

"I don't know, but he was certainly adamant about the physical results getting filed in Michael's school records," the nurse replied.

16.
A PLAN IN MOTION

Michael would never forget the good times he had fishing with Douglas Rodriquez in Texas. When he was fishing, something he was truly enthusiastic about, all his pain, fears, and negative thoughts disappeared. He enjoyed the solitude and melodic, comforting sounds of the water. The symphonic chorus of birds and frogs made him happy. There was nothing quite like the fresh outdoor fragrance of trees and water. Watching the hovering translucent dragonflies going to and fro, and the occasional florescent hummingbird darting hither and yon, transported him away from his worries. Fishing brought him peace of mind, whether or not he received so much as a nibble on a hook.

Michael saw a fishing pole standing in the corner of his new home, one he hadn't seen previously. *How long has it been there*, he wondered, *and who does it belong to*? *Does my new dad know how to fish?*

Excitedly, Michael asked, "Is that your fishing pole in the corner, Dad? Can we go fishing sometime, please?" Fishing was something Michael talked about non-stop ever since coming to the Riker household.

Leroy replied, "Sure, we can go."

"When?" Asked Michael, excitedly, just as Leroy expected.

"Well, I just happen to have some days off this Thursday, Friday, Saturday and Sunday. I think we can plan a little fishing trip one of those days. What day do you want to go?"

Grinning ear to ear, Michael said, "You know, I don't have school this Thursday or Friday. Can we, like, go one of those days?"

"I don't see any reason why not unless the weather changes for the worse," was the reply. "Is there anyone you'd like to invite to go with you? You can take one of your friends if you want."

"Max, for sure," Michael said, not wanting to leave his cocker spaniel behind.

"Of course, Max is coming. I meant that you can ask a friend from school too."

"Can I ask Danny?"

"I think you meant to say, may I ask Danny," Leroy corrected.

"Yeah, may I?"

"You may ask Danny and then I'll call his grandmother for her permission."

"Okey-dokey," said Michael. "I'll call him right now."

By dinner time, Leroy had authorization from Danny Williams' grandmother, Beverly Williams, to take him on a short road trip Thursday and fishing the following Friday. Michael slept only a few hours Wednesday night, as his excitement and anticipation grew by the hour.

That evening, while lying in bed, Leroy and Lora had a conversation.

"Don't forget the plan for tomorrow, Leroy."

"How could I? You've told me often enough already."

"Repeat it back to me, so I know you've got it."

"Oh, for Pete's sake, Lora," Leroy replied. "When I get to the bridge, I pretend to have a flat tire. I tell Michael not to show off by trying to walk on the bridge railing, knowing full well that he'll show off anyway because I told him not to."

"And if he falls into the river?" Lora asked.

"It will be a shock and tragedy," Leroy replied mockingly.

"And there will be three witnesses to the accident," Lora sarcastically added. "Let's cross our fingers. Then the fishing trip and Michael's accidental drowning scenario won't be necessary. Now, don't forget to play it up good if that happens."

On Thursday, Leroy loaded up Michael, Susie, Max, and a friend of Susie's, Karen, into his 1999 blue and white Chevy Silverado half-ton pickup, with an extended cab. Next, Leroy stopped by Danny's house to pick him up. Fortunately, the truck had bench seats, so all three of the guys rode up front, and the two girls and Max had the backseat to themselves.

Leroy explained to Beverly that they were first going to the old KPRK Bridge to check out the height and velocity of the Yellowstone River.

"Oh, how nice!" Beverly said. "It will be good for the kids to see that historic landmark. Please tell them that the KPRK Bridge was named after the radio station went on the air in January 1947. It operated until 1999 and was known for its Futuristic Art Moderne design. Then it was designated on the National Register for Historical Places on September 5, 1979."

"Wow," said Leroy. "I didn't know the backstory." He tried not to seem impatient while glancing at his watch.

"Yes, and even though it's been renamed the Veteran's Bridge, we locals still call it the KPRK Bridge. Promise me you'll fill the kids in on the hist—"

"I sure will," Leroy interrupted. "Now I better get on the road, or we might miss out on some sightseeing. And I want to have Danny home tonight before dark."

"Well, all right, then. Go with Mr. Riker, Danny. Have fun and be careful!"

Danny waved to his grandmother. After Leroy got him loaded into the front seat, he walked around the truck bed to get to the driver's side, muttering, "Crazy old coot. How am I supposed to remember all of that? Screw her history lesson."

There was minimal traffic on the KPRK Bridge that day. Leroy parked in the vacant lot of the old radio station and told the four kids he needed to check a tire on his truck.

Leroy told Michael, "Now, don't be a showoff, and don't let me see you trying to walk on that bridge railing."

As the four kids and Max ran onto the bridge to look at the river below, Leroy focused his attention on his supposedly flat tire. As the kids horsed around, Susie's friend, Karen, started goading Michael. "I bet you're afraid to walk on that railing," she teased.

"Oh yeah? Just watch me," Michael responded.

"No, Michael. Don't do it. It's too dangerous," Susie said.

"But Karen dared me, and Dad just said he didn't want to see me do it. He didn't say I couldn't. Besides, he's not even looking in this direction," Michael replied.

Michael's friend, Danny, spoke up. "Michael, your sister is right. You might drown. There is no way you'll survive falling into that river."

In want of more attention, Michael pretended that he was going to get up onto the bridge's railing. Max started barking.

Not knowing what else she could do to stop Michael, Susie let out a loud scream, which alerted her father. As he turned his focus from his truck's tire in the direction of the scream, he saw Michael retreating away from the bridge railing.

"You didn't need to worry about me, Max. I wasn't really going to do it," Michael told his companion.

Since there didn't appear to be anything wrong with the truck's tire, Leroy and the foursome proceeded onto Wilsall, a town with a full-time population of 227 residents. It consisted of one café, a combination bar and dining establishment located inside a former bank called The Bank Bar and Vault Restaurant, one vacant lot, and one general store closed more than it was open. This was the extent of the businesses in town, and they occupied the four corners of the only intersection. It was also the closest town to the campground for any services, emergency or otherwise.

Leroy drove towards the Shields River Campground, slightly more than an hour's drive from the bridge and a little under an hour from Wilsall. The forest service road to the campground was primitive under the best of conditions and downright inhospitable otherwise. Due to consistent and, at times, heavy rains that entire week and the week before, the road conditions on this day fell into the latter category.

Just outside of Wilsall, along the way to the campground, sat an all-volunteer fire station. This was picturesque cattle and farm country as far as the eye could see. It also happened to be one of the major tourist routes to Glacier National Park, another 290 miles northwest. To the casual traveler, the fire station looked like over-kill for the number of homes in Wilsall. However, range and barn fires caused by lightning or spontaneous combustion in stacked hay were a common occurrence, not to mention auto accidents involving deer, elk and antelope. There was also the occasional farm equipment versus farmer accident, where the farm equipment always won the battle of man versus machine.

The drive to the campground was hazardous and rough, not only on the truck's occupants but also on the truck. Many of Montana's rural roads are notorious for what the locals called "gumbo mud." When wet, not only does the gumbo mud roll up and pack into the wheel wells, but it's also extremely dicey to drive on, much like driving on thick grease.

Leroy made a mental note to leave the campground long before dark so as not to travel the road after sunset. He hadn't checked the weather forecast for that day, and although it was only lightly raining now, he didn't know if that would change for better or for worse later in the day. The following day, when he would return with the two boys, the forecast was for only cloudy skies, with no rain.

Once at the campground, Leroy was pleasantly surprised to find an empty campsite next to the river. There was no table, but it did have a rock-lined fire pit. He pulled into the site, turned off the truck, and told the four kids to sit tight, and that he'd be back in just a minute or two. The kids occupied their time joking and teasing each other, while Leroy walked towards the river and disappeared from their view. Max stood on Susie's lap and stared out a partially open window, which was down just far enough for his nose to fit. Just as he'd promised, Leroy reappeared in a matter of minutes, climbed into the truck, and started the engine.

Michael looked at his father and said, "I thought we all were going to get out and look around."

Leroy gave Michael one of those looks that immediately told Michael he'd already gone too far in questioning him and that it would be best to just drop the subject.

Leroy broke the silence a short time later by saying, "We need to get off this terrible road before it gets dark. Besides, I saw everything I needed to see, and with any luck, that same spot will be available for us tomorrow."

17.

CRIME SCENE

When Leroy and Michael arrived home that evening, Lora said, "Obviously, that didn't go according to my plan."

"No. That kid is smarter than we give him credit for. I think he was about to do it, but Susie screamed, and that made Michael back away from the railing."

"So, we go with plan B for tomorrow. Are you up to it?" Lora asked.

"I suppose. I'm not looking forward to it, I can tell you that"

"Just keep thinking about everything we've dreamed about having. Is Petrolli going to be there just in case?"

"That's the plan."

Leroy had been a guard on Donald Petrolli's cellblock for the past ten years, and Petrolli was now on parole. As an ex-con, he was the perfect backup for "the plan." The Rikers hired him to go to the campground before anyone else got there on Friday to pitch a tent along the river. That way, no one else could use that site. Later that night, he was to sneak back into the campground, grab his tent and take it across the road, and stow everything in his truck. He was promised $500 for just being there and another $500 if he had to kill Michael himself.

Excitement caused Michael to get very little sleep before Friday finally arrived. He was up, dressed, and had eaten his Cheerios long before his father woke. Now, Michael had to wait, which wasn't easy for a hyped-up ten-year-old.

By the time Leroy got the fishing pole, tackle box, and some food items loaded into his pickup, it was almost 10:00 a.m. when they picked up Danny.

Leroy told Danny's grandmother, "It shouldn't be very late when we get back, but don't hold your dinner for Danny. He's welcome to eat with us, and don't worry, I'll watch out for him," Leroy added.

The Shields River Campground was a primitive forest service campground with only four sites, none of which required reservations. The grounds were accessed by turning right off the dirt and gravel road and into a horseshoe-shaped area. A one-way road looped counterclockwise, past two outhouses and past the first of two campsites. Both campsites were not waterfront and didn't have a river view. Circling around to the other side, in the direction towards the main entrance, there were two more campsites, both on the river. The first one they passed had a tent occupying the site, where Petrolli had stealthily staked a claim, but no vehicle.

Leroy slowed and gave a quick glance at the tent, and continued. The last site was the one Leroy had checked out the day before.

The three amigos, as they started calling themselves, plus Max, arrived at the campground about noon. Both boys and the dog were out of the truck and down to the river before Leroy had a chance to turn off the ignition. The same riverfront campsite from yesterday was still unoccupied, and Leroy smiled to himself regarding his good fortune.

Leroy joined both boys down at the river, where they had discovered an ideal fishing spot. Someone had previously stacked rocks in a c-shaped half-circle to create a small eddy adjacent to the main river channel. The eddy created a small pond, about ten feet in diameter and about five feet deep. Of course, Leroy had seen the same thing the day before.

The three of them "horsed around," laughing and talking loudly over the rumbling noise of the river. They had a short competition to see who could throw rocks the furthest. Leroy suggested they all have something to eat before Michael and Danny started fishing, so they all walked back to the pickup, where Leroy produced cans of Dr Pepper and some jerky, cheese, and crackers.

After eating, both boys, with Max leading the way, went back to the river, and Leroy followed a short time later with one fishing pole, complete with line, hook and leader, and a red and white plastic bobber.

Michael asked, "Do we have any bait, like eggs or worms?" Before Leroy could answer, Michael said, "What's Danny going to use for a fishing pole?"

Leroy responded by saying, "While you fish, Danny and I will go look along the riverbank for discarded fishing line, and material to fashion him a pole. As far as bait, we don't have any, but I'm sure a smart boy like you will think of something."

Michael knew far too well, not to question his new father, especially in front of someone else. He was disappointed Leroy hadn't thought about getting fishing bait. Michael was also silently upset he'd invited his friend Danny to join in the fun, yet Danny might not be able to fish with him.

Michael looked around and noticed a bush with white berries. He recognized the shrub as the common "snowberry," native to North America. Michael learned about this plant during his time growing up in East Texas, and from the outdoor survival classes he'd attended. He knew the snowberry wasn't edible for humans but was okay for fish. Michael gathered a few berries and then used one to carefully bait his hook. Once done, he dropped his line into the water and commenced to fish in the small pond. The water was clear, and Michael could see the bottom. He strained as hard as he could in hopes of seeing a fish, but there were none in sight.

After only a few minutes, the snowberry bobbed to the surface. "Well, Max, I guess snowberries don't make the best bait after all." Michael remembered worms could often be found underneath rocks, especially close to water. "Okay Max, do you want to help me find a worm?"

Much to his surprise, the first rock he turned over revealed a large earthworm, ready and willing to entice any fish. Carefully, Michael worked the slippery fat worm onto his hook and readjusted the red and white bobber on his line. The mouthwatering bait sank deeper into the pond. *Now*, he thought, *I'm really fishing.*

As he intently watched his bobber, he could tell there was a small whirlpool in the pond, likely caused by the opening in the rock eddy perpendicular to the fast-moving river, because his bobber made a complete circle in the fishing pool every few minutes. Michael smiled to himself as he thought, *A fish might think the worm is moving around by itself.*

As he continued to stare into the water, his mind wandered. He listened to the rocks being moved by the current along the bottom of the river. They crashed and rolled and rumbled along, each one making its own distinctive sound according to its size and mineral composition. It sounded like an all-percussion band warming up behind a stage curtain before a concert started. Some of the sounds were like bass drums, others like cymbals, and still others were more like the deep sounds of a kettle drum.

The slight breeze made some tree branches rub against each other, giving off ghostly scratching and screeching sounds with their movement. Occasionally, a branch or pinecone became dislodged and fell to the ground. Michael jumped at the noise. Coupled with his fear of drowning, it was disconcerting being all alone alongside a fast-moving river and not knowing where anyone else was. This fishing trip was not as peaceful as he had envisioned.

To make himself feel better, he started a one-way conversation with Max, as he had often done before.

"Max, do you like your new home?" Michael asked as the dog moved closer. "Do you like my new parents? I suppose I know the answer to that question since you bark at both of them and nobody else. You know, if you didn't bark at them, maybe they would like you better."

Max cocked his head to the side as if he was hanging on Michael's every word. It flooded the boy's heart with love for his faithful companion.

"I know. You're just a one-person dog. You and me, Max, against the world." With that statement, Max moved even closer to Michael's leg and laid down on his feet.

His mind drifted back to his near-drowning incident in Tyler, only a few months earlier, when an older boy held Michael's head under water for what seemed like an eternity for Michael. That singular event caused Michael to have nightmares about drowning to death. The older boy never apologized to Michael, and none of the other kids who witnessed the event tried to intervene or say anything to Michael afterward. Michael felt so alone at that time in Texas, just as he did now, with the exception of Max's comforting presence.

The sounds of the rushing river and rolling boulders were enough to cover up almost every other sound, apart from the deep, raucous squawks of a raven. Michael noticed the raven in a nearby treetop, and soon a second raven appeared in another tree. Michael couldn't tell if the birds were talking to each other or to him. He remembered stories he had heard about ravens being a bad omen, associated with death.

This gave Michael a momentary chill. As he watched and listened to the birds, he was aware of other ravens soaring, squawking, and screeching in the sky above. *Maybe they found a dead animal nearby and are sending an alert,* he thought. Max, apparently, wasn't happy with the noisy ravens either, or at least that's what Michael assumed. The cocker spaniel stood up and started barking.

Trying to calm and reassure his buddy, Michael said, "Everything is okay, Max. They're just doing what ravens do."

As he continued to watch, he saw more and more ravens starting to land in treetops near the river, and they now were squawking excitingly, bobbing their heads up and down and making mournful sounds. *Are the ravens trying to tell me something? Or are the birds upset with Max?* Michael was so focused on the ravens that he was unaware of anything or anybody around him.

Max started barking and growling like Michael had never heard before. Just as he was about to reassure Max that the ravens meant no harm, a dark shadow cast over Michael's shoulder and reflected onto the surface of the rippling pool. The last thing he heard and felt was a heavy thud, and then his world went dark. He collapsed straight down on the very edge of the ice-cold swirling water.

18.

WILSALL FIRE STATION

Leroy Riker raced down the mountain on the hazardous forest service road toward the Wilsall Fire Station. It was now 6:30 p.m., and it felt like the road was slicker than it was a few hours earlier. Here, high in the mountains, darkness fell much earlier and more quickly. The ebony night was moonless, and cooler nighttime temperatures were apparent in the seasonal painted colors of the vegetation that glowed in his headlights. The needles of the firs and lodgepole pines took on brownish winter hues, and the shimmering of the golden quaking aspen leaves signaled an ominous warning. In another few weeks, everything would be buried in winter's soft, cold, ivory fleece.

Now, time was paramount as Leroy's half-ton Chevy pickup threatened to lose traction. His teeth rattled with every bounce, and it felt like he was driving down the center of railroad tracks. Leroy knew he couldn't risk losing control of his truck, nor could he risk a mechanical breakdown. As far as he knew, his newly adopted son lay dying or dead at the campground.

Leroy didn't know exactly what to expect when he arrived at the fire station, but his primary goal was to find an operable telephone. There hadn't been any cell service at the campground or anywhere along the road. His mind was troubled with anxious thoughts. *What have I done? What if Michael is already dead? What if Michael survives? Will there be a formal police investigation for an accidental drowning?* His mind returned to the one prevailing question — *What have I done?*

Leroy came to a stop in the middle of the pitch-black road. As he dwelled on that one question, a question somewhere between remorse and dread, he wanted to vomit. Soon, the outline of the unoccupied Wilsall Fire Station came into view. The fire station had four large bay doors. To the right of the four bays was the main entrance to the building. Another entrance was located between bays two and three. He pulled his now battered pickup into the parking lot, and away from the large doors reserved for fire and rescue vehicles. Then he spotted a red telephone on the wall outside the main entrance. Above the phone was a small sign that read, "For Emergency Use Only."

Leroy picked up the receiver and immediately heard the familiar refrain, "911: What is your emergency?"

Leroy took a deep breath and said, "A drowning at the Shields River Campground."

"Do you know the drowning victim and how long ago were you there?"

"The victim is my ten-year-old son, and I've been gone almost an hour. I did CPR for at least 30 minutes, and two other campers took over the CPR while I went looking for a telephone. Please hurry. I don't know if he's dead or alive."

"Do you know how your son got into the water or what he was doing?"

"He was just fishing, but I think he must've jumped from something high into the water because he also has a serious head injury. I'd only left him alone for a few minutes. Oh God, please hurry," Leroy pleaded.

"Please wait at the fire station for the fire department aid crew, and you can ride back to the campground with them."

It wasn't long before the eerie reverberations of sirens sounded in the distance, echoing off the night's darkness as they grew increasingly closer. The first person to arrive was the Wilsall Fire Chief, followed by a fire department aid car and very soon thereafter by a second medic in his personal vehicle. The fire chief told Leroy to get into the chief's car, and the two-vehicle caravan, with the aid car leading the way, proceeded into the darkness on the forest service road toward the Shields River Campground.

Leroy continued to dwell on his earlier thoughts, but now the road didn't feel as rough as before. Before long, they all arrived at the campground, where they found Michael still receiving CPR from Roger and Judy Sterling, a young couple camped nearby.

"The boy still has a weak pulse, but I'm most concerned about his head injury. It's still bleeding," Roger reported, without looking up from his life-saving efforts.

"Thank you, we'll take over from here," one of the medics said.

Upon hearing the news of Michael having a pulse, Leroy felt the sickening nausea rise from his gut and into his throat once again. And, as before, he stumbled into the darkness to vomit.

The two medics made a quick assessment of Michael's condition and decided he required rapid transport down the mountain to receive emergency treatment at Deaconess Hospital in Bozeman. After the boy was loaded into the aid car; they departed the campground with emergency lights flashing. Arrangements had already been made for a helicopter to meet the aid car at the Wilsall High School football field, for immediate helicopter evacuation to the hospital.

Leroy and the fire chief remained at the campground. The chief pretended he wanted to collect additional information from the people there. In actuality, he'd already asked the 911 dispatcher to send a Park County Sheriff's Deputy to his location.

Deputy John Peet and his partner, Deputy Gordon Morris, arrived just as the aid car was departing. The Shields River Campground was situated near the border of an adjoining county, and barely within Park County. The Park County Sheriff's Department had the jurisdiction to investigate all deaths in the county. At this stage, with only a suspected accidental drowning, patrol deputies Peet and Morris would make the initial determination to refer the matter to the detective division, if and when it rose to a possible crime.

Normally, Peet and Morris would have been in separate vehicles, patrolling different districts. The sheriff's department only had a total of eleven commissioned patrol deputies to enforce the laws in a county consisting of 2,803 square miles and a full-time population of about 16,000 residents. That equated to approximately 255 square miles within each deputy's patrol district.

On this Friday, however, the two deputies had ridden together to an all-day training event in Livingston. The class was about high-speed offensive and defensive driving and included performing pit maneuvers. They were still at the classroom when they received the 911 dispatch and responded to the Shields River Campground together.

Their patrol car's headlights revealed a man seated in a camp chair with his head in his hands. They both assumed he was the father of the drowning victim. As they pulled to a stop, the subject slowly raised his head with a look of surprise on his face. The two sheriff's deputies walked in his direction, but before reaching him, changed course when they saw the fire chief. After a brief conversation, they once again walked towards Leroy.

Leroy was stunned to see the sheriff's deputies. *Who called them, and why are they here?* he wondered with a panicky feeling in his gut.

The deputies introduced themselves to everyone and explained they'd be collecting general background information — police jargon for "conducting a preliminary investigation." The information they collected would be referred to the only two detectives employed by the Park County Sheriff's Department, and if there was reasonable cause to believe a crime was involved, the detectives would initiate a criminal investigation, in coordination with the Park County Prosecutor.

Deputy Peet led Roger and Judy Sterling away from the others and began to ask them basic questions. Deputy Morris went in the opposite direction to interview Leroy Riker. The questions started with the basics, such as names, dates of birth, social security numbers, addresses, and phone numbers. The questions progressed to the heart of the matter, such as "who, what, where, why, when, and how." Deputy Peet was the first to finish his interview of the Sterlings, so he then started to interview eleven-year-old Danny Williams. Due to the boy's young age, having a parent or guardian present for the interview would've been his preference. A follow-up interview with detectives, with a parent or guardian present, might be necessary.

19.

DEAD ON ARRIVAL

As everyone was preparing to leave the campground, Deputy Peet received notification by radio that Michael was pronounced DOA at the Bozeman hospital, despite the valiant efforts of the medics and Mr. and Mrs. Sterling. The sheriff's deputies now had the dreaded responsibility of informing Leroy that his son had passed and expressing their condolences. Next-of-kin notification is a job all law enforcement officers loathe. In this case, it was even more difficult because both deputies had children about the same age as Michael.

The task was also complicated because, from their years of experience, they had already formed an opinion that this wasn't just an accidental drowning, and it might very well become a homicide investigation. Expressing condolences to someone who might become a principal suspect in the death of his own son was going to be particularly difficult.

"Mr. Riker, I'm very sorry, but we just received word from the hospital that your son didn't make it. He was pronounced DOA at the Deaconess Hospital in Bozeman. We are very sorry for your loss," Deputy Morris said.

Leroy responded, "Do you know how soon my wife and I'll be able to claim his body?"

Peet and Morris exchanged a quick glance, with a look of disgust for the question even being asked. *How cold,* they both thought.

"That's going to be up to the medical examiner. There will have to be an autopsy," Morris said.

"What if we don't want his body autopsied? We just want to have his body cremated without a lot of fuss," Leroy replied angrily.

"Under the circumstances, an autopsy is required."

"Why is it required? Don't we have anything to say about it?" Leroy demanded.

"Your son drowned, and he suffered a blunt force trauma to his head that may have contributed to his drowning. There were no witnesses as to what caused his injuries or how he got into the water. For that reason, it is considered a suspicious death, and the law requires all suspicious or unexplained deaths to have an autopsy."

"But isn't it obvious? Michael slipped on the rocks, fell, hit his head, and then fell into the water and drowned," Leroy argued.

"That may very well be what happened," Morris said, "but an autopsy is still required unless you're able to obtain a court order saying otherwise. Again, we are very sorry for your loss. Please convey our condolence to your wife as well."

With that bit of news, Leroy wandered into the darkness to puke once again.

Both deputies were resigned to the fact that this was going to be another twelve-hour day. They'd taken a GPS reading to ascertain the proper county for jurisdiction, knowing that nothing kills a criminal case faster than filing in the wrong county. They'd also taken extensive photographs of the campground, the path through the woods and along the river's bank, and two specific areas along the river.

The first was the fishing hole where Michael was found floating, and the second was where Danny Williams had been left to wait for Leroy Riker to return with a custom-made fishing pole. Using the vehicle's headlights, they also documented the distance between where Leroy's truck had been parked and the vacant tent along the river, as well as the distances to the Sterling's campsite and to the downstream location. They completed their preliminary interviews with Leroy Riker, Danny Williams, and Roger and Judy Sterling.

When they drove down the mountain away from the campground, it was after 9 p.m. Now they finally had an opportunity to compare the results of their interviews as they headed back to Livingston.

"You first," Peet told Morris, who was driving. "What did you learn from Leroy Riker?"

"Well, Riker told me the three of them arrived at the campground around noon. He was glad to find the only campsite directly on the river unoccupied. Riker said he'd scoped out the campground yesterday with Michael, his daughter Susie, friend of Susie's by the name of Karen Klein, and Danny Williams."

"Was it his first time camping there?" Peet asked.

"Riker said he'd never been to this campground before and had only been told about it by people he worked with at the Deer Lodge State Prison."

"Got it," said Peet as he added to his notes.

"Yesterday," Morris continued, "he took the four kids to the KPRK Bridge over the Yellowstone River before driving up here to the campground. He said Michael wanted to see how close to the bottom of the bridge the Yellowstone River was because it had been raining hard that day and the entire previous week. When they arrived at the bridge; he parked his truck closest to the end of the bridge near the old KPRK radio station, only to discover his pickup had a flat tire."

"Any evidence of a bad tire?" Peet asked.

"No, I didn't see a flat. The spare, from what I could tell, hadn't been touched," Morris answered, turning his head and looking Peet in the eye. "While he attended to the tire, the kids walked onto the bridge to look at the river. Riker said the river was running near flood stage. He told me Michael was a daredevil and a showoff, so he told Michael, 'I don't want to see you trying to walk on that bridge railing.' He had his back to the kids as he worked on the flat tire, but his attention was drawn to the kids when he heard his daughter Susie scream. As he turned around and looked in her direction; it wasn't clear to him whether Michael had tried climbing onto the railing or what had transpired."

"Or, so he says," said Peet with a touch of sarcasm.

"My thoughts exactly," Morris agreed.

"When he reprimanded Michael for doing what he'd told him not to do, Michael responded by saying, 'You only said you didn't want to see me walking on the bridge railing. You didn't say I couldn't.'"

"Sounds like a smart kid, splitting hairs like that," Peet observed.

"Yeah, Riker said he wasn't happy with Michael's backtalk but decided to address it later. After he got the flat tire replaced, they drove to the campground to look around. He said the same campsite they looked at yesterday was still unoccupied today."

"Those campsites are almost always full with overnight campers," said Peet.

"Convenient, huh?" Morris responded. "When they arrived at the campground, a tent was pitched in the adjacent riverfront campsite. Riker said both boys jumped out of the truck and immediately ran down to the river. He followed the boys, and the three of them started throwing rocks into the river and just goofing around. After a short time, Michael wanted to fish, so Riker went to his truck and got the only fishing pole he had brought.

"Just one fishing pole? For the three of them?" Peet said.

"Odd, I agree," said Morris. "Riker said his wife, Lora, had purchased a second fishing pole specifically for Michael's upcoming birthday in three weeks, but they wanted to keep it hidden from him until then."

"What about tackle boxes?" Peet asked.

"Just one. Riker said Lora also purchased a child's tackle box, and he brought that on this trip."

"A poorly prepared fishing trip."

"Yep," Morris responded. "Riker prepared Michael's fishing pole with hook and bobber, and took it down to him. Someone had created a ten-foot diameter pool that was maybe five feet deep, using stacked river rocks."

"Like an eddy?"

"Yep, a small eddy. Riker said the eddy was round and had an opening in the rocks facing towards the river. When the river was much lower, the rocks acted like a dam, while also allowing an exchange of fresh water through the opening. With the river running as high as it was today, the river overflowed the upstream side of the dam by a few inches."

"Just spitballing here, but it sounds like a manmade drowning pool," said Peet.

"That's what I thought. But Riker felt it was safe to leave the boy alone as long as he stayed away from the fast-moving river. He and Danny messed around and threw rocks into the river even as Michael tried to fish."

"Seems like Riker was driving the fish away. That makes no sense," said Peet.

"Yep. Riker said it was Michael's idea for them to go someplace else and leave him alone. So Riker took Danny downstream about a hundred yards and around a small bend in the river that was out of sight of Michael. He directed Danny to stay there, while he looked for a tree branch to improvise a fishing pole."

"Most dads would have the kid help find a suitable pole."

"Yep. And get this — Riker said he changed his mind and decided to get into his truck and drive around the campground to look for a different location where both boys could fish together. He was gone only a few minutes, and then returned to the same spot to park."

"How convenient. He was out of eyeshot from Danny."

"Uh-huh. And he said that from his pickup, he was unable to see the location where he presumed Michael was still fishing. The bank down to the river drops off sharply from the campsite, and the only way to see the fishing hole was to walk to the edge of the bank."

"Did he check on Michael?"

"Nope. He assumed Michael was okay and still fishing, and walked downriver to check on Danny instead."

Peet scribbled a few more notes, shaking his head.

"Riker previously told Danny that he'd be back in just a few minutes, and he didn't want Danny to get scared if he was left alone too long. He said he was gone about five to ten minutes at most. Once he got back to Danny, Riker suggested they go look for Michael. He told Danny to look down by the fishing hole, and he'd walk towards the restrooms in case Michael had gone there."

"Let me guess. As he moseyed toward the restrooms, Danny yelled to him that Michael was in the water."

"Bingo. Riker told me he ran as fast as he could and jumped in to save Michael, who was totally submerged. Riker couldn't swim, or so he claims, and he was afraid of water, but he didn't think about that initially. He couldn't reach Michael on his first try because Michael's body was drifting slowly in a circle along the bottom. Riker thought the river's current was causing a small whirlpool, and there was a chance the current might discharge Michael's body from the pool and into the main river channel."

"So, Riker gave up?"

"No. He made a couple of attempts to reach Michael but then asked Danny if he could swim. Danny said he could, and Riker asked Danny to get a rope from his pickup and he tied one end around Danny's wrist, and then Danny could then go in after Michael."

"Pretty risky sending a little kid into a whirlpool."

"Maybe, but I think Riker wanted to delay Michael's rescue for as long as possible. He said Danny agreed to wade into the pool, but it was deeper than he thought, so the poor kid had to dive under the water. Riker said it took Danny several attempts before he success-fully reached Michael's arm and pull him to the edge. Riker was able to reach him and pull Michael from the water."

"Pretty traumatizing."

"Indeed," Morris agreed. "Riker then carried Michael part way up the embankment and started CPR. After a few minutes, he carried Michael farther up the bank to the flat area near his truck and started CPR again. He said it wasn't long before Roger and Judy Sterling became aware of the commotion and walked over to offer their help. Riker said he took turns with Roger performing CPR and trying to stop the bleeding on Michael's head."

"Meaning that Michael must have still been alive at that point because dead bodies don't bleed," Peet observed.

"Exactly. Roger Sterling offered to drive down the mountain to find a cell phone signal since there wasn't one at the campground. Riker insisted that he'd do that and would be back with help as soon as he could."

"Was that another attempt to delay getting help for Michael?" Peet asked.

"Very likely. Roger Sterling might have gotten help faster."

"Then…let me guess…Riker claimed he got into his pickup and drove towards the Wilsall Fire Station," said Peet with a touch of sarcasm.

"Correct! He said he was driving so fast that he nearly went off the road a couple of times. Once he got to the fire station, Riker used their red emergency phone to call 911. He left his pickup at the fire station and rode back up here with the fire chief."

20

NOT ADDING UP

"Well," Peet said, "that's a very interesting story and quite different from the version I got from Danny and both of the Sterlings."

"You don't say," said Morris, wryly.

"Danny told me it was Riker's idea to separate both boys, and Riker took Danny downriver and told him to wait there until he returned with a homemade fishing pole. Danny said during the time Riker was gone, he caught a glimpse of Riker squatting behind some bushes, watching him. He also said he never saw Riker drive around the campground."

"Not surprised," Morris said.

"Yep. The rest of Riker's story matches up to Danny's, except for the part where Riker said he jumped into the water," said Peet. "The boy said Riker told him he was afraid of water and couldn't swim and that Riker never entered the water other than to reach down to get a hold of Michael's hand. In fact, the boy said when Riker returned to Danny's location, his pant legs were already wet almost to his knees."

"Interesting."

"Yeah, and get this. Danny said Riker tied a rope around his wrist and asked him to go into the water after Michael. Danny told me he made several attempts trying to get a hold of Michael's hand or arm, but every time he would almost reach Michael, he felt a slight pull on the rope."

"Which prevented him from grabbing Michael," said Morris.

"Exactly. Danny said after he told Riker to stop pulling on the rope, he was able to reach Michael. He pulled Michael to the bank, and Riker lifted Michael out of the water."

"Any other inconsistencies?" asked Morris.

"Yes, Danny also said Riker was gone for at least fifteen or twenty minutes and not the five or ten minutes Riker told you. The other thing I find surprising is Riker never said anything to you about their dog," said Peet.

"No, he didn't mention that. What kind of dog?" Morris asked.

"According to Danny," Peet said, "it was Michael's dog, a black cocker spaniel named Max. Danny said Michael and the dog went everywhere together."

"Did either Roger or Judy Sterling say anything about seeing a dog?" Morris asked.

"Mrs. Sterling said she saw a small black dog run past the front of Riker's parked pickup just minutes before all the commotion began," said Peet. "She wasn't positive if the dog had something in its mouth before it disappeared into the woods. She assumed the dog belonged to the deceased little boy."

"I'm making a note to follow up on the dog's whereabouts," Morris said. "The Sterlings will be at the campground for several days, so the dog might show up. Hopefully, they will look out for him. What else did the Sterlings say?"

"Their plan was to spend several days at the campground, and they could tell Riker would be there only for a short time longer. Since the Sterlings wanted to relocate their campsite to his after Riker left, they kept a close watch on his pickup. They told me at no time did Riker ever move his truck. They also said when they came over to help with the CPR, Riker wasn't wet, except up to his knees and on the front of his shirt from carrying Michael," said Peet.

"All the conflicting stories just don't add up," Morris observed.

"Yeah, it strikes me as odd that Riker would gravitate to such a small and remote campground, with only four campsites and miles from town. He told me he'd never been here before yesterday when he came with the four kids. He knew yesterday there was no cell service available up here. But apparently, he liked what he saw. No pun intended, but it all sounds too fishy to me," added Peet.

"For what it's worth, I also believe he was much too quick to volunteer he works as a prison guard at the state prison in Deer Lodge," said Morris. "Like that was supposed to impress me or something. Maybe he thinks we're all on the same side of the "thin blue line" and that would give him more credibility."

"He should know that when it comes to the death of a child, it doesn't work that way," Peet replied.

"We have two different versions of events about separating the two boys and whose idea it was and why," said Morris. "Why not fashion a homemade fishing pole from materials found close to where Michael was fishing and let both boys fish together? Why separate them in the first place, especially since Danny was invited to come with Michael as his friend and presumably fishing buddy?"

"Yes, and what do you make of the contradiction between Riker saying he drove around the campground looking for another place where both boys could fish? He said the reason he separated them was at Michael's request, yet we have Danny saying it was Riker's idea to separate them," Peet responded.

"Let's not forget there is the fifteen to twenty minutes of unaccounted for time Riker was doing something, somewhere. We know he wasn't making a homemade fishing pole for Danny, and we also know he wasn't driving around the campground looking for a better fishing place. Hell's bells, the campground is so small, and the river only fronts two campsites, so it would've taken only minutes to walk the entire area," Morris added.

"Then there is also the contradiction between what Riker said about jumping into the water and what the Sterlings and Danny said. It might've been believable when Riker said he'd jumped into the water to save his son. What father wouldn't do the same thing, whether or not he could swim? He could easily tell how deep the water was. However, Riker obviously didn't go into the water since his pants were hardly wet. So, that begs the question, how did his pant legs get wet in the first place?" Peet asked.

"All very good questions, Peet. All the conflicting accounts are suspicious, and there's more to this story than we know. I hope the autopsy will shed additional light on the situation," said Morris.

"Let's get together with Detectives Wyatt and Judd next week and bring them up to speed. If anyone can find answers, they will," Peet replied.

21.

AUTOPSY REPORT

Notes

Detective Russ Wyatt on the Case

I, Russ Wyatt, have a reputation as a no-nonsense, seasoned investigator. But I do have my soft spots, namely kids and dogs.

I also have a somewhat bizarre sense of humor, mostly to mask all the emotional and haunting experiences I have had in my 27-year law enforcement career. For the past ten years, I've been the senior detective at the Park County Sheriff's Department. Being one of only two detectives for the entire department, me and my partner, Steven Judd, handle every type of investigation that comes our way — from check fraud, robbery, rape and to murder, and everything else in between.

Judd was an exemplary sidekick and partner. True, my once red hair was now white, which matched my well-kept small, white goatee. Our standing joke was that my white hair was a sign of wisdom, rather than age. But then my hair thinned to the point of almost being bald. I still tease my now 50-year-old daughter for my balding head of white hair.

Like most cops, I had a sweet tooth, mostly for pastries, and that was reflected in a slight bulge around my belt. Still, at 6'2" and 205 pounds, a little bulge was no big deal. I found that my physical stature and likability commanded respect from almost everyone.

Judd was ten years younger than me, and by the way, "Judd" was basically the only name he went by. We worked well together. Our mutual respect was obvious, whether we were together or apart. Normally, we each had our own caseload of investigations. Judd was smaller than me, both in height and weight. He was more conscientious about working out and staying in shape. I was close to retirement, and Judd knew he'd have some big shoes to fill once I left. I envied his full head of thick, jet-black hair, which contrasted with mine. Around the department, we were respectfully called the salt and pepper boys.

Judd and I have always worked closely with other law enforcement agencies, and, in fact, depended on them for vital information. We looked forward to a briefing from Deputies John Peet and Gordon Morris.

Peet and Morris had both been around for a while and were approaching fifty years of age. Both served with the sheriff's department for the same length of time, going on twenty years. Peet and Morris's sense of humor was sometimes undetectable to others but was always present, and easy to discern once someone got to know them.

Although they seldom worked together, this case was an exception. As patrol deputies, working alone with hundreds of miles of territory before any backup was available, they had to rely on their wit, their quick thinking, and fast reflexes. In many instances, they also had to rely on their brawn, and their mental agility to de-escalate a situation.

❀ ❀ ❀

The following Monday, Deputies Peet and Morris met with both Judd and me about the suspicious drowning of Michael Riker.

When I saw Deputies Peet and Morris approaching my desk, I said, "Look Judd, Peet's bringing us donuts. What do you think they want?"

"Relax guys," Peet said, "We're just here to bring you two gumshoes up to speed on what we learned about the drowning of a young boy you two Dick Tracy's might be interested in. Here's our preliminary investigation," Peet said while handing me a folder.

I took the folder and began flipping through it, with my partner, Judd, looking over my shoulder.

Peet said, "From our initial examination of the scene and preliminary witness statements, including the victim's adoptive father, there were things we discovered that made us think of you two. Now, if you don't want to hear about it or are just too busy, we'll take our donuts and leave."

"Not so quick there, Peet. Share the donuts, and I'll get some coffee," I offered with a grin.

Over glazed confections and steaming cups of liquid adrenaline, Peet and Morris laid out the interviews, suspicious contradictions, and crime scene notes. "Our guts told us that this was no accident — the boy was most likely killed," said Morris.

"But why?" Peet asked aloud.

"We've done some digging ourselves and have information to share with you too," Judd said. "First off, we just received the autopsy from Dr. Edwards with the Park County Medical Examiner's Office. Doc concluded the cause of death was accidental drowning, most likely from slipping on rocks, hitting his head, and then falling into the water. So, it sounds like the good doctor has already written this one off as accidental."

"However," I interjected, "if I were a betting man, which I am, I'd wager the M.E. is about to change his tune. I'm almost 100% positive this is about life insurance."

"Do tell," said Peet, who sat his cup on my desk and leaned forward, all ears.

"I got a heads up about this case over the weekend from a private investigator. I then called the insurance company and was referred to the insurance attorney. He asked if I was aware that Michael's parents were the named beneficiaries of two overlapping life insurance policies, to the tune of $650,000."

"No kidding!" Morris exclaimed

"Serious as a heart attack. The attorney said the most recent policy was written just three months prior to the boy's death. And the first policy was less than a year before that."

"It's odd for a boy that age to have two high dollar value life insurance policies," Peet stated.

"Exactly. According to the attorney, it's extremely unusual," I answered.

"And now, we can pass that information on to the medical examiner," said Judd. "Do you two flat foots want to stick around for that phone call?"

"What do you think?" Morris sarcastically responded.

"Dialing the good Doc now," I said, making sure the call was on speaker.

22.

MEDICAL EXAMINER

Notes

Detective Russ Wyatt on the Case

Doc answered the phone on the third ring, "Hello. Dr. Edwards, Chief Medical Examiner. Can I help you?"

Dr. Edwards had been the county's chief medical examiner for well over 50 years. His experience in that position was legendary. As the only examiner in the office, he had little time to spend on individual cases, and his budget was minimal. Thus, keeping current on new medical techniques, methods, and procedures was challenging, let alone acquiring state-of-the-art equipment. Still, Dr. Edwards always gave freely of his time and knowledge to law enforcement and put his best foot forward each and every day.

"Hi Doc. Detective Russ Wyatt here from the Park County Sheriff's Department. We just received your autopsy findings on Michael Riker, the young drowning victim from last week.

"Oh, yes. Always such a tragedy when children are involved," he said.

"Would you be interested in knowing some information we just received from an attorney for two life insurance companies?"

"Lay it on me," the M.E. replied.

"Their attorney told us Michael had not one, but two life insurance policies totaling $650,000, and his parents were the beneficiaries."

"Well, that certainly would be enough reason, under normal circumstances, to reexamine the body and double-check my conclusions."

"What do you mean, Doc, when you say under normal circumstances?"

"What I mean is as soon as I released my autopsy report, I had a request from his parents to release their son's body. I have since learned Michael has already been cremated. Obviously, I no longer have a body to reexamine. All I have are the photographs of his body, my notes, and the lab results."

"So, are you still confident the cause of death was by drowning? Or, do you now question if it was accidental?"

"That would be an accurate statement. I'm going to amend the autopsy report's conclusion to say, "Drowning, but under suspicious circumstances.""

"Doc, the attorney told us both insurance companies intend to open their own investigation, and I'm sure you'll be hearing from Dan Player, their contracted insurance investigator. As long as the Sheriff's Department and the insurance companies have open, ongoing investigations, they don't intend to pay any insurance money."

"I see," said Doc.

"Are you aware of the Slayers Act?" I asked.

"Explain," said Doc.

"The act basically says a person causing the death of another can't benefit from that death. Detective Judd and I have just opened a criminal investigation. In fact, we have the two deputies standing in our office who were the first responding officers to the scene, and they did an initial investigation."

"And under these circumstances, detective, I agree they shouldn't pay a dime," Doc agreed.

"If we hear anything regarding the insurance companies' inquiries, we'll let you know. Likewise, if you learn anything new concerning this death, please give us a call."

"I sure will," Doc promised.

"Oh, and would you send us all the photographs you have of the boy? Also, did you observe any signs of bruising on the boy's body that would be consistent with falling on rocks before falling into the water?" I asked.

"I'll get photos right over to you. I don't specifically remember where on the boy's head the skull fracture was located, whether it was on the back of his head or on the top of his head. I do remember there were no signs of any bruising on his body, which in hindsight, I would've expected to find if he'd fallen on river rocks before falling into the water. I'll double check my autopsy photos again for both the location of the head injury and for any signs of bruising."

"Doc, you just said the boy had a skull fracture. Does it strike you odd that a boy weighing about 70 pounds and about four and a half feet tall could fall on river rocks with such force as to cause a skull fracture?"

"Now that you mention it; that would be unusual. Also, while we've been talking, I have several photographs in front of me depicting the boy's head injury. It was on the upper center area of the parietal bone, near the zygomatic arch. In non-medical terms, that means the top portion of his head and not the back portion. In addition, the depression skull-fracture appears to be in a downward direction and not from the back of the head in a forward direction."

"That's valuable information, Doc," I said.

"Is there any evidence to suggest the boy might've jumped from some height and then hit the top of his head on a rock?" asked Doc. "If so, such evidence would be consistent with the photos. Absent such evidence, I don't know how a small boy could've suffered such severe injuries to the top of his head by falling backward."

"We'd like to see the complete report with your notes," I asked, more an order than a request.

"Certainly. But my report and the photographs also don't make any reference to bruising, and I'm confident if bruising had been observed, it would be noted in my autopsy report."

"Interesting. Anything else?"

"One last thing. As I am looking at the x-rays, the boy also had a neck compression between Atlas C-1 and Axis C-2.

"I see. Well, thanks for the information, Doc."

"Thank you for your call and the update, detective. I'll be amending my autopsy report accordingly. Good luck with your investigation."

As the four of us sat around the table discussing what we learned from the medical examiner, we were astounded. Most disturbing were the obvious bits of evidence that Doc had failed to note during the autopsy. For example, why didn't he pick up on the lack of bruising? Why did he fail to notice the downward trajectory and location of the skull fracture? And why didn't he perform additional tests and ask more questions before so quickly releasing the body?

During our phone conversation, Doc had asked if there was evidence to suggest Michael might've jumped from some height and then hit his head. Why hadn't he asked that very question earlier? Peet and Morris would have told him there was no location from which Michael could've jumped.

If Michael intentionally dove into the water and then hit his head, the water should've cushioned the effect of the injury and likely wouldn't have resulted in a severe compound skull fracture and compressed vertebrae in his neck. And how, we discussed, was it even possible for someone to fall backward on a level surface, suffer a skull fracture that would have surely rendered that person unconscious, and then somehow end up in the water? Wouldn't the unconscious person be situated in the same configuration where he or she had fallen?

And how did the boy's fishing pole end up in the water, along with his body, if he had fallen backward and not forward?

Lastly, we questioned why the parents were in such a hurry to have Michael's body cremated. We were all in agreement that no case was more disturbing and sinister than the suspicious death of a young child. No one wants to think parents are capable of such a terrible act... especially if the act included profiting from the death of a child. Now, it appeared the parents were in the clear after the coroner's accidental cause of death ruling, and that was that.

To complicate matters even more, the day after the medical examiner completed his investigation, Michael's body was released to his parents. The very next day, Michael was cremated. Even if we had sufficient reason to reexamine the body for evidence of a crime, we were thwarted.

23.

BETRAYED BY ALL

Detective Russ Wyatt on the Case

The all-important phone conversation I had with the insurance attorney changed the entire scope and direction of our investigation. Judd and I concluded there were sufficient facts leading a reasonable person to believe a crime may have been committed. That was the litmus test to initiate a thorough criminal investigation. Judd and I obtained every report we could find from local law enforcement about the Riker family and combed through all the witness statements obtained by Peet and Morris, as well as their initial case report.

So, with my obsessive-compulsive brain on high alert, I swore to the soul of the murdered boy that I would crack this financially motivated fraud, turned murder-for-profit scheme. Every child deserved my utmost, especially children who were cold in their graves and watching from above. But first, as any hardened detective will tell you, I had to get inside the dark and disturbed minds of Michael's parents — not just their motives and thoughts, but how they managed to work the system.

The criminal investigation now included me, other city and county law enforcement officers, a private insurance investigator, a certified fraud examiner, a CPA, and a forensic pathologist. I was pleasantly surprised how well we all worked together, which for me was the first-time law enforcement and the private sector had had such a close relationship, all striving to uncover the truth.

In order to be a successful detective, I've always made it my practice to know the victim in ways some would argue was not necessary. But that was how I conduct investigations. After all, someone must speak for the victims since they are no longer able to speak for themselves. And what better way to speak for the victim, then to know them intimately.

As I walk back through the case, I'm compelled to call out the county medical examiner. He quickly ruled the death an accidental drowning, which started a chain reaction. The school provided grief counselors to Michael Riker's 4th-grade classmates. His "parents" were sent condolence cards and money from a stunned public to cover the funeral expenses. For the first time in their worthless lives, the Rikers felt like heroes. After all, there weren't many other people they knew who fostered and adopted out of the largesse of their hearts. On top of that, Leroy was a law enforcement officer who worked within the prison system. He was thanked for his service as he and Lora posed for the media, choking back fake tears.

Choking back laughter was more like it. They had planned for months how they would go about spending the expected life insurance proceeds.

But I'm getting ahead of myself. The backstory was much more revealing. It's about the death of a child, and how the investigation worked its way through the legal system. I tracked the facts and, from my notes, put together what I *suspected* had occurred. Again, proving it was the challenge.

I continued peeling the onion one awful layer at a time. Judd and I wanted to know how Michael, a sweet, lovable, and intelligent boy, happened into the foster care system.

"Hey Russ, what's the background of Michael's adoptive parents?" Judd wondered out loud.

"That's a good question. What qualified them to be foster parents, let alone adoptive parents? And why did he die in their care?" I answered. "Let's find out."

We were about to do a deep dive into why Martha Maddox lost custody and how Michael came to be adopted by the Rikers. Those things don't just happen without a good reason. My first step was to contact the Livingston Police Department.

"This is Detective Russ Wyatt from the Park County Sheriff's Department. I'd like to speak to one of your detectives, please."

"I'll put you through to Detective Keith French," the Livingston Police dispatcher said.

Once I had Detective French on the phone, I said, "I'm working a potential child homicide in the county. Have you had any calls to Leroy and Lora Riker's residence, the victim's adoptive parents, or have they ever been suspects in criminal activity?"

"Can I get back to you on that, Detective Wyatt? It shouldn't take too long."

"Sure thing."

As I waited, my next step was to contact the Family District Court. If Michael had been removed from his mother, that's where the record would be. From there, I contacted the child services agency responsible for foster placement. I was confident there should be an application process and some type of a due diligence investigation into the background of the prospective adoptive parents.

What I learned was startling.

"Detective Wyatt, this is detective Keith French with Livingston Police. We've received several calls from school officials and neighbors regarding a "check on the welfare" of a minor. Michael Riker, it was reported, often came to school without a lunch or even money for a lunch. His clothes were described as hand-me-downs and most likely were his half-sister's clothes. Michael also had the appearance of being unkempt."

In other words, the care he received after adoption was no better than the care he received from his biological mother, Martha, I thought. It pissed me off.

Likewise, child protective services received numerous similar calls about the Rikers. CPS followed up with scheduled home visits when they could. Of course, the assigned case worker's records indicated that no issues were ever observed in the home.

I also discovered that the hands of school officials were often tied by statutes as to what authority they had to intervene or get involved with any issues outside of the classroom. Granted, they were considered mandatory reporters when it came to the health and welfare of children in their care, but that was the extent of their obligation and authority. Those reports often just fell into a deep in-basket of someone else.

The poor kid was neglected by all his caregivers. Every single one.

Much of what I learned came from public records, interviews with law enforcement officials, and from Martha Maddox. In other words, what I learned, or at least a great deal of it, was also available to the state agency responsible for foster child placement services. But did they look? Apparently not. What about the application to be a foster parent? What did it ask, and what information was verified by the state?

Again, not much. The application asked for less information than a job application. One important criterion was whether the applicants had sufficient financial resources to cover their existing personal and family expenses without the need for supplemental income from the state. In other words, the state wanted to make sure that all of the foster child support money would go directly to the support of the foster child and would not be used or needed for other purposes.

If the answer was yes, then the application asked about annual family income and expenses. There was no requirement to provide tax returns, payroll records, bank statements, mortgage or rental receipts, or any documentation to support the information provided in the application. Had there been, the state would have been able to readily determine that everything on the Rikers' foster application was a lie.

It made me sick to my stomach.

I learned that a few months earlier, the Livingston police and medic unit had responded to a 911 call from his biological mother's residence, which resulted in her being transported to the hospital for a drug overdose.

Michael's 911 phone call started the domino effect of what was to follow. Search warrants of Martha's apartment. Her arrest. Criminal court hearings for drug possession and child endangerment. Civil court hearings regarding the custody of Michael. And ultimately a guilty plea, loss of custody and a minimum six-month prison sentence.

❖ ❖ ❖

"Hey, Judd," I said as we sorted through the paperwork, "have you ever adopted a dog?"

"Yeah, several times. Why?"

"What was that like?"

"Well, they put me through the ringer. Paperwork, character references, prior veterinarian files, the layout of my house and yard, etc., etc."

"Yeah, same here."

"Oh, and I had one rejection."

"Rejection? Seriously?"

"Serious as a heart attack. It happened about ten years back. I already had a mutt and built him a dog door. Worked great because he went outside to do his business and didn't have to wait for me to come home. But the shelter insisted that I crate-train the new puppy. Didn't seem fair, keeping one in a cage all day while the other had a house and a yard. So, I argued on behalf of the dog's freedom, and they denied my application."

"Sounds like a lot of due diligence, just for a dog," I said. "If only the foster child agencies put that much effort into placing children, Michael might still be alive."

"The irony," said Judd.

"It's reprehensible," I added.

24.

CLUES FROM THE STERLINGS

Notes

Detective Russ Wyatt on the Case

On Tuesday, following the drowning death, Judd and I re-interviewed Roger and Judy Sterling, who were still camped at the Shields River Campground. Sitting at their campfire, they described the events leading up to performing CPR on Michael.

"No, we didn't see Leroy Riker ever move his truck, and we were watching closely," said Judy.

"Leroy seemed to be pacing around, going downstream and then upstream and in and out of the tree line. At one point, he seemed to be talking to himself in front of an empty tent," said Roger.

One thing Judy said that piqued my interest was that Leroy didn't seem to know how to properly perform CPR, and that he initially refused assistance from them.

While we talked, a black cocker spaniel slowly emerged from their tent.

"I'm guessing your name is Max," I said while gently taking a knee and speaking directly to the dog.

Max raised his head in acknowledgment of his name and wagged his tail.

"Have you two met before?" Judy asked.

"No, but the two sheriff deputies who were here the night of the drowning told us how Michael and Max were inseparable."

"Max has been in mourning since the night he showed up at our tent. He slept with us Friday night and hasn't left our sides since Michael's death," said Roger. "I had to make the trek to town to buy dog food and a leash."

"He even whimpers himself to sleep, and we have to wake him during the night because we can tell he's having a bad dream," said Judy.

"How so?" I asked.

"He tries to bark and growl in his sleep, and his little legs move around frantically," she responded. "It would be humorous, if it wasn't so sad."

"He's probably reliving some of the events he must have witnessed," Judd offered.

"That is really sad," Roger said.

"Did either of you see Max the day Michael died, other than when he appeared at your tent?"

"I saw him when the boys first arrived at the campground and while they were having a snack before fishing," Judy said.

"Any other time?" I asked.

"There was one other time I saw the dog flying past Riker's truck and running full speed downstream towards the trees," Judy said.

"Did you find that unusual?" Judd asked.

"It was unusual because Michael was nowhere to be seen. I should add, we both thought Max had something in his mouth, but he was moving so quickly it was difficult to see."

Roger spoke up and added, "Max has also been acting strange during the day. It's almost like he wants us to follow or chase him. We keep him on the leash during the day, but he tugs on it and whines and points."

"Have you ever tried to see what he wants?" I asked.

"No," they both said. "We just assumed he wanted to go find his master and we knew that wasn't possible."

"Actually," Roger added, "We don't want to encourage him to roam around. It would be terrible if he got lost or, God forbid, fell into the river. I don't think he could survive on his own."

I asked them if they saw anyone else at the campground that day or anyone associated with the tent. In response, they both said "No." I asked them if there was anything else they thought I should know, anything at all they saw or heard.

Roger said he couldn't think of anything else, but then Judy said, "What about those obnoxious ravens?"

"Ravens?" I asked. "What about ravens?"

Roger said, "It's probably nothing. It's just that there were about a half dozen ravens that landed in trees near the river and another half dozen soaring above. They were all making an obnoxious squawking and screeching racket, and we could hear Max barking. Then, after about ten minutes, they all stopped at once, and the ones in the trees flew off, and they lit out of here."

"That's odd," Judd observed.

"Well, like I said, it probably doesn't mean anything, but it wasn't long after when we saw Leroy Riker carrying the boy's body up the hill. Right out of some Alfred Hitchcock movie, right?"

"Yeah, that does sound weird. Too bad I don't speak raven," I said. "I'd like to know exactly what they saw from their bird's-eye-view, no pun intended. How long would you say it was from the time the ravens stopped making the awful racket," I asked, "and when you next saw Leroy Riker?"

"Less than five minutes," Roger said while looking in the direction of his wife for confirmation.

"Right around that, maybe slightly more," Judy added. Remember, dear, we saw Leroy walk downstream from near his truck in the direction where he had taken the other boy right after all the ravens left. Then we saw the other boy walking upstream in the direction where Michael had been fishing. Then, a few minutes later, we saw Leroy walk quickly across the campground from near the outhouses towards the other boy. The other boy was yelling at Leroy, all alarmed."

"You said a few minutes ago you heard Max barking while the ravens were making the noise," I said. "When did you see Max running into the woods with maybe something in his mouth?"

"Around the same time, the ravens stopped squawking, and before we saw Riker. Maybe the ravens scared him when they flew off," Judy speculated.

Or maybe something or someone scared him, I thought.

"We noticed a cardboard memorial for Michael on the tree by the river when we arrived today. Any idea when it was put there, and by whom?"

"The Riker family came by this morning and put that up. You didn't miss them by much. We got to meet Leroy's wife and their daughter for a short time. It was kind of odd though, that none of them seemed all that broken up about the death of Michael."

"How so?" Judd asked.

"Well, on Friday, we learned from the other young boy that he was the one who had gone into the water. Leroy told him that he was afraid of water. Then this morning, when they were all here, we watched Leroy wade into the water while his wife, Lora, videotaped him."

"So what did you find odd about that?" I asked.

"The whole time Lora was videoing Leroy, the two of them were joking and laughing. Leroy even made a joke about how cold the water was on his, well, his private parts."

"Do you know why Leroy went into the water today?"

"Yeah. He went in to get Michael's fishing pole. They said something about returning it to the store for a refund."

"Did they look for Max? Call for him?" I asked.

"No, not at all. And Max knew they were there. He hid in the tent, and we decided to keep him there and not say a word. Honestly, we think they'd just dump him."

"Why's that?" Asked Judd.

"Just a bad feeling. Something's off about that family."

"When do you plan to leave here? I asked.

"We leave this coming Friday, probably before noon. That will give us a full week being here," Roger said.

"Are you taking Max with you?"

"Oh, yes! He's pretty much adopted us, and we've adopted him back."

"I'm happy to hear that. You never know, we might need to revisit Max's part in all of this. We'll reach out if that's the case. Thank you for sharing these details."

"Happy to help," they both said. "And remember, you always have visitation rights with Max anytime you want."

"I might very well take you up on that someday," I said. "I feel a bond with Max, just like with Michael. They don't call me an ol' softy for no reason," I chuckled.

25.

FOLLOWING THE MONEY

Michael died one week short of a full year since his adoption was final. It was slightly over three months after his second life insurance policy went into effect. Five days after his death, Lora Riker filed a demand with both life insurance companies for payment of the full insurance benefits, including for accidental death, totaling $650,000. Six weeks after Lora's demand for the insurance death benefits, she also initiated a civil lawsuit against both insurance companies for their "bad faith" failure to pay the death benefits in accordance with the terms of the insurance contract and for the company's unnecessary delay.

Bad faith often involves an insurer's failure to pay the insured's claim, or a claim brought by a third party. The Riker's lawsuit initiated the civil discovery process allowing both the Rikers and the insurance companies to schedule depositions and issue subpoenas for documents. The civil investigative process, in the search for the truth, had begun.

Both life insurance companies wanted to know if there was evidence of foul play regarding the drowning death of the insured and if the beneficiaries had a financial motive or any involvement in

Michael Riker's death. The insurance companies noticed more than just a couple of red flags, and they wanted those issues addressed before they paid a substantial insurance claim. One critical question had to do with establishing whether Leroy Riker had any prior knowledge of the two life insurance policies in effect at the time of Michael's death.

Lora Riker swore she hadn't told her husband about purchasing either life insurance policy until the evening of Michael's death. Leroy said he was surprised Lora had purchased both policies without him knowing about them and said he only became aware of their existence afterwards.

The insurance companies told the Rikers that they wouldn't pay out the policies — not until the active criminal investigation into Michael's death was complete. Also, the Rikers were made aware that the insurance companies were initiating their own investigation that would also delay the payment. That investigation had been initiated immediately after learning of Michael's death.

The very first thing the insurance companies did was send a private investigator, Kevin Ross, owner of Comprehensive Insurance Investigations, to interview the Rikers. Ross was well-known by both insurance companies for his excellent work, and he knew exactly what information the insurance companies needed in order to evaluate a life insurance death claim.

Mr. Ross contacted Mr. and Mrs. Riker and set up an appointment at their residence for an "examination under oath," an EUO. This type of interview is required under the terms of the insurance contract. Failure to agree to a EUO interview would result in an automatic denial of an insurance claim. Providing knowingly false statements under oath during such an interview could result in even more serious charges, including fraud and perjury.

The information collected during the examination under oath is then evaluated and compared to other facts. If the information is corroborated, the insurance money is paid. During the course of the insurance investigation or any subsequent criminal investigation related to the insurance claim, it's common for insurance companies to withhold payment of insurance benefits. Insurance policies are a legal contract between the "insurer" and the "insured." An insurance company can be legally liable under the "bad faith doctrine" for unreasonably delaying and/or denying a legitimate insurance claim. Both insurance companies knew their legal obligation to promptly investigate a claim and to do so thoroughly and professionally.

Kevin Ross was also directed to check out the Shields River Campground and the surrounding area. At the campground, Ross observed a cardboard sign nailed to a tree that read, "Gone Fishing. Rest in Peace Michael."

Both insurance companies hired several top-notch professionals to assist in the insurance claim investigation. Dr. Kay Burkett, a nationally renowned Certified Forensic Pathologist in Louisville, Kentucky, was the first such expert hired. A forensic pathologist is a specific branch of medicine that establishes or interprets evidence dealing with causes of death, specifically looking for potential criminality. A pathologist's training is different from that of a medical examiner and is longer in duration and more focused. Dr. Burkett was tasked with reviewing the photographs, reports, and notes of Dr. Edwards, the Park County Medical Examiner.

Next to be hired were Greg O'Reilly, CPA, and an independent investigator and Certified Fraud Examiner, Dan Player. The insurance companies' theory was that the suspected insurance fraud would come down to the Rikers having a documented financial need for a windfall of money. Since Michael's suspicious death was a critical component of the insurance fraud scheme, the insurance companies knew they'd have to establish evidence showing Leroy Riker knew about Michael's life insurance policies prior to Michael's death. Without that evidence, Michael's death and the two life insurance policies would be nothing more than a coincidence, and they'd be unable to establish a motive or a cause and effect between the two.

26.

FRAUD TRIANGLE

Dan Player, CFE, had years of experience investigating financial fraud and white-collar crimes. These involved public corruption and complex drug and money laundering cases.

For much of his career, Player worked for the State of Montana and eventually retired from public service and started his own consulting business. Unlike most cops, Player loved a complex paper case. He often joked, the more documents involved, the more he would salivate like Pavlov's dog. Player's ability to speak the language of CPAs, prosecutors, and cops meant he got along with everyone. His biggest gift, he often quipped, was his "gift of gab." He said he inherited this gift to talk to people from all walks of life from his father.

O'Reilly and Player received boxes of financial and insurance records obtained by the insurance companies through the civil discovery process. From these records, O'Reilly and Player prepared multiple Excel spreadsheets, event chronologies, and link charts and did an analysis of all the information stretching back five years.

What O'Reilly and Player learned from these documents was Lora and Leroy's money woes had been piling up for years. During the fifteen years of their marriage, they'd filed for bankruptcy on three occasions. The year before Michael's adoption was final, they wrote over 300 bounced checks from three different checking accounts with associated bank fees in excess of $6,000. During that same year, their bank account began and/or ended with a negative balance for five out of twelve months. The year Michael was adopted, the number of non-sufficient funds checks increased to over 400, with associated bank fees in excess of $6,700. That year, their bank account began and/or ended with a negative balance for ten out of the twelve months.

O'Reilly and Player also found clear and convincing evidence that the Rikers were deeply in debt prior to Michael's adoption. A bank foreclosure resulted in the loss of their only home with a mortgage. Afterward, they had difficulty paying their house rent. Several banks took the unusual step of cancelling their bank accounts due to excessive insufficient fund check activity.

As a Certified Fraud Examiner, Dan Player, knew that the three cornerstones of the National Association of CFE's "Fraud Triangle" were: Opportunity, Rationalization (also called Justification), and Financial Need (also called Pressure, Incentive or Motivation). The hypothesis was first conceptualized by Leroy Cressey in 1953, whose widely used and accepted theory was that an otherwise honest person wouldn't resort to fraud unless and until all three elements of the fraud triangle were present.

An experienced CFE uses the fraud triangle model to analyze the evidence of a fraud case. In the case of Michael's drowning, it would be easy to establish Leroy Riker had the "Opportunity." He was the only known person near Michael at the time of his drowning. Leroy and Lora Riker could easily "rationalize" Michael's death because he wasn't their biological child and was adopted and then substantially insured only as a means to an end. Leroy and Lora's "financial need" was self-evident. Their wants and needs exceeded their income and ability to pay for even their basic household necessities. They hadn't been financially solvent for years and they wouldn't be eligible to file another bankruptcy to discharge their existing debt for several more years. Neither the foster child support money they received from the State of Montana, nor the money they received on Michael's behalf from his biological father's Social Security helped their financial picture.

Player prepared a spreadsheet of all checks, deposits, dates, amounts, and recipients, as well as who prepared and signed the checks. Dan Player noticed something curious about who was writing and signing checks. Player brought his conclusions to Greg O'Reilly's attention.

"Hey Greg, look at this spreadsheet. Check out who specifically was signing checks prior to Michael's adoption. You'll see both Lora and Leroy were actively writing and signing checks from each of their three accounts. However, the day after Michael's adoption, Leroy stopped writing or signing any checks. Now look what happened the day after Michael's death; suddenly Leroy resumed writing and signing checks. What do you make of that?"

Greg responded, "It looks to me like Leroy wanted to have plausible deniability concerning his knowledge of the checks Lora was writing for Michael's insurance. If he were to write any checks during that time period, it would be more difficult for him to deny having any knowledge of the checks Lora was writing, because those checks would show up in the check register or on the bank statements."

"But for someone like Leroy, that doesn't make sense! He had serious control issues regarding the amounts of money his wife was spending," Player responded. "That was a point of conflict between them for years. Suddenly, he's not paying any attention and doesn't have any interest in the family expenses? Given the timing, I don't buy that for a second!"

"Like I said, Dan, it's all about plausible deniability. It makes me think they coordinated this together and Leroy was more aware of the life insurance policies than either one of them wants to let on. Wasn't that exactly the point the prison inmate who worked with Lora mentioned? Something about having a plan and an alibi established in advance. I believe they hatched this entire, elaborate scheme long before Michael was a foster child in their home. There must've been some interesting pillow talks between those two."

One of the more interesting pieces of documentation in the boxes of documents was a prior burglary claim. Dan brought the claim information and the arbitration file to Greg's attention.

"Greg, here's documentation of a prior insurance claim for $75,000. It appears Leroy Riker filed a claim for the theft of personal property associated with a renter's insurance policy. Leroy purchased the additional personal property insurance only a few months prior to an alleged burglary of a set of collectible baseball cards. The insurance claim went to arbitration to establish an accurate value of the allegedly stolen cards. The arbitrator, Kenneth Lang, allowed into evidence documentation showing Mr. Riker had attempted to sell the exact same baseball cards for $750 shortly before the alleged burglary. Mr. Lang concluded the claim was fraudulent and the insurance claim was denied. What do you make of that?"

"It strikes me as evidence of a prior insurance fraud, at least an attempted insurance fraud."

O'Reilly and Player also reviewed tax returns filed by the Rikers. As Player examined an earlier federal tax return, he said to O'Reilly, "Look at this. There's a ten-year-old girl listed here as a dependent, but I have no idea who she is. I know she's not their daughter and I know she's not the same girl they had as a foster child for six months. Besides, it's entirely the wrong tax year for when the foster girl was there. We should make sure the insurance company attorneys know about this and can question Lora and Leroy about it when they take their depositions."

O'Reilly and Player continued their examination of the boxes. When Player came across another interesting document he said, "Hey, look at this Greg. What do you see?"

"I see a contract for the construction of a new home," O'Reilly said.

Player asked, "And what's the date on that contract?"

"I'll be damn. It's dated the day before Michael's death. The contract also references a security deposit for $1,000 along with a specific check number," O'Reilly responded.

"Yeah, and I don't remember inputting a check for $1,000, payable to D.J. Custom Homes or to Don Jackson, the owner, into the spreadsheet," Player remarked.

"Take a look at the check number and compare it to the sequence numbers of other checks to see if it matches up to the checks written on either side of the contract date. That'll help us nail down and confirm the date on the contract. Then we can go back and look at bank statements to see if the check was ever negotiated."

"Yep, the D.J. Custom Home check has the same date as the checks immediately before and immediately after. That confirms the date the check was written was the day immediately prior to Michael's death. So, it appears the Rikers were expecting a windfall of money when they started talks with D.J. Custom Homes and wrote this check. Let's get this information to the sheriff's detectives, and they can confirm this information with Don Jackson. Maybe Jackson has other records related to home construction meetings and negotiations and can shed some light on whatever happened to this $1,000 check and when the Rikers began their discussions with him. Any time prior to Michael's death would be highly suspicious. The check doesn't show up on any of the bank statements as ever being negotiated," Player said.

"Greg, look at this. It's a rental agreement for a camcorder, and it's signed by Lora Riker the day after Michael died. Why on earth would they want a camcorder then?"

"Beats me, but we need to let the detectives know about this also. Maybe there's a VHS tape in their house that will help answer that question when the sheriff's department serves a search warrant. It would be very interesting to see what they were recording the day after Michael died."

27.

WHAT A TANGLED WEB WE WEAVE...

Notes

Detective Russ Wyatt on the Case

Judd and I recognized several contradictions in the events related to the day Michael died. Most significant was Leroy Riker's version that he jumped into the water to save Michael. Other witnesses said Leroy Riker was only wet up to his knees. We also planned to interview the two fire department medics who were on the scene, as well as the fire chief who drove Leroy Riker to and from the Shields River Campground, and anyone else who might be identified as potentially having information about the events of that horrendous day.

Following our interview with Mr. and Mrs. Sterling, second on our list was Danny Williams. Since Danny was the very first person to see Leroy Riker, Danny's version of events was critical for us. The significant question we faced was why were Riker's pant legs wet when Danny saw him. Had he been in the water prior to returning to Danny and before they searched for Michael? Riker's explanation of falling into a mud puddle made no sense. Granted, it had rained all that week, but not the day Michael died. I thought it odd that

Riker was so quick to offer an explanation to Danny. Why did he feel the necessity of offering any explanation?

Beverly Williams told Judd and me that the Rikers had tried to convince her to not allow the police to interview Danny. The explanation was that Danny was much too fragile and young and the police interviewing him might damage him psychologically. Beverly said Danny wanted to talk to the detectives because he was very upset with some statements he'd overheard Leroy make about Michael's drowning.

Judd and I explained to Beverly she was more than welcome to be present during Danny's interview, and she was also welcome to add any information she was aware of at any time. We explained that due to Danny's age, we'd begin by asking the boy a series of questions to determine whether he understood the difference between the truth and a lie — standard procedure.

"Hi Danny, my name is Steven Judd, and this is Russ Wyatt. We are detectives with the Park County Sheriff's Office. How old are you, Danny? Do you prefer being called Danny or Daniel?"

"I prefer Danny, and I'm eleven years old."

"Okay, Danny. Now, it's very important you think carefully before you answer our questions. It's also very important you don't make things up and that you answer truthfully everything we ask. If a question confuses you or you don't understand the question, it's okay for you to ask either one of us to repeat the question. Or, if you don't know the answer to a question, it's okay for you to say you don't know. Please don't exaggerate or lie about anything. Do you know the difference between the truth and a lie?" Judd asked.

"The truth is what actually happened, and a lie is the opposite of the truth."

"So, if you were to say something that was only half true, would that be a lie or the truth?"

"If it was only half true, it would still be a lie because it wasn't the whole truth."

"That's exactly right, Danny. It sounds like your parents and your grandmother have taught you very well."

"Both my parents are dead."

"I'm sorry to hear that. Do you live with your grandmother?"

"Yes. I've lived with her for as long as I can remember."

"How long have you known Michael Riker and his parents?"

"Only for a short time since before school started. We ride, I mean rode, the same school bus together."

"Has anyone suggested to you what you should or shouldn't say to us?" Judd asked.

"No. My grandmother told me to just tell the truth. Mr. Riker didn't want me talking to you, but he didn't tell me what to say."

"Please tell us what happened the day before Michael drowned."

"Michael called me, like, you know, to say he was going with his father, his new sister and her friend to look for a place to go fishing the next day and asked if I wanted to come along. My grandmother said it was okay, so Mr. Riker picked me up."

"What did Mr. Riker tell your grandmother?" I asked.

"That we might be gone for several hours. She said that was okay, as long as I was home in time for dinner."

"And then what happened?"

Only a few miles from my house, Mr. Riker said he wanted to go look at the Yellowstone River to see how high the river was. There's an old bridge that goes over the river down by the old radio station.

When we got to the bridge, Mr. Riker parked his truck at one end of the bridge, and us kids and Max all ran onto the bridge to look at the river."

"Did Mr. Riker say anything about having a flat tire?"

"Maybe. He said, like, he needed to fix something on his truck. I didn't pay much attention. We all just headed for the bridge and Mr. Riker stayed behind."

"Did Mr. Riker say anything else you remember?"

"He told Michael not to climb on the bridge railing and you know, like, not to show off."

"Do you remember Mr. Riker's exact words to Michael?"

"He told Michael, I don't want to see you showing off and climbing on the bridge railing."

"What did Michael say or do?"

"Michael said okay," Danny responded.

"Did Michael do as his father said?" Judd asked.

"You know, we were all goofing around. Michael looked back towards his father, who was kneeling on the ground looking at his truck or the tire. Michael said his father wasn't looking and wouldn't see him walking on the bridge railing. Michael said, like, if his father didn't see him, you know, he wouldn't be doing anything wrong."

"What did Michael do then?"

"Michael said, 'Watch this! I bet I can climb up there and walk on that railing.' The friend of Michael's sister started to dare him to do it, and Michael's sister was telling him not to. But Michael pretended like he was going to climb onto the railing and his sister started screaming at him. Mr. Riker must've heard her, and he yelled at Michael."

"What happened next?"

"We all got back into the truck, and Mr. Riker drove to the same campground where Michael drowned the next day," Danny said.

"What happened when you all got to the campground on Thursday?"

"Mr. Riker told us to sit in the truck, and he walked down to the river to look for a good fishing spot for Michael and me the next day."

"How long were you there that day?"

"Not long; maybe just a few minutes. I still needed to be home in time for dinner."

"And then what happened?"

"Mr. Riker drove me home and, like, asked my grandmother if I could go fishing with him and Michael the next day. She said that was okay with her, but I didn't have a fishing pole. Mr. Riker told my grandmother he'd take care of that."

"What happened the day Michael drowned?" I asked Danny.

"Mr. Riker picked me up, and the three of us drove to the campground. I don't know the name of it. When we arrived at the campground, Mr. Riker parked in the same spot we had been at the day before. Me and Michael went down to the river and started throwing rocks. A few minutes later Mr. Riker also came down and started throwing rocks with us."

"Did Max go with you that day?" Judd asked.

"Yeah."

"Were you all having fun?" I asked.

"Yes, we were all, you know, kinda horsing around. Michael said he wanted to fish, so Mr. Riker went to his truck and came back with a fishing pole for Michael. There was a small pond someone had made by stacking rocks next to the river, and Michael started fishing in it."

"All right. What happened right after that?"

"Mr. Riker and me kept throwing rocks and messing around. After a few minutes, Mr. Riker said we should leave Michael alone to fish in peace, and he'd take me to another good spot so I could fish alone," Danny said.

"Where did Mr. Riker take you?"

"Downstream and around a bend in the river. I don't know how far it was, but I couldn't see Michael from there. Mr. Riker told me to wait there, and he'd go make me a fishing pole from a branch or something."

"Did you see Mr. Riker again before he returned to your location?" I asked.

"I saw him kinda like, you know, kneeling in the woods halfway between me and Michael. He was just, like, watching me."

"When did you see him next?"

"When he came back and asked me if I'd seen or heard anything."

"Was there anything about Mr. Riker that seemed odd to you?" I asked.

"Well, he didn't come back with a branch or a fishing pole like he said. I noticed his pant legs were wet up to his knees, and he told me he'd fallen in a puddle of water. Mr. Riker said we should go look for Michael, and I should go check near the river where Michael had been fishing, and he'd go check near the bathrooms, or maybe I should say outhouses, to see if Michael was there," Danny said.

"What happened next?"

"I walked towards the river, past the pickup and as I started down the bank, I could see Michael in the water. He was kinda floatin', you know, like near the bottom of the fishing pond. I ran back up the bank and yelled to Mr. Riker that Michael was under the water."

"Where was Max at that time?" I asked.

"I don't know. I didn't see Max, but I wasn't thinking about him then."

"Do you now think it's odd that Max was nowhere around?"

"Oh yeah. They are, sorry, were always together. Max walked to school with Michael, on the days Michael walked to school, and then Max was always there to walk Michael home again. I still don't know what happened to Max, but I really hope he is okay. He is really a very smart dog."

"What did Mr. Riker do then?" I inquired.

"Mr. Riker walked quickly, but he didn't run. We went down to the edge of the river where Michael was. Mr. Riker said he was afraid of the water because he couldn't swim, and he asked me if I could swim. I told him I could. He walked back to his pickup and got a rope. He tied one end of the rope around my wrist, and I went into the water and tried to reach Michael."

"That's very brave of you," I said, praising the poor kid who was obviously still shaken by the chain of events.

"Yeah, but whenever I reached out to Michael, the rope around my wrist pulled me back just enough so I couldn't get a grip on him. I finally was able to get a hold of Michael's hand and pulled him towards the bank."

"What did Mr. Riker do?"

"He lifted Michael out of the water and laid him on the bank. He started trying to get Michael to breathe," Danny said.

"What was Mr. Riker doing to get Michael to breathe?" I asked.

"He was breathing into Michael's mouth like I learned in school."

"Did Mr. Riker have any help from anyone else?"

"After he carried Michael further up the bank to a level area, some other campers saw what was happening, and they offered to help."

"Do you know who the other campers were?" I asked.

"I don't know their names, but it was a man and a woman on the other side of the campground across from where Mr. Riker had parked."

"Did you see anyone else around the campground that day?"

"No. Wait. I did see a man dressed in all black."

"When did you see this man, Danny?" Judd asked.

"I saw him after Mr. Riker left the campground and while the man and woman were giving CPR to Michael."

"Do you think anyone else saw him?"

"I don't know, but I don't think so. There was only me and the man and his wife who were trying to help Michael."

"What do you remember about this person?" Judd asked.

"He was a lot taller than Mr. Riker. He looked like he could've been a professional football player because he was very big, but not fat. He was wearing a black knit hat, black jacket, and black jeans. His boots were the kind soldiers wear sometimes, tan and green."

"Was there anything else you noticed about him?"

"He had pictures or something like pictures drawn on the back of his hands," Danny said.

"How were you able to see something on the back of his hands?" Judd asked.

"While the others were giving Michael CPR, the guy walked up and was standing next to me and looking down at Michael. His hands were almost level with my eyes. When the fire chief and the ambulance arrived, their headlights beamed on his hands. That's when I noticed."

"Those were probably tattoos. Do you remember anything about them?"

"The right hand had what looked like a spider web. The other hand had what looked like a flower, kinda like a rose."

"Did you ever see his face?"

"Not really. I saw his hat and his hands."

"Do you know if he was white or black?"

"He was definitely white."

"How can you be so positive if you didn't see his face," I prodded.

"Because I saw his hands in the headlights."

"Did the man say anything?" I asked.

"No. He just stood there next to me, and when the cars showed up, he kinda just disappeared."

"Do you know where he went or where he came from?"

"No. I didn't know he was gone until he wasn't there anymore."

"Okay, Danny. Now, this is important. I want to make sure you really saw this person and are not just making it up," I queried.

"I promise. I really saw him, honest I did. He was standing next to me."

"Do you think you would be able to recognize those same tattoos again?" Judd asked.

"I think so. I've never seen anything like those before. They were kinda cool, in a spooky way."

"Did you mention seeing the man in black to either of the sheriff's deputies the night of the drowning?" I asked.

"No. I forgot."

"That's perfectly understandable, Danny. Don't worry about it," I reassured. "Okay, we'd like you and your grandmother to follow us to our office when we're done here, and we'll show you some tattoo pictures. Does that sound okay to you, Danny?"

"Sounds like fun to me," the boy said.

"How did you get home the day Michael died?"

"I rode with the fire chief and Mr. Riker to the fire station, and my grandmother picked me up."

"Beverly, do you have anything you want to add or clarify, and do you have the time to come to the sheriff's department now?" I asked. "It sounds like what Danny is describing are prison tattoos, and we have a book of prison tats we'd like him to look at."

"That's no problem. We'll just follow you. I also want to mention again that Leroy didn't want Danny talking to the police or any investigators. I don't know what his issue is other than him saying he thought Danny might not do well being interviewed. I personally don't think that had anything to do with his reluctance. Leroy also asked me if he could take Danny fishing on a boat. I told him no. There is no way under God's green earth I'm going to let Danny get close to that man ever again."

"Understood. What is your impression of Leroy Riker?"

"I wouldn't trust him as far as I could throw him."

"Why is that?"

"Because I believe Danny. He told me he is afraid of Mr. Riker and doesn't believe Riker told the truth the day Michael died."

"And you trust Danny's instincts?"

"Yes, Danny has been diagnosed with autism. The AMA, the American Medical Association, says most autistic children can recall facts and details easily. That's probably why he remembered the man with the tattoos in such detail. I don't know if Leroy Riker knows that or not," Beverly Williams said.

"Did you have any occasion to observe Michael in his house or outside his home?" I inquired.

"I've seen the poor boy standing outside his house and staring down the street. He always appeared lonely and unkempt. Other than Danny, I don't think Michael had any other friends. That's why I agreed to let Danny go with Michael and his father the day before and the day Michael drowned. I've watched Michael play with the cats and dogs in the neighborhood, and he always appeared very caring and gentle with them," Beverly responded.

"Is there anyone else you suggest we talk to?" I asked.

"If you haven't already done so, I suggest you speak to Leroy Riker's aunt, and Lora Riker's mother. I also think Leroy told his pastor some things the pastor wants to share with investigators. It would all be hearsay for me to repeat those things to you," Beverly said.

"Generally, what relevant information do you believe each of those individuals has to share?"

"Leroy's aunt told me she gave some clothing to Lora for Michael and Michael told the aunt he never received them."

"I see. And what else?"

"Lora's mother said Leroy Riker wasn't a nice man. I have no idea what she meant by that, but I agree with her."

"All right. What about the pastor?

"The pastor supposedly heard an entirely different version about how Michael drowned from a neighbor of the Rikers. The neighbor told the pastor that Riker said Michael fell out of a boat while fishing with the Wilsall fire chief and drowned," Beverly Williams said.

28.

TATTOO HUNT

As the detectives drove away, Judd said, "Wow, what do you make of that bombshell Danny dropped about this man in black with the prison tattoos?"

"When's the last time you've ever encountered a witness who had a memory for such detail, Judd?" I asked.

"Never," Judd replied.

"That's why I believe the kid," I said. "His description of prison tats was almost spot on, and he'd have no reason to know anything about those."

"So, in addition to the father, if this accident turns into a homicide, we now have more than one suspect to focus our attention on," Judd replied.

"Bingo. After Danny has an opportunity to look at prison tattoos, and hopefully he is able to identify one or both, why don't you follow up with Probation and Parole to see if they have anyone in our general area who matches Danny's description."

"Sure thing," Judd replied.

"I'm going to play a long-shot and contact The Bank Bar in Wilsall."

"Why there?"

"If I had just killed a kid, I might want a stiff drink. Wilsall is the closest and only place around to get that. I also know the owner, and they have video surveillance inside and out," I explained.

"It's certainly worth a shot. As they say, it's better to be lucky than good," Judd added.

"If either Probation and Parole or The Bank Bar pan out, it won't be a matter of luck; just good old detective work," I said.

"I'll drink to that," Judd said emphatically.

"Hello. Officer Keith Foster speaking, Montana State Probation and Parole. How can I help you?"

"Officer Foster, this is Park County Sheriff's Detective Steven Judd. I'm hoping you can match up some prison tattoos to one of your clients."

"If the subject is in our system, it should be an easy matter. Our database tracks everyone by their unique tats. What do you have?"

"We are looking for a white male, about six-foot one or two, probably around two-hundred-eighty pounds, with a tattoo on the back of each hand. The first one was of a spider-web and the second one is a flower, possibly a rose."

"Do you know which tat was on which hand and if the rose had thorns?"

"Our witness is a young boy and although he described which hand each tattoo was on, I don't want to assume his memory is accurate, so if you can search first for the tattoos and then we can match them up to our witness's statement. He said it was dark and he only got a quick glimpse of the tats in headlights, and he didn't say anything about seeing thorns, but he wasn't sure if it was a rose or just some kind of flower."

"A rose with thorns is a common prison tattoo for someone with an eighteen-year or longer sentence. I'm not aware of any other flowers used by inmates. Using an eighteen-year or longer sentence as a parameter, along with the other descriptions, will also help. Do you want to hold or have me call you back?"

"If you can search while I hold, that'll be great. This is a potential homicide we're investigating, and time is critical."

After holding on the phone for fifteen minutes, Keith Foster said, "You're in luck, Detective. We have only one subject in our entire database matching all the descriptors you provided. Your guy is Donald S. Petrolli, six-foot, two-inches, and three hundred pounds. He's a white male, with a spider-web tattoo on the back of his right hand and a rose with thorns on the back of his left hand. He was serving a thirty-year sentence for killing a man in a barfight with his bare hands. He is now on parole and is one of my parolees."

"Do you have a good address for him and any vehicle descriptions?"

"Yep, I have an address in an apartment in Livingston and he drives an old 1967 Ford pickup, green in color. I can't guarantee how current the address in Livingston is, however. I'll send you all his particulars, including a photograph and his last known address under one condition."

"What's your condition?"

"If you intend to bust him, I want to be there. There might be a parole violation or two I'll be able to identify for you. In fact, I see he didn't keep his appointment or check in with me last week, so technically he's in violation."

"You got it. We first need to get an arrest and search warrant prepared for his truck and apartment. Then we'll be ready to rock and roll. There is one more thing we're checking out before we're ready. I'll give you a call when it's time."

29.

VIDEO

I next called my friend Art Beebe, owner of The Bank Bar and Vault Restaurant.

"Hi, Art. This is Russ. Can you meet me at your bar? I really need to speak with you, and it's important." Art Beebe lived a couple of blocks from The Bank Bar in Wilsall and walked to meet his old friend — me. It was mid-week and early in the morning, so there were no other customers present.

Art and I proceeded into his office where we had privacy. "Art, are you aware of the drowning last Friday at the Shields River Campground?"

"I read about it in the newspaper. Terrible tragedy. I feel bad for the boy and his parents."

"My partner and I are investigating it as a possible homicide, and we're hoping you and your staff might be able to recognize an individual." I showed Art the photograph and the tattoos of Donald Petrolli. "He might have been in here last Friday or a day or two before."

"We had a stranger in here last Friday night from about 10:30 to closing. He was getting a little hammered, and Lola cut him off. She described a fellow about his size with those same types of tattoos on the back of both hands. Lola said he was the type of person she wouldn't want to meet in a dark alley, or anyplace else for that matter. He was very intense, like a guy who didn't have any social skills and someone who was most comfortable being left alone. He didn't cause any problems for us Friday night, unlike the commotion he and two others did two nights earlier."

"You mean to say he was here with two other people earlier in the week?"

"Yeah. I was working last Wednesday when he came in with a woman and another man. They got loud, and I had to tell them to take it outside. They were having a heated argument, about what, I have no idea. Strangers tend to stand out around here this time of year, and when they start acting the way those three were, they stand out even more. I can pull up our security video for you if that might be helpful."

"Thanks, Art. That would be very helpful. I'd like to know who the other people were with him. Your system doesn't pick up audio, does it?"

"No, not on the inside, but it does on the outside," Art replied.

"That could be helpful. Let's look on both days you know our subject was here and then we can check your outside video for those days while we're at it. How much do you capture with your outside camera?"

"We have one camera on the side of the building and one camera near the entrance. Both cameras will capture some parked vehicles, but not everything. It depends how close to the intersection someone parks."

While Art advanced the video to the appropriate time for the previous Friday night, I said, "Stop it right there. That looks like our man sitting alone at the table in the bar. Now advance it slowly, I want to see his hands. Do you know how much he had to drink?"

"Like I said, he was here for almost four hours. It looks like he was drinking beer. If you need a precise count, I can pull that up off the cash register, or we can watch and count each drink," Art offered.

"I'm more interested in his appearance and demeanor when he arrived than when he left. I don't intend to jam you for over-service."

"From what Lola told me, he appeared moody and seemed upset about something. That's why, after several hours, she decided it was time to cut him off, although he never gave the appearance of being intoxicated. You can see what a big man he was. Undoubtedly, he would be able to hold his liquor."

"What was the other night you said he was here with another man and woman?"

"That was last Wednesday night while I was working. I would say sometime between 1:00 and 2:00 a.m. It will take just a couple minutes to pull up that night and scan that time period." It took only a minute for Art to find the three individuals entering the front door and taking a seat in a corner booth. The time was 1:13. "Art said, "I don't recognize either the man or woman with your subject. It appears the two men know each other, so this might have been just a business get-together, and they wanted to eat and drink while discussing business."

My eyes opened wide as I stared at the video and the three individuals. Finally, I said, "I believe I know the other man and woman." I was having difficulty controlling my excitement and feeling of good fortune as I continued to watch the video for nearly an hour. As the video progressed, it was easy to see how the three individual's demeanor changed from being friendly when they first entered, to being hostile, agitated and aggressive towards each other.

Art said, "Here is where I went over to their booth and told them if they couldn't hold down their voices, they'd have to take their discussion outside. I told them this ain't no logger's or a biker's bar, and their language was not acceptable."

"Did they do as you told them? Were you able to make out anything they were saying?"

"For the most part, they did. I heard the big man with the tattoos say, 'I won't do it.' And the other man said, 'Yes, you will.'"

"Did you ever hear the woman say anything?"

"She was very much part of the conversation, but she kept her voice down and appeared more in control of herself. What she lacked in volume, she made up for with her arms and hands. There was more than one occasion I thought she might hit one or both men."

"What about your outside cameras Art? Can you pull them up to the time when they arrived and when they left?"

"Sure, I can pull up both outside cameras and put them on the screen side-by-side. On the left side of the screen is the camera on the side of the building facing north towards the intersection. The image on the right is the camera near the entrance facing west towards the same intersection. It looks like the couple arrived 1:12 and they parked right in front of the bar facing east, after making a U-turn in the intersection, so I would say they came from the west. The man arrived at 1:13 and he parked his pickup along the side facing north. Here, you can see and hear them greeting each other before entering the bar. If I advance the outside cameras to when they left, I'll be able to show you what direction they all went."

"That would be helpful," I responded. I was interested if they all went west in the general direction of the Shields River Campground. If so, the couple would need to make another U-turn and head out of town towards the Wilsall Fire Station.

"Thanks, Art. Will you make me copies of these tapes and send them to me via email?

"I hope that was helpful, Russ. You'll have the videos and outside audio by the time you get back to your office."

"More than you know, Art. I'll be in touch. If you see any of these individuals in the future, please call me immediately."

I was eager to share the news with my partner and called him once I was outside and in the car. "Judd, I'm just leaving The Bank Bar in Wilsall. I reviewed their security video for two different days; both times Donald Petrolli was there. I bet you can't guess who was with him last Wednesday."

"From the excitement in your voice, Russ, I would venture a guess Leroy was with him."

"And you would be half right. Who else do you think was there?"

"Surely, not Leroy's wife!" Judd said.

"Don't call me Shirley, but you'd be right about Leroy's wife," I replied with a laugh.

"Wow. That was some long shot that panned out. We can place all three of them together two days before the drowning and Petrolli in the area the night the boy drowned," Judd said.

"That's just the half of it," I said. "When they left from The Bank Bar on Wednesday, they all headed west towards the Wilsall Fire Station in two vehicles."

"You don't suppose they were going to the Shields River Campground, do you?"

"I think that was exactly where they were all going," I replied.

"That's great information for the affidavit for the search and arrest warrant for Donald Petrolli and his apartment and his pickup. Cross your fingers, Russ, that Petrolli will play ball with us. He's on parole for ten more years. If there is enough evidence to violate his parole, that might be just enough to flip him into a cooperating witness," Judd remarked.

"Let's regroup at the office and get the arrest warrant and search warrants in hand. Then we'll call Keith Foster at Probation and Parole. He said he wanted to go with us and considering how big Petrolli is, we might just want his backup."

I was doing my best to keep my feelings under control, as usual, and not let those feelings interfere with doing my job professionally. Every now and then, a case like this one comes around. Any time a young child is involved, as a father and grandfather myself, the facts tore at my heart. The evidence pointed toward his adoptive parents being directly involved in his death.

Worse yet, their son's death was premeditated based solely on greed. The thought repulsed and infuriated me. I wanted nothing but justice for Michael. Yet, I knew that unless I did my job professionally and by the book, there would be no justice. I was committed to following every lead and the last shred of evidence to make that possible. Then, and only then, would I have peace of mind, knowing full well I did everything I legally could. Me, being a man of faith, truly believed greed was one of the seven deadly sins.

30.

FIRST RESPONDER INTERVIEWS

Notes

Detective Russ Wyatt on the Case

Later that day, I called the Wilsall fire chief.

"Hi, Chief. This is Detective Russ Wyatt. Detective Steven Judd and I would like to come by the fire station and talk to you and your medics. Would you set that up for us, please? It's regarding the drowning death of the young boy at the Shields River Campground."

"Sure thing. I'll set that up for later today if the two of you are available. How about 2 p.m.?"

We arrived at the Wilsall Fire Station promptly.

"Thanks for setting this up, Chief. Being able to talk to all three of you during one visit will be very helpful. We know you were one of the first people to see Leroy Riker when you met him at the fire station the night of the drowning. What do you remember?" I asked.

"He was obviously very upset, but in a different way than what one might expect from a distraught father," the chief replied.

"I expect you have some experience and expertise in judging people's emotions under these types of difficult circumstances. In what way did he seem different?" I inquired.

157

"He came across as someone who was worried for himself more than worried for his son. He kept mumbling, "What have I done?" I never asked him what he meant because I don't think he thought I'd heard him. There also seemed to be a lack of urgency for him, as if he was in perpetual slow motion. That might have been due to stress," the chief said.

"Did you notice anything about his clothing that stuck out in your mind?"

"He told me he'd jumped into the river to save his son, but only his pant legs and the front of his shirt were wet. That's consistent with wading into the water to reach his son and with carrying his son's wet body up the bank. His clothing showed no indication he'd jumped into the water."

"I see. Anything else?" I asked.

"You might also want to talk to the 911 operator, Sharon Mills. When we first received the dispatch call, Sharon said the 911 caller reported that a young boy had jumped from a considerable height into a pool of water, hit his head, and drowned. I assume you've both been to the campground and observed for yourselves that there are no places from which someone could jump from anything high into the water," the fire chief responded.

"Chief, was there anything he said while riding in your vehicle, either on the way to or from the campground?" I asked.

"He was quiet most of the time. Like I said before, he kept mumbling the, "What have I done" statement. I don't know what he was referring to, whether he was questioning his decision to separate the two boys, his decision to bring both boys to such a remote campground, or something else. Riker didn't know how much information I'd received from the 911 dispatcher, so his explanation about the events leading up to Michael's drowning was to the effect that Michael slipped on rocks near the fishing hole, fell backward, hit his head, and then somehow ended up in the water."

"You didn't personally see Michael's head injuries?" I asked.

"I never had a reason to inspect Michael's head injuries since I knew the medics would do that, as would the medical examiner. I do remember him asking me, 'What happens next? Will there be an autopsy or an official police investigation?' When I told him both were very likely since there were no witnesses to Michael's drowning or the circumstances leading up to his drowning, he got very quiet. While I'm thinking about it, you might also want to speak to Riker's pastor. When we all got back to the fire station, I called Danny Williams' grandmother, and Riker called his wife. While he was waiting for his wife to arrive, the pastor told Riker he had some dry clothes he was welcome to change into. I believe the pastor will be able to confirm the condition of Riker's clothes and I know they also had a casual conversation while he waited," the chief added.

We next met with the two paramedics. Since we only had one or two questions for them, there was no reason to interview them separately.

"Hi guys, you obviously know we're investigating the drowning death of Michael Riker. There are a few issues that have come to our attention we're hopeful you can shed some light on. The first issue has to do with your observations of Leroy Riker's clothes. Also, is there anything he might have said after you arrived at the campground, and would you both please comment as to your professional medical opinions regarding Michael's drowning and his head injury?"

The first medic stated, "The 911 dispatcher said we were going to a drowning incident of a ten-year-old victim who'd jumped into a pool of water and hit his head on rocks at the Shields River Campground. We both have fished that river from the campground both upstream and downstream and we weren't aware of any place from which someone might jump into the water. We all met at the fire station and Leroy Riker rode to the campground with the fire chief.

"Do you recall any statements that Mr. Riker made?" I asked.

The second medic stated, "He said his son obviously slipped, then hit his head and fell into the pool of water that had been created by stacking river rock. The pool was about ten feet across, but we couldn't see a place from which the boy might have jumped. Riker told us when he first found his son underwater, he'd jumped into the water, yet his shirt was only wet in front, and his pant legs were wet to his knees, which would coincide with someone carrying a wet child, but it was at odds with someone who'd jumped into the water. The water was certainly deep enough that he should've been totally wet."

"What about the head injury?" I pressed.

"He had a fractured skull. The fracture and a substantial depression were on the top of his skull and presumably caused by an impact with a rock. I say presumably because there was no other obvious answer of what might have caused the skull fracture. The location for the skull fracture would be expected for someone jumping into shallow water, but it wouldn't be expected if someone had just slipped on round river rock, fell backward, and then hit his or her head. For that to have happened, the injury would've been on the back of the skull. The medical examiner, Dr. Edwards, will have more detail and opinion regarding the skull fracture following the autopsy," answered the first medic.

"When you first arrived at the campground, who was in the front vehicle?" I asked.

"We were both in the medical van and the fire chief was behind us?

"Did either of you notice anyone standing near the boy's body when you first arrived, other than the other boy?" I inquired.

"Not really. Our attention was immediately drawn to the woman who was motioning for us to follow her. As we turned slightly to our left, we saw a young boy standing looking down towards the victim and a man performing CPR," one medic said, as his partner nodded his head in agreement.

"So, neither of you saw another man that night?" I asked.

In response, they both shook their heads "no."

"Thanks, guys. If either of you thinks of anything else, please call us."

31.

CLUES FROM THE
INSURANCE ATTORNEY

Notes

Detective Russ Wyatt on the Case

Judd, who had listened closely and taken notes, asked "Who's next on our list, Russ? We already have the transcript of the 911 call and the transcript of the fire department dispatch. The original recordings will be retained as evidence should we need them in the future. We also have the medical examiner's report, so currently, I don't see the need for a formal interview with Dr. Edwards."

"Agreed. I'll check with the attorney representing the life insurance companies and then call their Certified Fraud Examiner, Dan Player," I responded.

After calling the phone number of Dan Player, I said, "Hello, is this Dan Player?"

"Yes. Who is this?" came the reply.

"I'm Detective Russ Wyatt from the Park County Sheriff's Department. My partner, Detective Steven Judd, and I were told by attorney William Kimble, who represents Northwest Life Insurance and Montana Life Insurance, to reach out to you and CPA O'Reilly.

It's my understanding we're all working on the same case related to the drowning death of Michael Riker but from different angles. I believe we all have a common interest of conducting a full, fair, and thorough investigation into the events of that day and determining if there were any criminal activities involved."

Player, half-joking responded, "It's good to finally have an opportunity to speak with you, Detective Wyatt. Under most circumstances, I'd ask for more information from you to assure myself that you are whom you claim to be. However, I was provided your name and the name of Detective Steven Judd by attorney Bill Kimble. In addition, my caller I.D. shows me your office phone number. That's good enough for me. And please, you can call me Dan."

"I thought only the feds were that cautious," I said jokingly.

"It's an occupational hazard I developed after 45 years. Better safe than sorry. Whenever I'm working on a high-profile case such as this one, there's always a potential for unscrupulous lawyers on the other side, I never know what they might be capable of doing. I hope you don't take offense," Dan Player said.

"Not at all, Dan. I totally agree with you. What can you tell me as to where you and Mr. O'Reilly are in your investigation? Have you started your analysis of any documentary evidence yet?" I asked.

"As a matter of fact, we're well into our analysis. Attorney Bill Kimble has already issued subpoenas to all the known financial institutions, and I've received most of those offsets. Both Northwest Insurance and Montana Life Insurance provided all their documentation, and I've already interviewed both insurance agents."

"How did that go?" I asked.

"The insurance agent who is most relevant is the one from Northwest Insurance, Mr. Ray Heath. That's the company who provided the accidental life coverage and whose insurance overlapped the second policy from Montana Life."

"Do you mind if I interrupt you for a minute? I want to make sure I understand all the insurance terms and legalese. You said you've received 'offsets' from the banks. What exactly is an offset?"

"Sorry about that," Player apologized. "An offset is nothing more than a microfilm or digital copy of a financial transaction. For example, when a bank customer deposits money into an account, there is a deposit slip prepared either by the customer or the teller, which supports the transaction. So, the deposit slip and any corresponding documents associated with the deposit, like checks, are considered offsets. Similarly, when a bank customer makes a withdrawal from the account and writes a check; the negotiated check goes through the bank clearing process and images of the check are also considered offsets."

"Got it. I just never heard them called that before. So, you were telling me about your progress."

"Yeah. And I also want to make clear we are conducting a civil investigation, as compared to your criminal investigation. In no way, shape or form do we want to interfere with your criminal investigation or step on any toes. We are more than happy to share with you anything we legally develop, but we recognize your legal limitations to reciprocate."

"Thanks for your understanding. You really have been doing this for a while," I said.

"I've almost completed entering all the financial records into an Excel spreadsheet, which I'll send you when finished. Spreadsheets are always a work in progress as new information becomes available. My spreadsheet tracks the financial transactions by an assigned Bates number, date of the transaction, the date the transaction cleared the bank, whether the transaction cleared or not, the dollar amounts of all transactions, including deposits and withdrawals other than by check, the purpose of the transaction," Player stated.

"Meaning the name of the payee and any memo notes on the check itself?" I asked, just to clarify.

"Yes, and the name of the person who prepared and signed the check as the payor. That information can then be sorted based on multiple parameters. The initial information for the spreadsheet starts with the bank statements. I use the bank's beginning balance for the first month in the spreadsheet, and then I maintain a running bank balance on the spreadsheet that allows me to crossmatch my running balances with the balances on the bank statements. That process quickly identifies any data entry errors on my part. Once I receive copies of the canceled checks, I then go back and fill in more detail on the spreadsheet."

"That should be helpful. Thank you," I replied, my eyes glazing over a bit with the number of details Player was sharing. And there was more to come.

"I've also begun an event chronology that tracks all significant events by date and person(s) involved so I can track all events chronologically. The chronology helps me identify false or misleading statements of the plaintiffs, or suspects in your case, and helps to identify missing events in the chronology. I can then access specific documents noted in the event chronology, again by the Bates number, for additional examination if necessary. All the insurance documentation has now been entered into the spreadsheet."

"Can you explain to me what is meant by a Bates number?"

"I certainly can. A Bates number is nothing more than a sequential number assigned to each document. Bates numbers have been around since the late 19th and early 20th centuries. The number might be generated by a computer program and is applied by a printer when the document is photocopied, or the number might be applied manually to the original, either by a self-inking stamp or by peel-and-stick labels. A fellow by the name of Edwin G. Bates was the one who came up with the self-inking stamping device that automatically advanced by one number each time a document is stamped. Once a document receives a unique number, the document goes into a three-ring binder, organized by that sequential number, and then the document can be easily retrieved later for further examination."

"All right, good. Do you have a law enforcement background, and have you ever testified in criminal court before?" I asked.

"Yes, and yes. I worked in law enforcement for over 27 years before retiring and starting my own business, which specializes in white-collar and organized crime. I'm considered an expert witness in multiple county and federal courts. You might also be interested in learning I interviewed one former and one current inmate who worked with Lora Riker at the Billings State Prison for Women. One of them is now out of prison, and both are willing to talk to you. The one who's still in prison has years left on her murder-for-hire conviction," Player said.

"Interesting," I said.

"And it gets even more interesting," Player continued. "One of the things both inmates told me was Lora Riker expressed interest in learning from them how to commit the perfect crime without getting caught."

"Interesting," I said.

"Get this, the former inmate was recruited by Lora to go into a house cleaning business with her and Lora wanted that person to purchase a life insurance policy naming Lora as the policy's beneficiary. There's also a man with whom Lora Riker intended to go into a janitorial business. Like the former inmate, Lora convinced him to also purchase a life insurance policy naming Lora as beneficiary, and she told him she would do likewise. I can provide those names to you if you are interested," Player offered.

"I certainly would be interested, thanks. I can almost venture a guess how much the intended life insurance policies were for," I chuckled.

"And I would bet your guess would be right," Player responded. "Hey, have either you or your partner had an opportunity to review the rental agreement for the camcorder we sent to you? You'll notice it was rented the day after Michael died," Player said.

"We reviewed it, thanks. Big help," I said. "What's CPA Greg O'Reilly's role in all this? I had him on my list to call, but now I don't know what it is he's doing that might be different from what you're doing."

"Greg is a certified public accountant. CPAs tend to look at financial numbers differently than someone who is a Certified Fraud Examiner. The insurance attorney, Bill Kimble, asked that Greg and I put our heads together, collaborate and double check each other's work and opinions. I'm taking the lead, but you're more than welcome to give Greg a call. I'm sure he'd enjoy speaking with you."

"Great. I'll enjoy speaking with him too," I replied.

"Honestly, this case is taking an emotional toll on both of us because we each have grandsons the same age Michael was," Player admitted. "As white-collar crime investigators, we're not accustomed to working cases involving the death of a child. Speaking for myself, I don't envy the work you and your partner do."

"Funny you mention that. This has been a tough one for all of us, it seems. I have a grandson the same age too. And on a personal note, I was a young red-headed adopted boy myself. Hits close to home."

"Wow, that's heavy. You have my admiration for maintaining your objectivity. It can't be easy." Player paused, exhaled, and inhaled.

"These cases are never easy. We're preparing an affidavit for a search warrant of the Riker residence. Is there anything you would recommend we include in the affidavit and warrant?" I asked.

"Other than the obvious," Player said, "such as all financial documents and insurance documentation. I suggest you include their computer and all external computer drives, such as thumb drives. Include all audio and/or videotapes, and any documentation and research concerning life insurance, including books on the topic.

"Just so you know, we also found information that suggests the Rikers were interested in a custom home. There should be a contract and postdated check in the possession of a Don Jackson, of D.J. Custom Homes. Finding that contract and the returned post-dated check in the Rikers' possession would help show their mutual intent and potential knowledge of the two life insurance policies, which up until the day Michael died, Leroy Riker has denied any knowledge about," I said.

"The same would be true if you found any type of research they were doing on new home construction and/or land purchases prior to Michael's death," Player responded.

"We'll keep an eye out," I assured him.

"Are you aware of a prior insurance claim Leroy submitted several years ago under their renter's policy? An insurance arbitrator ruled their claim was fraudulent. That prior insurance claim and decision are not necessarily helpful to prove fraud in this life insurance case, but it does show a prior pattern and practice and could be used for impeachment purposes. You should also be aware of a prior federal tax return wherein the Rikers, under penalty of perjury, claimed a fictitious dependent, in order to receive a larger tax refund. That tax return could also be used for impeachment purposes, assuming their attorneys ever allow them to testify."

"I was vaguely aware. Good to know," I said.

"If you're looking for a financial motive, we have that documented in aces and spades. They filed for Chapter 7 bankruptcy three times during their marriage. During the time Michael was a foster child, Lora wrote 304 bad checks from three different checking accounts for a total cost in bank fees of $6,080. After Michael was adopted, the number of bad checks increased to 403 for a total bank fee cost of $6,735. That year, their bank account began and/or ended with a negative balance ten out of twelve months."

"Yes, Judd and I both noted that they were in obvious financial straights," I said.

"On top of all that, we can establish circumstantially that Leroy Riker had knowledge of Michael's life insurance policy, despite his denials to the contrary."

"How's that," I asked.

"The spreadsheet I've prepared shows who in the household was writing and signing checks. Leroy ceased his practice of writing and signing checks the day before Michael was adopted, and then resumed his check writing and signing routine the day after Michael died. Riker's so-called 'ostrich defense' of putting his head in the sand and saying he didn't know, see or hear anything is total BS," Player opined.

"Wow. You really have been busy. It sounds like you've already received all the financial and insurance records, so you're ahead of us in that regard. We still have to jump through hoops to obtain our documents using the criminal process. I'm envious that you get to obtain your information via civil discovery. We're already aware of some of the evidence you mentioned. At the appropriate time, we'd appreciate you sharing with us your event chronology and your spreadsheets and summaries," I said.

"I'll help any way I can," Player responded. "Speaking of testifying, I'm scheduled to give a deposition related to this case next week. I doubt the Rikers' fourth attorney will stick around much longer after that. He's supposed to be this highfalutin' attorney who specializes in bad faith lawsuits against insurance companies."

"Let me know how that goes, if you would?" I asked.

32.

THERE ARE NO COINCIDENCES

Notes

Detective Russ Wyatt on the Case

After receiving a veritable information dump from Dan Player, the next on our list was Don Jackson, of D.J. Custom Homes. The timing of his initial contact with Lora and Leroy Riker was critical. If our information was accurate and they reached out to Don Jackson before Michael's death, that would be very important, especially since they had no money and were having difficulty making rent or even making the life insurance payments. In addition, if Leroy Riker was involved in those initial contacts with Jackson and not just Lora, that would destroy Leroy's defense that he knew nothing about the life insurance until after Michael died.

"So, do you want to call Jackson first, or just show up at his door?" asked Judd.

"I think we'd be safe just showing up. It's already late in the day and the weather isn't very conducive to home construction, especially with two inches of snow on the ground," I said.

"Hi, Mr. Don Jackson? My name is Detective Steven Judd, and this is Detective Russ Wyatt. We're investigating the drowning death of Michael Riker. I believe you had a business relationship with his parents, Leroy and Lora. We have a couple questions for you if you have some time now. If not, we could make an appointment to speak with you later, say at the Sheriff's Department?"

"Now's as good a time for me as any. Please come in detectives. How can I help you?" Don Jackson replied.

"For starters, how well do you know the Rikers?" Judd asked.

"They contacted me a short time ago about building a new home for them near Livingston. I didn't know them prior to that time."

"When you say 'they,' was that Leroy or Lora Riker who made the first contact with you?" I asked.

"My notes show I received the first phone call from Lora on the 7th and then again from Leroy on the 8th. We met in my office also on the 8th and the contract was also signed on the 8th," Jackson replied.

"Would it also be possible for us to get a copy of your file without the need of a subpoena or search warrant?" I asked.

"I don't know why not," Jackson responded. "Let's do it this way. I'll make you a copy of everything I have today, and if you end up needing the information for court, you give me a subpoena at that time."

"Thank you, Mr. Jackson. You've been very helpful and if you are able to make us copies of your file while we wait, that too would be much appreciated. If you think of anything else, anything at all that might be helpful to our investigation, please don't hesitate to call either one of us," Judd said.

"So, Judd, what do you think? Does this sound like the boy's drowning and the life insurance and a new home are just a coincidence?" I asked.

"You know how I feel about a coincidence," Judd replied.

"We need to write up an affidavit for a search warrant and get a warrant served on the Rikers' home ASAP, Russ. While we're at it, we need warrants for bank records and insurance records from all their financial institutions and for both insurance companies. Much of that information might be found during our search of their residence, but I don't want to assume we'll find everything there. They've had more than sufficient time to destroy or hide a lot of evidence by now."

"I couldn't agree more. I think we should also broaden the scope of the search warrant to include their computer and any audio/video tapes, external hard drives or other storage devices, as well as any books or other documents related to life insurance and insurance fraud. We already have reason to believe there might be tapes associated with a rented camcorder around the time of the boy's drowning."

The following week, after the civil depositions concluded, Dan Player called me.

"Detective Wyatt, we spoke last week. I thought you might be interested in knowing the life insurance civil case is over."

"Well, that was kind of sudden, wasn't it? Did the insurance companies decide to settle? How much did the Rikers receive?" I asked

"Zip, zilch, zero. The Rikers dropped their lawsuit entirely and they won't receive a penny. After my deposition and the deposition of the forensic pathologist, Dr. Kay Burkett, the Rikers packed it in," Player said.

"Wow. What happened with their highfalutin' insurance attorney? I thought he was going to be their ace in the hole. Doesn't sound like he helped them at all," I said.

"Actually, I think he did help them. The civil case against them was building with such momentum; I think their attorney saw the handwriting on the wall. Meaning, the more they pushed their civil case, the more and more facts would keep coming out that a criminal prosecutor could use against them. So, not knowing any of the details, I think their highfalutin' attorney told them it was best to cut and run," Player said.

"I'm glad the civil case ended at least with them not profiting from the death of their son. Unfortunately for them and just between you and me, we are going to arrest both parents very soon. So, their dropping the lawsuit is not going to benefit them in the slightest. The criminal charges are going to be insurance fraud, homicide and conspiracy. When it happens, you will read about it in the local newspapers," I said.

"So, the prosecutor has decided this is a circumstantial case she actually wants to file?" Player asked.

"The prosecutor not only wants to file, but she also feels she must file it. This case could really help her politically, if you know what I mean. I don't think there is a parent or person who wouldn't reach a guilty verdict and hold the parents accountable for the death of their adopted son. Trying to profit from the boy's death is a big deal. If they are convicted that is bound to be a vote getter," I responded.

"Thanks for the heads up on their soon-to-be arrest. I'll look forward to that. I might even attend their arraignment if you let me know," Player said.

"You've been a great help, and I'll let you know about their arraignment. If this goes all the way to a trial, I'm sure we'll be working closely together and with the prosecutor," I said.

33.
PROSECUTING ATTORNEY PAULA JENNINGS

Notes

Detective Russ Wyatt on the Case

The Rikers had planned the perfect crime. Or so they thought. The medical examiner's impromptu findings were odd to those of us in law enforcement, and my job became much more difficult as a result. Now, all evidence had to overcome the presumption of accidental death.

The media always had their doubts, as did I. The swell of suspicion heightened after the information about two life insurance policies became widely known.

Judd and I sat at facing desks in our tiny office, working on the search warrant affidavits of probable cause. And in my gut, I knew we were missing something. Little did I know then that it had everything to do with Michael's dog, Max.

My phone rang at 8:30, jolting us both from our focused tasks.

"Detective Wyatt," I answered, and immediately recognized the voice of Paula Jennings, the elected prosecutor of Park County. I punched the speaker phone button so Judd could hear.

"Hi, Russ. Is Judd with you?"

"Paula, hi. You're on speakerphone, so we both can hear you," Judd said.

"Great. I'm hoping you're both available for a short meeting in my office to bring me up to speed on your drowning investigation."

The prosecuting attorney's office has jurisdiction for all felonies committed within the county. It was also common practice for detectives to keep their local prosecutor in the loop on a major investigation and seek input and direction. I was happy to oblige.

"Sure thing, Paula. We're almost done with our search warrant affidavits and would love to get those all approved by the judge today," I responded.

"I am available anytime this morning until 1:00 p.m., and I know the judge is in her chambers until that time," Paula said.

"We both should be finished with our affidavits within the hour," I said while looking at Judd, who nodded his head in agreement.

"Come down to my office when you're finished. Once the actual warrants are finished, I'll call the judge to make arrangements for her approval," Paula responded.

"Okay. We'll see you within the hour."

Judd and I put the finishing touches on the search warrant affidavits, grabbed our investigative materials, and walked down the short hallway to Paula Jennings's office. The sheriff's department, the prosecuting attorney, and the fire department all occupied the

City of Livingston/Park County government complex, a one-and-a-half-story modern building located on East Callender Street.

"Thanks for coming down, detectives," Paula said. "Coffee, anyone?"

"No problem, and yes, I would love some coffee," Judd said.

"Make that two," I added.

"Both black?" Paula asked.

"You know it. If coffee's not good enough to drink black, it's not good enough to drink," I quipped.

"So, where are we on your investigation? The media has lots of interest in the suspicious drowning death of this young boy. All I've been able to tell the media is our two best detectives are on the case," Paula said.

"That's funny, since there are only two detectives in the entire sheriff's department," I said.

"What have you learned so far? Is the drowning death going to end up being an accident or a homicide? Paula asked.

"Without a doubt, at least in our minds, a homicide," I said. Judd nodded his head in agreement.

"Okay. You have my attention. Tell me why."

"To start, we know the parents were deeply in debt. Lora Riker has been writing insufficient funds checks for several years. Not long after the boy's death, I had a phone conversation with an attorney representing two life insurance companies. He told me about two very large life insurance policies Lora had taken out within days of the boy's adoption being final. At the time of the drowning, both policies were still in effect," I offered.

"Wait. There were two policies in effect at the same time? That's not supposed to happen, is it?"

"Nope and yep. They overlapped. The first policy was scheduled to expire for non-payment of the insurance premium three weeks after the boy died, but it was supposed to expire right after the second policy was issued, according to the understanding of both insurance companies," Judd chimed in.

"What was the value of each policy?"

"The first policy had a value of $400,000, including the accidental death rider. The second policy was for $250,000.

"So, the parents stood to gain $650,000 if the boy died of accidental death before the first policy expired?"

"You got it."

"What else do you have?"

"Lora Riker once worked as a custodial supervisor at the women's prison in Billings. We spoke to two inmates, one former and one current, who said Lora would sit around and ask them questions about how they would go about committing the perfect crime. She seemed interested in this topic."

"That's smart. Nothing like asking convicted felons how to commit the perfect crime. What else?"

"There are a lot of contradictions in Leroy and Lora's versions of what happened leading up to and on the day of the boy's death."

"Okay?"

"The insurance companies hired a private insurance investigator who interviewed both Rikers almost immediately after the boy's death."

"Was that an EUO interview?"

"An examination under oath? Yes."

"Give me the condensed version of the contradictions."

"Riker said it was his son's idea to separate Michael and his young friend, Danny Williams. Danny said it was Riker's idea. Riker said he only left Michael alone for five minutes while he went looking for something to make Danny a fishing pole, yet Danny said Riker was gone for about 20 minutes. Riker said when he learned Michael was floating in the water, he jumped in to save him. Danny said Riker did not go into the water and it was Danny who got Michael. And lastly, Riker said he drove around the campground to find another fishing spot for both boys, yet a couple camped nearby said Riker's pickup never moved."

"That's all interesting and suspicious, but all very circumstantial thus far. What did our county medical examiner say about the death?"

"Dr. Edwards initially said the cause of death was from accidental drowning. Once he learned about the life insurance policies, he had some second thoughts," Judd said.

"Is Dr. Edwards going to conduct a new autopsy?"

"Michael Riker was cremated the day after the first autopsy was completed," Judd said.

"So no DNA?" Paula asked rhetorically.

"None so far," I answered. And as the words came out of my mouth, a light bulb went off. Somewhere, back in a report, Deputy Peet mentioned that Michael's dog, Max, ran into the woods with something in his mouth. I had never followed up on that potential lead and made a mental note to do so.

"We're waiting to hear back from insurance attorney William Kimble concerning the finding of a forensic pathologist he hired. Kimble also hired a certified fraud examiner and a forensic CPA.

We've spoken to the fraud examiner. That's why we know about the Rikers' financial problems," said Judd.

"Were there any other witnesses in the campground the day Michael drowned, other than the other couple you spoke of?"

"There might have been. Danny Williams described a man dressed in all black with what Danny described as pictures on the back of both his hands. We showed Danny a bunch of prison tattoos, and he picked out two from the book. We were then able to match the prison tats to a former inmate, so we have a name," I said.

"What was this guy in prison for and where was he incarcerated? Paula asked.

"Until recently, he was in prison for second degree murder. Coincidentally, the same prison and cell block where Leroy Riker worked. He was serving a thirty-year stretch but was released after twenty years only a few weeks ago. He killed a guy in a bar with his bare hands."

"Wait, I think I remember that case. I was a deputy prosecutor at the time. By any chance is his name Donald Petrolli?"

"Bingo, Paula. That would be him," I said with a smile.

"Have you found or interviewed him yet?"

"Not yet. It appears he has gone into hiding," I said.

"Do you think he might be the killer, a witness or a co-conspirator?"

"Not sure yet. We are trying to keep an open mind," Judd said.

"Find Petrolli and let me know what he has to say, if anything. If he's not the killer but knows who is, I'm more than willing to offer him some considerations. Then let me know when you get the results from the forensic pathologist and the CPA and CFE finish their forensic analysis. I'll get you all the search warrants you need, but I need more conclusive evidence before I can file charges against any-one. Good work you two. Get out there and don't leave any stones unturned. If someone murdered Michael Riker, I want hard evidence to put them away for a really, really long time," Paula said.

"You got it. We have some leads we're following to find Petrolli, and we'll continue to talk to other potential witnesses," I said, think-ing of Max the cocker spaniel.

"What was Lora doing while Leroy and Michael went fishing?" Paula asked.

"From what we were told, Lora and their daughter and her friend, all went to the mall shopping," I replied.

"Have you tried to verify that, like interviewing the daughter's friend?"

"Not yet. We didn't think it was critical at this time."

"You're probably right. Sounds like you have some other good leads to follow up on," said Paula. "Maybe since the guys were hav-ing an all-guys day, the girls were having an all-girls day," Paula commented.

"We'll keep you posted, if you don't have anything else to ask us."

"Great. Please do," Paula replied.

<h1 style="text-align:center">34.</h1>

THE PETROLLI PROBLEM

Notes

Detective Russ Wyatt on the Case

A week after the drowning, Leroy and Lora were at home having another heated argument. Lora tried to convince Leroy that Petrolli couldn't be trusted.

"If you only had the balls to do something yourself, we wouldn't have to worry about Petrolli," Lora said. "Instead, you insisted Petrolli be at the campground to give you a backbone, just in case you lost your nerve."

"But I didn't lose my nerve, did I? I got the job done without Petrolli's help."

"That may be true, but Petrolli was there, and he saw everything. Now, he might say you hired him to kill Michael," Lora responded.

"One thing you're forgetting, my dear, is that I didn't hire him; we hired him. And you were the one who promised him money regardless of what role he had to play last Friday. I wouldn't be surprised if you also hired him or someone else to kill me so you could have all the life insurance money for yourself."

"Don't be stupid, Leroy. Don't you see? Everything is working just as I planned. No one is going to know Petrolli was even there, and neither the cops nor the insurance company can prove Michael's death was anything but an accident. Now, you'll call Petrolli and tell him to meet you at the campground so you can give him the money we promised."

"We don't have any money to give him. What do you think he's going to do if we stiff him on the money?" Leroy asked.

"Oh, Leroy. You're so stupid sometimes. He can't very well say he was hired as a hitman and didn't get paid, can he?" Lora declared.

"Look, Lora. You don't know him or other cons like him the way I do. I worked on his cellblock for the past ten years. He was released on early parole and has ten years left to serve if he gets violated. He's learned to be naturally suspicious. That's how he's survived all those years."

"Leroy," Lora countered, "that's even more reason you're going to call him and set up a meet at the campground. Tell him you have his $500; except you're going to be hiding just inside the tree line with your Glock. Do I need to spell it out for you any clearer than that? You take care of Petrolli, and that takes care of our problem."

"Are you asking me to kill someone else now? Where does this all stop?"

"I'm not asking you; I'm telling you," Lora said emphatically. "Just keep thinking about that $650K and nothing else. Petrolli was never part of my plan. You were the one who brought him in, and now he is a potential liability for us because of you. You caused this mess, so now you go clean it up."

"Okay! But don't you ever talk to me like that again," Leroy said angrily. "And don't ask me to kill anyone else. I'll call Petrolli and get him to meet me at the campground this evening, and then, whatever happens, it's best if you know nothing."

35.
THE SET UP

"Hi, Don. I have the money my wife promised you. Meet me tonight, around eight at the campground, and I will pay you what you have coming," Leroy said.

"Why at the campground, Leroy?" Petrolli questioned. "Can't we meet someplace a little more convenient?"

"It has to be at the campground. We can't afford to be seen together. And Don, come alone. Lora is having an absolute hissy-fit that I involved you to begin with, so I want to make sure you and I don't involve anyone else."

"Okay," said Don. "This better not be a set-up."

"Look, Don," responded Leroy. "You don't need to worry about that. I have as much to lose as you do. If you don't turn on me, I have no reason to turn on you."

"Is your wife going to be with you?" Don asked.

"No. I told her to stay as far away from all of this as possible."

"What if there are other campers there?"

"If there are, I'll meet you across the road in the parking area where you parked your truck last Friday. That's another reason for meeting after dark. We shouldn't have any difficulty finding each other. I'll have my pickup, and you'll have yours, right?"

"Yeah, I'll have my truck. So, eight tonight?" Petrolli confirmed.

"Yeah. See you soon."

Before Leroy left home, he dressed in all black and grabbed his model 19, Glock 9mm, from his gun safe. He doubled-checked the magazine, slammed it home into the magazine well, and jacked a round into the chamber. He put the gun into his behind-the-back holster and was out the door to his truck. Leroy wanted to be sure he arrived at the campground well ahead of Don Petrolli.

No words were exchanged between him and Lora as he left the house. Leroy was still too furious to speak to her. The drive to the campground was now familiar, having driven it on Thursday, Friday, and Saturday. Still, although it was familiar, the drive brought back all the memories of what he had done the previous Friday. Leroy knew Lora was right and he should have just manned up and not involved Don as a backup last Friday. Killing a child for money and shooting someone else to cover up the crime was something he struggled to wrap his head around.

In his mind, he quietly wished Petrolli had been the one to bash in Michael's head with a rock concealed inside a boot sock. He got the idea from inmates who used a bar of soap inside a sock to inflict severe injuries on other inmates, like broken jaws, cracked cheekbones, and sometimes smashed skulls. Swinging a weighted sock would inflict more damage than just a rock held in someone's hand.

Leroy arrived at the campground an hour early. He first drove through the parking area across from the campground. Seeing no vehicles, he next circled through the small campground. As he had hoped, there was no one there either. Riker then mapped out the perfect ambush in his mind. He had chosen the campsite where Petrolli previously pitched his tent because it was closest to the tree line. Next, he wanted to make sure when Petrolli arrived, there would be only a couple of options for him to enter the site and no more than a couple of places he could park. Either option had to leave a clear and easy shot from the tree line.

In another hour Leroy knew it would be very dark and he had to make sure Petrolli would have to exit his pickup and walk through a no-man's kill zone. He'd have only one chance to get it right. With all his planning, it never occurred to Riker that Petrolli might be armed himself. After all, Petrolli was a convicted felon and should not have access to any firearms. He also didn't think Petrolli would take a chance of having a firearm in his possession while being on parole.

More importantly, Petrolli had no reason to be suspicious of their meeting. After all, it made perfect sense why they shouldn't be seen together, and meeting at the scene of the crime was the ideal location. However, unbeknownst to Leroy, Lora had called Petrolli just as soon as Leroy pulled out of their driveway, thereby giving Petrolli advance notice of Leroy's intentions.

Now satisfied with his planning, Leroy backed his pickup against the tree line, with his passenger side door positioned next to the embankment closest to the Shields River and his headlights pointing downstream. A large boulder would prevent Petrolli from parking next to him, and Petrolli's only option would be to park nose-to-nose with Leroy's pickup. His plan was to sit in the passenger seat of the truck with the engine running.

No sense being out in the cold and laying on the damp forest floor for the ambush when I can easily sit inside my comfortable truck with the heat on, Leroy reasoned.

When he saw Petrolli's headlights approach the entrance to the campground, Leroy reached across the front bench seat and turned on his headlights. He then slipped out the passenger door before Petrolli could see what was happening. Petrolli would have to approach Leroy's vehicle through the glare of his headlights, providing Leroy with a clearly lit target at close range.

Leroy's planning might have worked, except for a couple of important details he failed to take into consideration. The first being that Petrolli was a survivor. He had survived twenty years in prison, and he had survived his entire life on the streets before entering prison. As a con, Petrolli had a sixth-sense Riker couldn't comprehend without having been a con himself.

By nature, Petrolli was suspicious, cautious, and paranoid. He was also smart enough to realize he was the only eyewitness to Michael's murder. Although he was not the person who had delivered the fatal blow, he would have a hard time explaining what his role had been if the authorities ever became involved.

Petrolli put that thought out of his mind as he pulled into the campground and noticed Leroy's headlights were already on. *That's curious,"* Petrolli thought. *There's no good reason for Riker to light up the campground, regardless of whether anyone was there or not.*

Petrolli hadn't seen Leroy slide out the passenger's door and disappear into the darkness. He kept his focus on the driver's door, assuming Leroy had turned on his headlights while seated behind the wheel. With Petrolli's headlights shining towards Leroy's truck and Leroy's headlights shining back in his face, Petrolli was unable to see if anyone was seated behind the wheel. He sat and waited to see if Leroy was going to approach his pickup.

Twice, Petrolli flashed his headlights on and off, yet didn't receive any response from Leroy. He was reluctant to leave the relative safety of his pickup and approach Leroy's truck. After several minutes, which seemed like a lifetime, Petrolli slowly opened his driver's door with his left hand while keeping his right hand under his left armpit where, in a shoulder holster, Petrolli carried a borrowed semi-automatic Colt .45 pistol.

"Leroy," Petrolli shouted, "we don't have to do this."

"What do you mean?" Leroy responded. "Do you want your money or not?"

"You know what I mean, Leroy. Lora called me tonight right after you left the house. I know you're here to kill me. Just thought I'd tell you I didn't come without protection of my own. Your wife is hoping I'll kill you first, or we kill each other. So, we don't have to do either. Leave me the money and drive away, Leroy."

That bitch, Leroy said to himself. *That dirty, double-crossing bitch!*

36.

BY THE SKIN OF HIS TEETH

Shooting at paper targets or metal silhouettes to qualify at work was much different than shooting a real person. Leroy waited as he saw Petrolli cautiously step from his old truck. Petrolli held his Colt 45 along his right side, concealed by the shadows. Leroy couldn't risk waiting any longer. If Petrolli was armed, he didn't want to give him the chance to shoot first.

Leroy fired his Glock at the largest part of his intended target as he had been trained. Petrolli collapsed immediately to the ground and remained still. Riker was reluctant to approach to make sure Petrolli was dead. He was sure his shot hit exactly where he wanted it to hit, in the center of Petrolli's chest.

Petrolli played dead, with his right hand remaining on his weapon now concealed under his body. He could feel what he presumed was blood running down his left side. He remained where he had fallen until he was sure Leroy had driven away. Had Leroy approached his prone body, Petrolli was prepared to kill him.

The distinctive sound of Leroy's pickup scraping the side of the large rock filled the night air. It was replaced by the screeching sound of metal against metal as Leroy glanced off Petrolli's pickup. Leroy had backed his vehicle against the tree line and Petrolli had pulled up to within two car lengths in front of Riker's truck, so there was little room to negotiate between the rock and the front of Petrolli's pickup. Another familiar sound, this time of breaking glass, pierced the darkness as Riker accelerated out of the campground.

Once Petrolli was sure Leroy was gone, he crawled to the front of his truck and using the bumper for support, brought himself into a standing position. He wasn't exactly sure where he'd been hit but was confident his condition was not immediately life-threatening. Although he was bleeding, he was able to breathe without difficulty, which meant neither lung had been hit. However, he was unable to move his left arm and his ribs hurt like hell.

He had to stop or slow the bleeding. Direct pressure along his side and under his left arm would accomplish that. He wrapped his black woolen cap around the Colt .45 and placed them under his left arm. By applying pressure against his side with his arm, he successfully slowed the bleeding as he made the long drive to the Livingston General Hospital.

Petrolli debated whether to stop at the Wilsall Fire Station and summon help there. However, he didn't want to leave his truck at the fire station with his gun inside. Prior to his release from prison six months earlier, he had a phony Montana State Driver's License made in the prison print shop. Only under a black light would anyone be able to tell it was not legitimate.

His old farm pickup, held together with baling wire and years of rust was a beater he'd purchased from a rancher shortly after his release. Although the truck didn't look like much, the engine was strong and had very few miles on the odometer. Petrolli never bothered to get the registration transferred into his own name since the license tags were good for another eight months. In the parking lot of Livingston General Hospital, it would look like any other old beater farm truck.

As Petrolli carefully drove down the mountain road he remained aware of his breathing and bleeding. He was confident the bullet had missed an artery. If not, he would have bled out long before now. He also felt confident the bullet had missed other major organs. He made the decision if he felt worse or if the bleeding resumed when he got close to the Wilsall Fire Station, he'd stop there. If not, he'd continue to the hospital with a story about accidentally shooting himself.

As he drove, Petrolli thought about all the ways he might exact his revenge against Leroy and his wife. He decided that after he successfully arrived at either the hospital or the fire station, he'd remove his shoulder holster and hide it and the Colt .45 in the springs behind the seat and then reposition the old Army blanket that covered up the tears in the backseat cushions. The blanket provided the perfect place to conceal his firearm and holster. In the meantime, he knew he needed the gun, along with his wool cap, to keep pressure on his wound.

As all of this ran through his mind, he smiled at the thought, *I must not be hurt too badly if I can still think this clearly.*

Thirty minutes past the Wilsall Fire Station, Petrolli arrived at the hospital. He took the time to place his Colt .45 and shoulder holster behind the seat in the exposed springs. Then he lifted the Army blanket and placed the car keys into a slit in the seat upholstery. He didn't want to lock the truck just in case he needed to ask a friend to pick it up.

With his wool cap still firmly pressed against his side, he walked into the emergency room. It didn't take any time before the admitting nurse recognized that he was pale from blood loss. She asked what happened as blood dripped on the hospital's pristine white linoleum floors.

As soon as Petrolli uttered the words, "Shot my..." he lost consciousness and was whisked into an emergency treatment room. His outer garments were cut away by the ER nurse, and an IV drip was started. The ER doctor entered the room and immediately noticed two points of entry from a bullet or part of a bullet. The doctor surmised a bullet had ricocheted off a rib and into the bicep muscle of his left arm, narrowly missing the brachial artery.

Only a small piece of shrapnel was recovered from the hollow-point bullet, and the remainder of the round had obviously exited without a trace. The piece of shrapnel was too small to identify the caliber, other than to positively determine it was from a copper jacketed hollow-point bullet.

37.
ALSO KNOWN AS

Before Petrolli was admitted to a hospital room for observation and blood transfusion, standard hospital protocol required the hospital to contact the Livingston police for all gunshot victims.

When Livingston Police Officer Crawford arrived, Petrolli was conscious and still in the emergency treatment room. He confidently handed Officer Crawford his fake driver's license with the alias of Austin Shoemaker, and a date of birth close to his own. The address on the ID was 625 Main Street, Deer Lodge, Montana. Deer Lodge was in Powell County, located to the West of Park County.

Officer Crawford had been assured by the ER doctor the patient was strong enough to answer a few questions.

"Mr. Shoemaker," Crawford began, "can you tell me how you were shot?"

"It was one of those dumb mistakes you hear about other people making, except I never in a million years thought I would be one of those other people. I was out target practicing with my Colt 45. I thought the chamber was empty. The stupid gun fired while I was putting it back into my shoulder holster."

"Was anyone else with you or anyone who can verify these facts?"

"I'm afraid not, Officer. I was alone and didn't see another living soul."

"The doctor tells me you are a very lucky man. The bullet missed your artery. How long did it take you to get to the hospital and how did you control the bleeding?"

"I must be lucky. I was about 45 miles west of Livingston. I knew Livingston had better hospitals than Deer Lodge, so I drove here. I used my wool knit cap to apply pressure to my wound. It must have worked, at least until I got here. The nurse tells me the bleeding started up right after I arrived. The next thing I remember is being treated."

"Well, Mr. Shoemaker, I'm told you'll likely be admitted for observation and more blood transfusions since you apparently lost a great deal. Detectives from the Park County Sheriff's Department might also want to follow up to ascertain where precisely your accident took place. After I leave, the hospital wants to take X-rays of your ribs to make sure no bullet fragments are floating around to cause more internal injuries. Is your vehicle still in the hospital parking lot or will you be making your own arrangements to have it secured while you're here?"

"As soon as I'm admitted, if not before, I'll make all the arrangements regarding my vehicle."

Officer Crawford knew he didn't have sufficient probable cause for a search warrant of Shoemaker's vehicle. Nor did he have any reason to ask Mr. Shoemaker for his consent to search. However, Crawford felt that something about Shoemaker's story didn't add up. Maybe, after he spoke to the ER doctor in more detail, he'd have an opportunity to run Shoemaker's driver's license through their system. Then he could contact his police academy buddy who now worked for the Deer Lodge Police Department, and maybe he could glean more information to forward to the Park County Sheriff's Detectives.

For now, Crawford wanted to maintain jurisdiction since the Livingston Hospital was inside the city limits. Plus, he wanted to make detective in the police department someday. This was his chance to demonstrate what he could do to further his career goals.

Austin Shoemaker (aka Donald Petrolli) was admitted to the fourth floor of the Livingston General Hospital. Shoemaker asked his nurse about the procedure for making local phone calls from his room. The nurse told him if the call was not long distance, all he had to do was dial 9 first, and then the full number he wanted to call. There was no charge for any local calls, and a record of his calls would not appear on his discharge paperwork.

Shoemaker next inquired if the nurse had any idea how long he'd be in the hospital, to which he was told "just one or two days at the most."

Crawford called his buddy in Deer Lodge Police Department.

"Hey, Demmon, this is Crawford with Livingston PD. What can you tell me about the address 625 Main Street in Deer Lodge? We have a subject in our hospital with an alleged self-inflicted gunshot wound, and he is using the Main Street address on his Montana driver's license."

"Have you made detective already, Crawford?" Demmon asked jokingly. "I can tell you that's an apartment building with eight units, and it's leased by the state as a halfway house for paroled inmates."

"You don't say. So that suggests that my gunshot victim is likely a former felon. As for making detective, I could only wish. I'm just doing some preliminary follow-up on this shooting before turning it over to an assigned detective. You know how it is."

"If he really shot himself, that's a problem for him, now isn't it?" Demmon replied. "And yeah, I know it never hurts to demonstrate initiative, up to a point."

"I hear you. Have you had any bad interaction with anyone from that Main Street location?"

"Nah. Most of the ex-cons play it careful when they get released to the halfway house. What's your suspect's name?" Demmon asked.

"He goes by Austin Shoemaker, but I suspect his driver's license is a fake."

"That's a good possibility. The prison has an excellent print shop with the ability to turn out legitimate-looking Montana IDs. Prison officials have only recently been able to shut them down."

"Thanks. I'll pass that along to Detective French with the City of Livingston Police. He might follow up with you or one of your detectives."

Crawford next contacted the police dispatcher in Livingston and provided her the information from Shoemaker's driver's license. Not surprisingly, no record existed. Crawford next asked dispatch to conduct a search for all vehicles registered in the name of Shoemaker. Again, the response came back with nothing found.

Armed with this information, Crawford decided to speak with the ER physician about Shoemaker's gunshot wounds.

"Hey doc, I'm doing some follow-up on the self-inflicted gunshot victim that was admitted. What can you tell me?"

"I can tell you his wounds are not consistent with a self-inflicted shooting. There was no powder marks on Shoemaker's clothing or skin or any sign of flash burns. If Mr. Shoemaker had a shoulder holster, he was not wearing it when he arrived in the ER. It would have been very difficult, but not impossible, for him to take off a shoulder holster, considering his condition."

"Doctor, would you please bag Shoemaker's clothing? I'll have Detective French follow up with you," said Crawford.

It was obvious that Austin Shoemaker was not the patient's real name and he was most likely a former inmate from the Deer Lodge Men's Prison. That meant, if Shoemaker had shot himself, he would be in violation of the law prohibiting felons from possessing a firearm, and also in violation of the terms and conditions of his probation and parole.

This is all the preliminary investigating I can do, thought Crawford. *Now it's time to turn the case over to Detective French. Hopefully, he'll be able to get the truth from Shoemaker… or whatever his name is.*

Crawford knew that any future promotional opportunities hinged on him treading lightly within a pecking order. If he wanted to advance, he could not venture too far afield from his patrol officer role and into the realm of a detective. That would piss off the detective division, and complaints might be sent to the Chief of Police. Crawford knew perfectly well he'd hear about it from his sergeant, who would have heard about it from his lieutenant, who in turn would have heard about it from his captain. Regardless, everything flowed downhill and would land on him.

38.

PLOTTING REVENGE

Petrolli's first phone call was to Roy Puzzo, his former cellmate and someone he knew he could trust.

"Hey, Puzzo. This is Don, and I need a favor. Are you up for it?"

"Hell, yeah," Puzzo said, "Considering everything you did for me in the joint, I owe you."

"Great," Petrolli continued, "I'm in the Livingston Hospital for the next day or two, and I need someone to get my pickup out of the hospital parking lot and move it to a secure location. Under the old Army blanket on the driver's side, there's a slit in the seat, and inside the slit are the truck keys. Take it to your barn and stash it out of sight until I call you. Okay?"

"What in the hell are you doing in the hospital? I figured someone as tough as you would never be in a hospital," Puzzo said.

"It's a long story, and I'll tell you in person when I pick up my truck," Petrolli replied.

"Where in the parking lot is your truck?" Puzzo asked. "I know I'll recognize it when I see it, but I don't want to draw unnecessary attention to myself by driving around."

"It's in the visitor's parking lot, close to the main entrance into the hospital."

"Is there anything else you want me to do for you?" Puzzo asked.

"As a matter of fact, there is. I need someone trustworthy to get a message to Gaspipe on my old cellblock," Petrolli said.

"It just so happens I know Gaspipe's old lady. I hear she visits him at least once a week," Puzzo replied.

"Just be careful how well you get to know Gaspipe's old lady while he's on the inside. He didn't get that name from being a pipefitter, you know," Petrolli said with a chuckle. "Tell her this message is urgent and she needs to deliver it as soon as possible."

"What's the message you want delivered?" Puzzo asked.

"Just tell her that I have proof badge number 40 and his wife murdered their adopted son and number 40 just now tried to kill me in an ambush. That's all she needs to say. Gaspipe will know what to do. Make sure she gets the badge number right: Number 40! Also, tell her to let you know when the message is delivered."

"Sure thing. I'll call her right away," Puzzo said. "Is that the long story you were going to tell me the next time I saw you?"

"That's it for now. I want Gaspipe to put the word out to The Prison Brotherhood. I have some other loose ends to take care of once I get out of the hospital," said Petrolli.

Don Petrolli knew the longer he stayed in the hospital under his alias, the sooner the cops would return and his story of shooting himself would fall apart. He couldn't risk that because if he stuck with his story and the cops figured out he was an ex-con, he'd be back in prison in a heartbeat. He didn't want to rat out Leroy and Lora Riker, at least not before he exacted his revenge against them.

They both had double-crossed him and tried to kill him. If he had to give them both up to the police to save his own skin or to get a plea deal, he was willing to do that. But he wanted to get his pound of flesh first.

As Leroy drove home from the campground Friday night he was enraged over Lora's double-cross and her devious plan to have Petrolli kill him. *Why else would she call and warn Petrolli? Now, the question was what was he going to do about her?* Leroy thought. He felt like strangling the life out of Lora as soon as he got home, but he knew he needed to think and plan his course of action more carefully. *No,* he told himself, *I'll go home, wake her up, have sex, and tell her how everything worked out with Petrolli at the campground. I'll tell her she has nothing to worry about.*

39.

ACTS ONE AND TWO

Just witnessing Lora's reaction to seeing me alive will be worth the price of admission to Act One of my little play, thought Leroy.

It was late when he arrived home, and the house was dark. Leroy was surprised to find the front door unlocked. He first looked into Susie's room, and she was fast asleep. He quietly opened their bedroom door, and Lora was, or at least pretended to be, asleep. The room was totally dark, and Leroy wasn't sure if Lora was expecting Petrolli to slip into bed with her or if she was really expecting him. Either way, he somewhat noisily undressed, threw back the covers, exposing Lora, and climbed on top of her.

Lora's only words were, "Is that you, Leroy?"

"You weren't expecting anyone else, were you?" He said sarcastically.

"Of course not, dear," she replied. "Do you want to tell me how everything went tonight before or after we make love?" Lora asked.

"I'll tell you everything after. I've some adrenaline I need to work off first," Leroy said.

Act Two was going to be his toughest role in his play; making love to someone he despised and wanted to kill while hiding his true feeling of abhorrence. *Every move in the sex act has to be a perfect per-formance*, Leroy told himself.

Afterward, Lora said, "Did that work off your adrenalin? Now, tell me how everything went at the campground; according to the plan I hope?"

"Yeah, everything was according to plan. Petrolli showed up, and I caught him off guard."

"Are you sure he's dead? What did you do with his body?"

"I'm sure. The last I saw of his body it was floating down the river. In just a few weeks, the river will start to freeze over, and there will be several feet of snow up there. Petrolli's body won't be found until next spring. After the animals have their way, it won't be recognizable."

"What if someone finds his car? Won't the authorities search for the owner?"

"Don't worry about his car. The keys are still in the ignition, and they will be found someday in Timbuktu considering all of the joyriders that dump stolen cars up there. Besides, Petrolli told me the truck was purchased with cash and was still registered to an old farmer he bought it from. So, if the cops find his truck, it will lead them to a dead end."

"I told you everything would work out, and now all we have to do is sit back and wait for the life insurance money to flow in," Lora said.

Almost everything Leroy had just told Lora was a lie, including the part about Petrolli floating down the river. However, there was always a slim chance that Petrolli was alive.

Maybe," he thought, "*I should have dragged his body to the river.*

As Leroy lay in bed wanting his exhaustion to put him to sleep, his mind second-guessed his every move. He was confident that the ballistics from his gun would not be matched to the fatal round in Petrolli's chest. That's when he remembered the shell casing from his 9mm. He was in such a hurry to get away, he forgot to pick up his brass that could potentially be matched to his firearm. If the police made a connection, he'd be a suspect in the death of Petrolli and they'd get a warrant for his gun to test it for ballistics. *Maybe I should get rid of my gun*, he thought. Yet, he couldn't do that because the 9mm was his work duty weapon, and the firearm had to be available for inspection and secured in his locker whenever he was at work. *I could always just replace it with an identical make and model*, he told himself. *After all, what's the likelihood anyone would compare serial numbers during an inspection?*

The more pressing topic on his mind was, *What about Lora's betrayal?* He had to plan something, and soon. Lora's fate, whatever that might be, would have to give him a perfect alibi.

Lora's question about Petrolli's pickup also reminded him that he had scraped the side of his truck against Petrolli's. Paint would most certainly have been transferred, which would tie his truck and Petrolli's truck to the same place and time. He also knew the crime lab could determine make, model, and vehicle color in the paint trace. He promptly got dressed and went outside to look at his truck.

"Damn it," Leroy said out loud. Not only had there been a transfer of paint, but he obviously had broken a large portion of his taillight. He told himself, *Just as soon as Lora is asleep, I'll drive back to the campground and do what I should have done while I was there, and what I told Lora I had done. Petrolli's body must not be found next to my truck, and I have to find my spent shell casing and any broken taillight glass. Then I'll figure out what to do with my pickup.*

40.

OFF AND ON THE RADAR

Notes

Detective Russ on the Case

The following day, Petrolli called a lady friend and asked her to stop by his apartment and bring him some clothes. When she arrived, he asked her for a ride to Puzzo's house so he could get his truck. There were no police holds on him, so Petrolli signed himself out of the hospital, over the strenuous objections of the head nurse. He walked out of the hospital and fell off the radar.

Once Petrolli arrived at Puzzo's farm, he found his truck; the keys and gun were just where he had left them. He now needed a place to crash. He couldn't go back to the address on his driver's license in Deer Lodge and he couldn't go to the apartment in Livingston that his probation officer had on file. The cops and his probation officer would be looking for him every place else he might go. Petrolli didn't know it then, but he was soon to be back on the radar. An outstanding arrest warrant was about to be issued and his name would be entered into NCIC, the National Crime Information Center's database, available to every law enforcement agency in the country.

The following Monday, Livingston Police Officer Crawford forwarded his report to Detective Keith French. However, he did not receive Crawford's report until Tuesday. As soon as French read the report, he told Crawford he would contact Shoemaker at the hospital.

"Obviously," French said, "this guy is not who he says he is and his story about accidentally shooting himself doesn't hold up."

Detective French arrived at the hospital at 9 a.m. on Tuesday, only to learn Austin Shoemaker had a visitor the previous day. The fourth-floor head nurse said the visitor brought Shoemaker clean clothes, and Shoemaker had discharged himself against medical advice. French was pissed Shoemaker was no longer there and now he really wanted to get to the bottom of whatever was going on.

French decided to call the Park County Sheriff's Department, and wouldn't you know it, the Wyatt and Judd detective duo were about to receive a lead.

"Detective Wyatt?" French asked as I picked up the phone.

"Yes, Wyatt here."

"This is Detective Keith French from Livingston PD. Is the name Shoemaker familiar to you?"

"Hey, Keith. It sure is. Shoemaker is an alias for Don Petrolli, who is involved in a suspicious drowning death of a young boy, Michael Riker."

"You don't say!" exclaimed French.

"Yeah, Petrolli's probation and parole officer told us about the Shoemaker alias. Based on the information we both have, I'm thinking there is probable cause to obtain an arrest warrant for, at the very least, a probation violation, felon in possession of a firearm, and suspicion of murder."

"Agreed," said French.

"Great. I'll enter the necessary information into NCIC and issue a county-wide BOLO," I announced.

Then I filled Judd in about this latest development.

41.
ACT THREE

Leroy called his sergeant on Sunday morning. He was expected back to work the next day after taking the previous two days off to take his son fishing.

"Hey Sarge, this is Leroy. You're probably aware by now that my son died last Friday. I'd like to take the next two weeks off. Lora and I have a lot of things to work out. We need to plan for his memorial, arrange for his cremation, and a dozen other things. Lora is also having problems coping with his death. I'm concerned about her mental health, and I feel I need to be here to watch over her and give her my support."

"Yeah, I read about his drowning. My condolences to you both," the sergeant said. "Take as much bereavement leave as you need, and I'll keep your shift covered."

"Thanks, Sarge," Leroy said.

Now that Leroy had two extra weeks of leave arranged, he could spend more time strategizing on what to do about Lora. *If she was dead,* he thought, *her personal life insurance and Michael's will come to me, and I'd get my revenge against her*. He was still working out the details of how to make her death look like an accident or suicide.

Her life insurance would be held up if there was any semblance to a homicide, just like Michael's insurance was.

Finally, Leroy decided how to get his vengeance against Lora. She would die by suicide. He had been repeating the same lie about Lora being mentally unstable, drinking heavily, and suffering from depression to his parents, their neighbors, Lora's parents, and anyone else he could think of. As the week progressed, he was careful to selectively slip in the term "suicidal" when talking about Lora. He also made several phone calls to the National Suicide Prevention Hotline to get advice concerning his wife. He wanted a record demonstrating he had an ongoing concern for her.

Whenever Leroy spoke to Lora's parents, he cautioned them against confronting Lora about her depression. "Please don't talk to Lora about her mental health or use the word 'suicide' around her. That will likely put her over the edge, and she might carry through on her suicidal tendencies," he told them.

At the end of his second week of leave, Leroy called his sergeant again.

"Hey, Sarge, as I feared, Lora's getting worse. I've taken her to counseling and she is on depression and anxiety medication. Her doctor said she should be admitted for a day or two, but she was against that. I'm hopeful the meds will work for her, and she can get back to being her old self. Our daughter, Susie, has been staying with Lora's mother since the memorial service. That's probably a good place for her to be for the time being."

"I'm sorry to hear that, Leroy. You have plenty of sick and vacation leave, so just let me know when you're ready to come back to work, and I'll keep your shift covered in the interim."

The stage was now set for Act Three of Leroy's little play. All he had to do was to convincingly make Lora's death appear to be a suicide.

42.
ANY WORD FROM PRISON?

While Leroy worked out the details in his head for the demise of his wife; Don Petrolli was getting impatient. It had now been three weeks since he received confirmation his message had been delivered to Gaspipe, yet there had been no news of any correctional officer being killed at the Deer Lodge State Prison.

Why haven't I heard or read something by now? he asked himself. *What if the plot has been thwarted, or worse, detected?* His greatest fear was having something traced back to him. Petrolli wanted his revenge against Leroy and Lora, but he didn't want to go back to prison either.

Petrolli had been lying low and avoiding places the cops might think to look for him. He thought maybe he was just being overly cautious or paranoid. After all, he hadn't received any word from any of his friends that the police were looking for him. Perhaps the cops and doctors had accepted his word about the accidental gunshot wound. He was starting to feel more comfortable that his Shoemaker alias had held up, and no one had made the connection between him and the mysterious man in black at the campground the night the young Riker boy drowned.

He was also confident that neither the cops nor anyone else would make a connection between him, Leroy, or Lora Riker. The only time they were ever seen together was on one occasion, by one employee, at The Bank Bar and Vault Restaurant. *Hardly anything for me to worry about,* he told himself. Petrolli decided he would call Puzzo again and find out what the hold-up was with Gaspipe and The Prison Brotherhood.

"Hey Puzzo, what's the word from prison? It's been three weeks, and I've heard nothing. Are you sure Gaspipe's old lady delivered the message?" Petrolli asked.

"Don't worry, Petrolli. The message got delivered. The problem is Riker hasn't been back to work. The word on the cellblock is Riker's wife isn't coping with their son's death, and Riker has been taking time off to care for her," Puzzo responded.

"Yeah, I bet! That's total bull. His wife was involved in all of this, including my attempted murder, up to her not-so-beautiful eyelashes. She's the one that wanted the boy dead to begin with, to collect on the life insurance, and she forced Riker into everything. So, there is no way in hell she's upset about the boy's death. Do you know if there have been any leaks at the prison?" Petrolli asked.

"The only leak was the inmates publishing an article in the prison newspaper about Riker and his wife being suspects in the death of their son," Puzzo said.

"Well, that could be a good thing or a bad thing. We know the general population despises child killers, especially by a C.O., and they might decide to take things into their own hands when Leroy returns. The Brotherhood might not have to get involved at all, or at a minimum just stoke the flames a little bit. The bad thing is if the administration comes to the same conclusion and assigns Leroy to a desk job for his own protection. That would isolate him from the general population." Petrolli replied.

"If Riker hasn't returned to work yet, the administration probably won't do anything," Puzzo remarked. "So what if The Brotherhood started stoking those flames now?"

"No," Petrolli said. "Listen, if the general population starts getting riled up too soon, the administration is bound to get wind of it and take protective action. Let things play out until after he returns to work. I've waited this long for my revenge, and I can wait a few more weeks."

"Got it. We'll wait," agreed Puzzo.

"But I wonder if Riker's cooking something up for his wife. Right before he shot me, I told him his wife tipped me off about his motives, and I'm betting that really pissed him off. Maybe all this crap about his wife being upset, depressed or suicidal is just his con for setting the stage for her death. I sure wouldn't put that past him."

43.

AT HOME IN THE BAR

Petrolli's restlessness at being cooped up was getting the better of him. It was now late fall, and there shouldn't be many people around Wilsall mid-week. He decided to make a road trip to The Bank Bar to shake off his stir-craziness. After all, no one knew what his truck looked like, and almost no one knew what he looked like.

It was two in the afternoon when he rolled up, with no other cars in front or on the side of the building. *Like most good ranchers, they're all still hard at work*, he thought.

Once inside, Petrolli's eyes had to adjust to the dim lights. No other patrons were inside, and he sat down at the long bar. He noticed a piece of history on the back bar wall in front of him — a huge vintage mirror in the process of de-silvering, framed in a discolored black oak frame. He remembered that his grandparents had a much smaller, yet similar mirror hanging in their home.

The bar's tin ceiling was made from old, stamped tiles. The former bank building dated back to the early 1880s and was converted into a bar after the railroad stopped regular runs through town. Petrolli relaxed as he sat on the bar stool, feeling incognito and comfortable in the midst of the nostalgia.

Directly in front of him perched an antique cash register, tended by a woman every bit in her eighties. She approached and welcomed him.

"What's your pleasure?" she asked.

"Just whiskey. Neat," Petrolli said.

"Any particular brand?"

"Jack Daniels, Black, if you got it."

"Good choice. Direct from Tennessee," she replied with a smile. "Welcome. I'm Elsie. I try to get to know my customers. What's your name?"

"Just call me Don," he replied.

"Glad to meet you, Don."

"Yeah, same here."

As Elsie brought his drink, she momentarily glanced at the tattoos on the backs of his hands. She then quickly diverted her eyes to not draw attention to herself. Under the bar, visible only to staff, was a picture and a description of Petrolli and his tattoos.

Elsie told Petrolli to take his time, and she'd return shortly to see if he wanted another round. In the meantime, she had some paperwork to do in the back office. "Just holler if you need anything," she told him. Once in the safety of the office, Elsie called Art Beebe, the bar's owner.

"Art," Elsie said, "the guy the police are looking for is in the bar now. I know you said to call the police first, but I wanted to let you know before I did."

"Thanks for calling, Elsie. Is the guy alone?" Art asked.

"Yeah, he's just sitting at the bar minding his own business. Seems nice enough," she said.

"Try to keep him there. But don't let on that anything is wrong," Art instructed. "Tell him the bar is running a special. Buy two drinks and get a free lunch. If he goes for it, take your time fixing his meal. I'll call the sheriff's detectives and let them know. If he leaves, try to get his license plate number and his direction of travel. Just don't let him see you doing it. Got it?"

"Got it. He's asking for a second round now, so I better go," she replied.

As soon as he finished talking to Elsie, Art Beebe called the Park County Sheriff's Department. "Please put me through to Detective Russ Wyatt. It's urgent," he said.

"May I ask what this is in regard to?" was the response.

"Just tell him it's Art Beebe from The Bank Bar and Vault Restaurant in Wilsall and that it's urgent. He'll know."

44.

BAR STING

Notes

Detective Russ on the Case

"Hey, Wyatt," hollered my partner, Judd. "You've had a call holding for two minutes."

"Can't a man go to the John around here?" I shot back, chuckling on my way out of the men's room.

"It's Art Beebe," said Judd, serious as a heart attack.

"Oh, crap! I better grab that."

"He's here," Art blurted out as I picked up the phone. "Your guy with the tattoos is in the bar drinking. I don't know how long we can keep him occupied. I told Elsie, the bartender on duty, to offer him free food as part of a promotion. I don't know if that's going to work or not. He's on his second drink now."

"Okay, good job, Art. I'm on my way. Your phone call is being transferred to my cell phone so we can keep in touch while I drive. I'll tell dispatch to send a uniform car in your direction, but without lights or sirens."

"Got it," said Art.

"We don't want to put anyone in jeopardy. This man is a suspected murderer and a former prison inmate. If he wants to leave, let him. Tell Elsie to play it safe and don't make him suspicious," I directed. "Tell her to make an excuse and stay in the kitchen in 20 minutes. Either me or uniform deputies will be there around that time."

"I'll send a text to her cell phone," said Art. "Elsie's good at responding quickly. I'm glad she's working the bar today and not one of the younger ladies. She knows how to play it cool and keep her head."

"Good," I said. "If he leaves, just let me know what direction he goes. We don't have his license plate number, so if you can get that for me, I'd appreciate it."

"No problem. I'm able to monitor both our indoor and outdoor security cameras from home, and his vehicle is parked right in front of the building."

"One more thing, Art. Apart from the door into the bar from the street corner and the entrance into the restaurant from the side street, is there access to the kitchen area from outside, and is that door locked?" I asked.

"Correct. We normally keep the kitchen entrance locked when only one person is working. Do you want Elsie to unlock it?" Art asked.

"Yes. If I can get more than one uniform there, I'll direct a deputy to enter through the kitchen," I said. "Are there any weapons inside?"

"There is a short-barrel 12-gauge in the back office. I've seen Elsie drop pheasants like a pro, so she definitely knows how to use it, if necessary," Art responded.

"Let's all hope that won't be necessary... hello, Art? Are you there?" A combination of a bumpy road and a cell phone dead zone temporarily cut us off. "Art?"

"Yeah, yeah, I'm here."

"Just so you know, two uniformed deputies in separate cars will arrive in about five minutes, and I'm not far behind. No one will enter until we're all in position. Was Elsie successful in serving him food?" I asked.

"She just sent me a text saying she's in the kitchen finishing up chicken fried steak. And he's switched over to Moose Drool. At least he has good taste in beer," Art quipped.

"Okay. Tell Elsie to serve his food and then retreat to the kitchen. Tell her to stay there until a deputy comes in through the back door. Then she's to exit out that same door."

"Just FYI, Russ. This guy seems to be favoring his left arm, like maybe it's impaired in some way," Art said.

"Thanks. Good to know," I replied.

With one deputy outside, another silently located in the kitchen, and Elsie safely out of the building, I gave direction by radio. "We'll go on my command. Remember we don't know if this guy is armed or not. There are no civilians inside, and there is no place for him to go. Also, I'm told his left arm may not be usable, but don't take any chances either. Everyone double-click your mic if you are in position. Kitchen entrance?"

Click, click.

"Restaurant entrance?"

Click, click.

"Okay, we go on the count of three. *ONE, TWO —*"

45.

GOODBYE, LORA

Leroy devised a plan concerning his wife as he drove to the Montana State University in Bozeman, 26 miles west of Livingston. As he casually strolled fraternity row, his intent was to approach any guy who looked like a jock. Having been a jock in high school, he thought he was a good judge of that type.

"Hey, got a minute?" Leroy asked the first guy he saw. "Are you a student here? My friends and I are looking to score with some women this weekend, and we're looking for some drugs to improve our chances if you get what I'm saying."

"You some kind of cop or something?" was the reply.

"Hell no," Leroy responded. "Do I look like a damn cop? If you can't help me, just say so."

"Hold your horses, pops. Did I say I couldn't help you? What you're looking for is GHB, Liquid G, Liquid Ecstasy, or Gamma 10. Do you want it in liquid, pill, or powder? It's colorless and odorless, but you gotta be careful using it. Too much and it's fatal. And too much, it shows up in toxicology results. Not a good thing. Use as directed and you're golden."

"How much is too much?" Leroy asked.

"Anything more than two drops of the liquid, one pill, or one pinch of the powder. No more."

"Got it. How much for the liquid GHB and how soon can I get it?" Leroy asked.

"I can get you a small container in about 20 minutes. Forty bucks. Does that work for you?"

"Sure. Meet back here or someplace else?" Leroy asked.

"See that pub across the street? Meet me inside by the pool tables in twenty minutes. And pops, bring cash and no cops."

Twenty minutes later, Leroy slipped the date-rape drug in his pocket. "How do I know this is the real thing and not just water?"

"You don't. But you have enough there for twenty good times, so go try it out. I personally stand behind it."

Leroy smiled to himself as his plan was one step closer to fruition. He'd put two drops, just to be sure, into Lora's nightly bourbon, just before she went to bed. After he was sure it had taken effect, he'd undress her and take her and her clothes out to her car. Then he'd drive her car down to the KPRK Bridge and dump her body into the murky Yellowstone River. It wasn't running as high and fast as it was a few weeks earlier and was now a few feet below flood stage.

There was some kind of poetic justice that Lora should drown from the same bridge that she planned their son, Michael, would fall to his death from. Leroy thought it was providence that the Shields River was a tributary to the Yellowstone, so it was even more fitting for her to drown in a similar way as Michael.

He was surprised at how heavy Lora's dead weight was when he loaded her into the back of her Jeep. It was 3 a.m. when he arrived at the bridge — totally dark, except for a half-moon that shed some light. The air was cold and still and had the unique sweet fall-like smell of decomposing vegetation. Riker parked Lora's car on the bridge.

He removed Lora's unconscious body and her clothing from the car and leaned his wife's limp body against the cold, metal bridge railing, with her arms dangling over the edge and partially support-ing her dead weight. The hard part was lifting her lower body mass up and over the bridge railing, but a surge of adrenalin made the task easier. Leroy heard the satisfying splash of her body as it struck the surface of the cold water. She disappeared into the golden hue of yellow moonbeams reflecting off the surface of the fast-flowing river.

Leroy next placed her clothes haphazardly on the bridge to make it appear that a woman had hastily undressed and then jumped to her death. He smiled to himself about how he had laid the ground-work the past three weeks about Lora being suicidal. He left Lora's car keys in the pocket of her jeans to avoid running the risk of some-one stealing the car.

Then Leroy walked the two miles home, where he went to bed, and waited for the phone call from the police. He was pleased with himself about how carefully he planned everything, including leav-ing his cell phone turned on at home, and wearing gloves when he drove Lora's car. If the cops tried to determine where he was that night by using the pings to his phone from cell towers, it would show he was home all night.

The expected phone call came at 5:10 a.m.

"This is Livingston Police dispatch. Is this Mr. Leroy Riker?"

"Yes, this is Leroy Riker."

"Sir, do you know where your wife and Jeep are?"

"Until you woke me, I thought my wife was in bed with me. I assume her Jeep is still in the driveway. Why do you ask?"

"Sir, would you please check your house now to see if you wife is someplace inside."

"What's this all about? You're starting to freak me out."

"Sir, I'll be happy to explain, but first check the house for your wife."

"Okay. Give me a minute or two." After a short pause, Leroy said, "there is no sign of my wife or her Jeep. What the hell is going on? Tell me right now," Leroy demanded.

"A patrol officer found your wife's Jeep abandoned on the old KPRK Bridge. Woman's clothing was also located on the bridge near the railing and car keys in her pant pocket."

"Oh my God. She's actually done it. I can't believe she would do this."

"What is it sir you can't believe she might have done?"

"We lost our only son recently to an accidental drowning. My wife took his death very hard and has been talking about committing suicide because she didn't want to live any longer without him," Riker said.

"At this time sir, we don't know if that's what happened or not. At first daylight, we'll have a boat on the river, along with Park County Sheriff's Department dive team, looking for your wife. She might be on the riverbank someplace, or she might have staged the entire thing as a cry for help.

"When did you last see your wife?"

"We went to bed together around midnight. We both had a night-cap, and we usually sleep soundly after that," Riker said.

"Once the detectives arrive to work later this morning, I'll have them contact you for more details and hopefully with some positive news. They'll want to talk to you anyway."

"Of course. Not a problem. I'm awake now, so anytime is okay. I'm alone in the house so they will not wake up anyone else," Riker said.

Leroy hung up the receiver and thought to himself, *that went well.* He had purposely tossed the vile of GHB into the raging Yellowstone from the bridge. He was content in his belief it was the perfect crime, something Lora always sought to accomplish. *Maybe now, she would finally be proud of me, he thought.* It would likely be months, if ever, before her body was recovered. Since she was alive at the moment she hit the water, there would be water in her lungs and no trace of the drug in her system. Leroy knew there was a certain length of time before a person could be declared legally dead when there was no body. He would just have to be patient before receiving her life insurance.

46.
BUSTED

Notes

Detective Russ on the Case

Back at the Wilsall bar, I gave the command… "*THREE!*"

At that moment, Petrolli saw one deputy enter the bar from the kitchen. From his peripheral vision, he saw another deputy enter the dining room from his far right and approach the bar. In the gilded antique mirror in front of him loomed an imposing figure of a man in plain clothes, with thinning white hair and a neatly trimmed white goatee, approaching him from behind.

We all had our firearms pointed directly at him. "DO NOT move and keep your hands on the bar!" I ordered. "If you make any sudden movements, we will SHOOT you! Do you understand?"

"There has to be some mistake," Petrolli complained.

"No mistake, Donald Petrolli. You are under arrest for violation of your parole, and suspicion of murder. Now, slowly take your right hand and put it on top of your head. Take your left hand and inter-lock your fingers. Then stand up and move away from the bar. Do it now, but slowly."

"Okay. Okay. Do you mind lowering your weapons? I can't raise my arm over my head or put it behind my back because I accidentally shot myself in my left bicep a while back," said Petrolli.

"We'll see about that in a moment," I replied. "Stand up with your right hand on your head and walk backward to me, Petrolli."

Without moving a muscle, Petrolli said, "My name is Austin Shoemaker, not Petrolli. Check my driver's license."

"Pat him down for weapons, deputy," I directed my team. To Petrolli I said, "I know who you are, and your fingerprints will confirm it. Your counterfeit prison driver's license won't change that. I've seen a dozen of those over the years if I've seen one."

"You've got the wrong man! I...I know my rights!" Petrolli stuttered.

I'm sure you know your rights, but I'll read them to you anyway." After reciting the Miranda warning, I said, "Now, do you understand your rights as I have explained them to you, and do you wish to speak to me?"

Petrolli sucked on his teeth, obviously caught between a rock and a hard place. "Okay. Okay," he finally responded. "Yes, my name is Donald Petrolli, but I've never killed anyone except the dude in the bar over twenty years ago. I served my time for that, and that was an accident. I've certainly never killed any kid."

"Who said anything about a kid?" I asked.

"Ah, I was just saying I would never hurt any child in general. I wasn't speaking about any specific child," Petrolli stuttered.

"How well do you know Leroy and Lora Riker?"

"Who? Never heard of them," Petrolli said.

"Don't lie to me. I wouldn't have asked the question if I didn't already know the answer. Now, let's try that again. I didn't ask if you knew them, I asked you how well you know them," I demanded.

"Honest. I never heard those names before."

Impatiently, I said, "I told you, don't lie to me. Now, unless you want these deputies here to twist your left arm behind your back, I suggest you start being honest with me. I want you to look straight ahead and above the mirror on the back bar. Tell me what you see?"

"Ah, is that a security camera?" Petrolli asked.

"Very good observation. It has a complete view of the entire bar. There's another camera in the dining room and two other cameras on the outside of the building. I know you met with both Leroy and Lora Riker in that very booth in the corner just a few weeks ago. You're on video having a very intense conversation with them. Now, once again, how do you know them?" I demanded.

It was now time for Petrolli to pull the ace he had up his sleeve to save his ass.

"If I tell you what I know, what's in it for me?"

"That all depends on what you say and whether you can prove what you say. Right now, you're lacking in the credibility department."

"I can prove everything, and I'll also testify to everything I know. I just don't want to go back to prison."

"Look, Petrolli. You have ten years left of your original sentence. Violation of your parole and probation is enough to send you back right now. On top of that, you are our primary suspect in the murder of Leroy and Lora Riker's adopted son or at least a co-conspirator in his death. If you truly shot yourself, then the prosecutor could add being a felon in possession of a firearm. You don't hold many cards to negotiate with, but if you tell the truth about everything, and I mean everything, I'll speak to the prosecutor on your behalf. That's all I can do for you now," I responded.

47.

THE CONFESSION

"Okay. I've known Leroy Riker for at least ten years. He was the C.O., I mean correctional officer, on my cellblock most of that time. When I was released on parole, Leroy approached me about helping him do something. I then met with Leroy and Lora in the bar. I told them I didn't want any part of what they were planning, but Lora was very unrelenting and pushy," Petrolli said.

"Let's start with what it was they wanted you to do," I replied.

"They were going to kill their adopted kid for his life insurance money. Lora wasn't confident Leroy had the nerve to go through with it. She wanted me to be at the Shield's River Campground, and if Leroy lost his nerve, I would kill the boy for them."

"Did they offer to pay you?"

"They were going to pay me $500 just to be there in case Leroy didn't go through with it and another $500 if I had to do it for him."

"What happened at the campground?"

"I was hiding in the woods near my tent next to Leroy's campsite. From there, I was able to see the boy fishing and would be able to tell if Leroy lost his nerve or not. At one point, Leroy walked close to my tent and told me to stay put and that he was going to do it himself. I watched Leroy take a large sock from his truck and put a rock from the fire pit into the sock. He walked down the bank and hit the boy over the head." Petrolli took a deep breath.

"What happened then?" I asked.

"The boy dropped right away and was partly in and partly out of the water. Leroy took a couple steps into the water and pulled the boy deeper in, and then threw a fishing pole in after him. Afterward, I watched as Leroy walked downstream to get the other boy," Petrolli explained.

"What did Leroy do with the rock and the sock?"

"He put the sock on the ground right before he pulled the boy farther into the water. That's when the dog bit him," said Petrolli.

"Where did he get bit?" I asked.

"On the forearm. The dog must have bit him good because Leroy hollered and grabbed his arm."

"Then what happened?"

"The dog picked up the sock and ran for his life."

"Can you describe the sock and where the dog went with it?"

"Dark grey. Red stripe near the top. All I know is the dog got out of there fast and ran downstream into the trees."

"How do I know you're not just blaming Leroy for everything you did? What proof do you have?" I questioned further.

"For one thing, I can't use my left arm because Leroy tried to kill me. He told me to meet him at the campground a week after the boy died to pay me for just being there. That was part of the conversation in the bar. Instead, Leroy set up an ambush. He thought I was dead. Lucky for me, the bullet ricocheted off my rib, and a small fragment embedded in my left bicep. The hospital records will confirm all this," Petrolli replied. "And a Livingston police officer took the report."

"That doesn't prove you didn't kill the boy yourself," I challenged.

"How about a tape recording of our conversation at the bar? How about a recording of the phone call telling me to meet Leroy at the campground the night he tried to kill me? Is that enough proof?"

"It's a start," I replied. "What else?"

"Look at my truck and you'll see where Leroy hit the passenger side when he was gettin the hell out of Dodge. His truck should show damage on the right. He also scraped his truck's left side against a boulder and broke his taillight or headlight."

"Good. What else?" I pushed.

"He didn't pick up his brass after shooting me, so look hard around the campground. He thought I was dead, but he wasn't going to stick around to find out," Petrolli said.

"Where did this all take place?"

"Where I pitched my tent the day the boy died. Leroy backed in alongside the large boulder, with the front of his truck pointing downstream. I was parked a couple car lengths in front and facing toward him. He would have been standing close to the tree line when he fired. His only escape path was to squeeze between the front of my truck with his. I'm sure you will find tire tracks there," Petrolli explained.

"If what you say is true, and I can confirm the hospital records, I'll present everything to the prosecutor and recommend leniency on your behalf," I pledged. "But you better have what you say you have.

No more lies. You'll also have to testify to everything you told me, and to anything else you might say. Is that clear?" I asked.

"Crystal."

"Where are these tapes?"

"In my truck," Petrolli said.

"Tell me where in your truck and I'll get them," I said.

"On the driver's side in an envelope taped under the front seat. The cassettes are in the envelope. The tapes will confirm everything and are my insurance policy," Petrolli stated.

48.

GOOD OL' MAX

Notes

Detective Russ Wyatt on the Case

I found the envelope where Petrolli said it was. He was taken into custody, and his truck was impounded. An inventory search at the police department also revealed a hidden Colt .45 in a shoulder holster behind the front seat.

I listened to both tapes that evening and concluded they supported everything Petrolli said. His pickup also showed signs of body damage with sufficient paint transfer as to get a match to Leroy Riker's blue and white pickup. On the tape recordings, Lora and Leroy implicated themselves in the murder conspiracy, and Leroy admitted on tape that he delivered the fatal blow to the top of his son's head.

There were still a few loose ends I wanted to wrap up before presenting all the evidence to the elected prosecutor, Paula Jennings.

"Judd, can you put your hands of the inventory and photographs of Leroy's truck?"

"It's right here," Judd said. "What are you looking for?"

"Remember Petrolli's description of the sock? I think we documented the mate to that sock when we did the inventory and there should be a photo of it."

"Do you mean this grey, wool boot sock with a red stripe across the top?" Judd asked while holding up a photograph and the inventory slip.

"Exactly. What are the odds since we did the search that the sock is still in the truck?"

"I'd guess pretty good. There's no reason Riker would have done anything with it."

"That's why I want to get a new warrant for his truck specifically for that sock. We didn't have probable cause the first time to take the sock," I said. "We are also going to impound his truck for other evidence, since we can now place it at the scene of Petrolli's shooting."

"Okay. I'll start working on that and get it to Paula ASAP," Judd said.

"After we get the warrant, I want to take a road trip to hopefully wrap up another loose end," I said.

With the search warrant in hand, we went directly to Leroy's house. He apparently had worked the night before, so we had to wake him up. Needless to say, he was pissed.

"Leroy Riker, we have a search warrant for your truck. Is it locked?" I asked.

"Are you kidding me? When is this harassment going to stop?"

"Just give me your keys and stand right there to the rear of your truck."

Leroy kicked the truck's tire but did as directed. While Judd watched him, I began looking inside the pickup. When we found the sock the first time, it was under the front seat on the driver's side. And that is where I found it this time.

"Judd, will you hand me an evidence bag, please? This is going with us," I said. "We are also going to impound your truck as evidence."

"Wait," he said. "You can't do that. How am I supposed to get to work?" He protested.

"That's up to you to figure out. As of now, we have probable cause to believe your truck was involved in a crime, so until we can establish otherwise, it is going with us," I responded. "Now give me your keys and a tow truck will be here shortly."

Riker's face lost all color, but he didn't say another word. We left him a receipt for the sock and truck, and drove away just as soon as the tow showed up.

"That went well," Judd said. "Now all we have to do is match this sock to the murder weapon. How do you propose we do that?"

"That's where Max comes in. Remember, Petrolli said the dog grabbed the sock and ran into the woods. That's also exactly what the Sterlings said, and I believe that is what Max was trying to tell them."

"I get it. Kind of like the Lassie movies. *Follow me, Timmy's in the well.*"

"Something exactly like that. But Max wanted to take them to the sock, not a person."

"Let's just hope that Max hasn't forgotten and still wants to help," Judd said.

"The next thing I want to do is pay a visit to the Sterlings and borrow Max."

"I'm not following, but count me in," Judd said.

"You will soon enough."

When we arrived at the Sterling's small rental house, we found them home with Max, all sitting comfortably in front of a nice fire. I explained our idea, and both Sterlings enthusiastically wanted to follow Judd and me in their vehicle. There was still plenty of daylight, so we headed to the Shields River Campground. When we all arrived, Max was the first to put feet on the ground. It was almost like he understood why he was there.

I looked at Max and said, "Search."

Max let out one bark and headed into the trees. It was almost as if he was saying, *I thought you'd never ask.*

Roger and Judy Sterling stood there with their mouths ajar. As Judd and me followed Max; Roger and Judy stayed behind and were engaged in a serious conversation.

Judd and I were quick to follow the cocker spaniel. We didn't need to worry about losing him because he occasionally stopped and looked to see if we were still following.

Less than a hundred yards into the trees, and under a downed log, Max stopped and started barking.

"Did you find it, Max?" I asked. "Good boy. You might have a new career ahead of you as a police dog. Would you like that?" In response, Max let out another bark.

There it was, the perfect mate to the sock we had just removed from Leroy's truck, except this one had a rock inside. We carefully took several photographs before moving it, being careful to not disrupt the location or position of the heavy contents.

"Wow," the Sterlings said. "So that's why he wanted us to follow him. Smart dog."

"Now that we have the suspected murder weapon, how do we link it specifically to Leroy?" Judd asked.

"Let's first bag and tag this and get it into an evidence bag. Then, let's check out to see what kind of rock we might be dealing with. I don't want to handle or remove the rock from the sock yet. We'll leave that to the crime lab."

"Okay, I'm still with you, but I'm still not following," Judd said.

"If you remember, the forensic pathologist said the boy's head wound was irregular. That rules out round granite river rocks. If there are other basalt or fractured granite rocks at the fire pit, I think it is likely a good guess this murder weapon will match, by rock type one of those."

"And you think we can get fingerprints off a basalt or granite rock?" Judd asked.

"If we are really lucky, yes. The rock has been inside the sock and thanks to Max, they've both been protected from the elements under that log. If my assumptions are right, both basalt and granite, have smooth surfaces. Since fingerprints consist of sweat secretions, which are composed of fat, oils and amino acids, there's a good chance the lab can find identifiable prints. There is also a chance the lab will be able to detect DNA from both Michael and Leroy on the inside and outside of the sock," I optimistically added.

"I understand why Michael's DNA might be there, but why do you believe Riker's DNA might also be there?" Judd asked.

"Remember how Petrolli said that Max bit Riker on his forearm? There might be a transfer of Petrolli's blood from Max's teeth to the sock."

"We can only hope," said Judd.

"Yes, and there's also a chance that Leroy's skin cells or hair might have been left behind on the inside of the sock when he inserted the rock."

"So, you are hoping for a trifecta of fingerprint evidence on the rock, biological evidence from Riker on the inside of the sock, and DNA evidence from both Michael and transferred DNA evidence of Riker's, courtesy of Max, on the outside of the sock. Is that what I'm hearing?" Judd asked.

"Correct. If everything goes our way, we will have two witnesses who have Leroy delivering the fatal blow. We'll have his fingerprints and DNA tying him to the murder weapon, and we'll have the tape recording Petrolli provided. If the judge allows it, I'm sure Max will also testify against Riker."

"Wait. You'll need to explain that last one. You expect Max to somehow testify?" Judd asked.

"In a manner of speaking, yes. That's exactly what I'm thinking."

As we all were preparing to leave the campground, Judy said, "we'd like to talk to you about Max." Her voice trembled and sounded so serious, that I was momentarily afraid there was something wrong with Max.

"Sure," I said. "What about Max, is he okay?"

"Oh, yeah, Max is fine. Sorry, if I caused you to think otherwise. It's just that, well, you and Max have a special bond, and our landlord is not going to allow us to keep him," Susan finally said with a tear starting in the corner of her eye.

"I see, I think. So, what are you planning on doing with him?"

"We were actually hoping you would be able to take him if that's okay with you."

"Okay? It's more than okay. I would be delighted to do that, but only on one condition," I replied while making no attempt to withhold my enthusiasm.

"What's that?" Roger asked.

"That the two of you come to visit him often, and I do mean often."

"Would you be okay with us doing that? We wouldn't want to be a disruption to his bonding," Judy said, as Roger nodded in agreement.

"I insist on it. Any time. Any time at all. Max's casa is your casa. As far as being a disruption, I'm sure Max would love to see you both. He's going to have lots of one-on-one time with me and my grandson. Now that I think about it, I think he'd be a good candidate for the police canine academy. Max can't replace Judd, I don't think," I joked while looking directly at Judd with a smile on my face, "but Max will still make a great partner. Once trained, he will become a drug or explosive-sniffing dog, or maybe a tracker. That will all depend on how his training goes, and what his instructor believes is the best fit. The best part is, he'll live with me."

Judd spoke up at that moment and added, "Yeah, he's always trying to replace me. Good luck with that, partner."

"Great," Judy said, "this sounds like a win win for everyone, including Max."

It was easy to tell from the sound of her voice she was attempting to maintain her composure, as we all were.

49.

NO TO A PLEA BARGAIN

Notes

Detective Russ Wyatt on the Case

When I presented all the evidence to the Park County Prosecutor, Paula Jennings, she was beyond ecstatic. She agreed charges were in order for Leroy and Lora Riker for the deliberate homicide of their son, conspiracy to commit deliberate homicide, attempted murder of Donald Petrolli, two counts of attempted insurance fraud, and two counts of conspiracy to commit insurance fraud.

Even though Lora was missing and presumed dead, Paula treated the charges against her as if she were still alive. She offered Petrolli a reduced sentence and waived the parole violation in exchange for his cooperation and testimony against Leroy Riker.

Paula made out arrest warrants for both Lora and Leroy Riker. Judd and I personally served the warrant on Leroy and took him into custody. The warrant for Lora Riker was entered into NCIC, in the event she was still alive and hiding somewhere.

The news regarding the arrest of Leroy Riker in connection with the death of his adopted son, Michael, was big news not only in the Livingston area but throughout Montana and beyond. Michael's drowning and all the speculation about his death drew national attention and was picked up by the Associated Press and widely distributed. NBC Dateline carried an exclusive exposé on the drowning death. Riker's arrest renewed the media spotlight on the small towns of Wilsall and Livingston.

When a trial date was set and an actual trial was about to begin, the streets around the Park County Courthouse begin to buzz like a movie set. Every major, and some not-so-major media outlets wanted to get the inside scoop of what was happening each day in the courtroom. The judge authorized only two TV cameras to carry live coverage during the trial and conditions were set down to which everyone readily agreed. Channel 5, from the college Town of Bozeman, located due west of Livingston, was selected as one of two media outlets to carry the trial live. "Courthouse Live Coverage" was the other, a show that normally aired in the evenings but would film live during the trial.

The substantial pre-trial publicity featured pictures of Leroy Riker and his now missing and presumed deceased wife, Lora Riker, along with photographs of their adopted son, Michael. The publicity caught the attention of the University of Montana student who remembered selling GHB to the person identified as Leroy Riker. He didn't know how relevant it was, but he contacted me.

Without implicating himself, the student told me the guy in the newspaper was the same man who appeared on campus wanting to purchase a date-rape drug just days before the papers said the man's wife went missing. Absent any direct evidence linking Leroy to Lora's death, it was time to turn up the heat on Leroy Riker. I suggested to Paula Jennings that she play hardball with Riker's court-appointed attorney, Douglas Cannon.

❁ ❁ ❁

"Mr. Cannon, this is Prosecuting Attorney, Paula Jennings. There are some new witnesses and corroborating evidence against your client, Leroy Riker, that I want to make you aware of. I intend to add the new charge of deliberate murder of his wife, Lora Riker. The new evidence is Riker's purchase of a date-rape drug known as GHB from a college student at Montana State University shortly before Lora Riker's disappearance and presumed drowning. This student has identified Riker from a photo montage and is prepared to testify," Jennings said.

"How do you intend to prove corpus delicti without a body?" Cannon asked.

"I'll argue that in court. I also want you to be aware I intend to pursue the death penalty against your client. You and he should discuss his options, and I'll accept a plea of guilty in exchange for life in prison without the possibility of parole. That might be his only chance to stay alive."

"You know as well as I do a prison sentence for a correctional officer in the same facility where he worked would be a death sentence," Cannon said.

"I would be open to him serving his life sentence at a different facility," Jennings countered.

"How would that protect him?" Cannon asked.

"He could serve his entire sentence in isolation if you prefer," Jennings said.

"Not much of a deal if you ask me," Cannon responded.

"I'm not asking you to make that decision for him. That's a decision Riker needs to make. Life in prison wherever the Department of Corrections decides or life in prison in isolation. What I am offering is life in prison at a facility in another part of the state, or he can take his chances with a jury. Remember, the evidence will prove he and his wife conspired to murder their ten-year old son, conspired to murder Donald Petrolli, and most likely he murdered his wife. The two of them also conspired to commit life insurance fraud in order to profit from the death of their adopted son. How do you think a jury will decide this case with that overwhelming evidence, including DNA evidence and tape recordings of Leroy Riker admitting to one murder and one attempted murder and to the insurance fraud?"

Cannon was silent as he processed this information, and Paula continued. "If Riker makes me go through the time and expense of an entire trial, I'll be less inclined to offer any leniency for him whatsoever. You have 24 hours to deliver his decision. Talk to him and let me know," Jennings said. "Just remember, the clock is ticking on my offer."

Prosecutor Paula Jennings meant what she said to Douglas Cannon. The clock was indeed clicking, and the clock finally ran out when she did not hear back from Cannon after 24 hours. Apparently, Leroy Riker, or his attorney, was willing to roll the dice and take their chances with a jury trial.

Now Paula Jennings prepared for a long trial. The case against Leroy Riker was a slam-dunk, as far as the evidence went. She was also experienced enough to know there were no guarantees when it comes to juries. It only took one juror to return a hung jury. Still, she was willing to go that extra mile because the victim in this case deserved no less.

50.

STATE V. RIKER — DAY ONE

Notes

Detective Russ Wyatt on the Case

Park County District Court
December 3, 2001, 9:00 a.m.

Finally, the time had come for the trial to commence.

"Ladies and gentlemen of the jury, my name is Paula Jennings, the prosecuting attorney for Park and Sweet Grass Counties. The defendant, Leroy Riker, and his wife, Lora Riker in absentia, are charged with two counts of life insurance fraud, two counts of conspiracy to commit life insurance fraud, and two counts of conspiracy to commit deliberate homicide. Additionally, Leroy Riker is charged with one count of deliberate homicide and one count of attempted deliberate homicide. Unlike most murder cases, this case is all about greed, the primary motive behind all frauds. It was greed that caused the defendants to obtain $650,000 of life insurance on their newly adopted son, Michael Riker. It was greed that caused them to plan an elaborate alibi, years in advance. As part of that alibi, the Rikers purchased life insurance for their biological daughter just prior to Michael's adoption and then purchased an identical amount of life insurance for Michael. By doing so, it was part of their plan and scheme to demonstrate there was nothing unusual when they purchased Michael's insurance. Greed necessitated that Michael must die and was made to look accidental for them to collect on his two life insurance policies."

As all prosecutors did, Paula surreptitiously eyed the jury and quietly gauged the general mood in the courtroom.

"You'll hear compelling and emotional testimony from several witnesses," she continued, "and you'll have an opportunity to examine bank records, insurance records, and other documentary evidence. You'll hear from a private investigator, Kevin Ross, who conducted a sworn, recorded interview with both defendants, shortly after Michael's death. You'll hear testimony about how the Rikers had been involved in other insurance fraud matters and about their detailed knowledge of the insurance industry and insurance policies."

Again, she paused slightly to let the gravity of her words sink in.

"Importantly, you'll also hear testimony proving the parents were financially strapped for money prior to, and after Michael's adoption," she continued. "A Montana State Insurance Commissioner representative will testify about how uncharacteristic it is for a ten-year-old to have $650,000 in life insurance from one, let alone two over-lapping insurance policies. You'll also hear testimony that will establish the first policy valued at $400,000, including its accidental death provision, was scheduled to lapse 22 days after Michael's death. Since both policies were "whole life" policies, they accumulated a set amount of money in a "cash reserve" account, from which premiums could be withdrawn. In the event insufficient funds were available in the "cash reserve" account, Lora needed to make a payment by money order or cashier check. The insurance company had declined to accept her personal checks any longer due to the high frequency of bad checks."

Another short pause.

"You will also hear testimony from an independent certified fraud examiner, Dan Player, who analyzed years of bank and insurance records. One very important piece of evidence you'll see from the defendants' bank records is a change in Leroy Riker's practice of writing checks. Prior to Michael's adoption, Leroy Riker was regularly involved in writing and signing checks, including insurance checks for his daughter. Immediately after Michael's adoption, Leroy Riker stopped writing checks, and he didn't resume writing checks until the day after Michael's death.

Another pause, but this time Paula looked into the eyes of each and every member of the jury. Her voice was somber but tinged with determination.

"In addition, you'll hear testimony that establishes a timeline of events leading up to Michael's murder and a timeline of events shortly after his death. Included in these events is a phone call and meeting the defendants had with a custom home builder only two days before Michael was killed. The custom home builder will also testify about a post-dated check he received from Leroy Riker the day before Michael's skull was crushed."

At this point, audiences at home were riveted to their TV sets. Prosecutor Paula Jennings was using stronger terms such as "homicide" and "murder" and "crushed skull" to drive home points.

"You'll then hear testimony from two Park County Sheriff's Deputies and two Park County Sheriff's Detectives," she continued.

"Collectively, they'll testify about what they discovered at the crime scene, and how they determined the crime scene was in fact located within Park County. You'll hear further testimony from Park County Sheriff's detectives concerning evidence found in the defendants' residence, such as a long and detailed list of everything they intended to purchase for their new, expensive home from the life insurance proceeds. We will prove they murdered their adopted son, Michael, for money and a grand lifestyle."

From a row in the courtroom, Judd and I looked at each other. The air seemed electric as Paula asserted her case. "She's in it to win it," whispered Judd, and I nodded.

"They also executed a search warrant on the defendant's pickup truck and located a grey wool boot sock that was an identical match to the murder weapon, which was a grey wool boot sock with a basalt rock inside," said Paula.

On the rock, the Montana State Crime lab was able to identify fingerprints matching those of the defendant. The same crime lab identified DNA evidence on the outside surface of the sock matching the victim's DNA as well as DNA evidence matching the defendant, which had been transferred to the sock when the victim's dog bit the defendant and then picked up the murder weapon.

"Good ol' Max," I whispered to Judd.

"Keep in mind the evidence will show a previous Riker home was foreclosed on and that they were frequently behind on the rent for their present home. The detectives will also testify concerning a videotape found during a search of the defendant's residence. That video shows Leroy Riker wading into the same pool of water the day after Michael's death, totally without fear, in order to retrieve Michael's fishing pole.

"A second videotape was found in the master bedroom depicting several adult sex scenes between Lora and Leroy Riker and other adult participants. The police also found a handwritten note, presumably written by Leroy Riker that read: 'You bitch. I'll see you in hell. I'm going to the police, and I'll get immunity. I'll tell them it was all your idea and that you made me do it. I hope you rot in prison bitch.' You'll also hear testimony from eight-year-old Carol Brannon, who was the first foster child in the Riker household. A few months after she arrived in their home, Carol told her caseworker she wanted to leave because Lora and Leroy Rikers' talk about sex made her fearful. The orgy video tape appears to confirm her statement."

A gasp erupted from the audience, both in the courthouse and in homes across the state. "And the system allowed the Rikers to foster and adopt Michael after that shit went down," hissed Judd, shaking his head.

"You'll hear testimony from a former residential cleaning customer of Lora Riker. The customer will tell you about a phone call she received the day after Michael Riker died. She will testify that Lora Riker called her to cancel her cleaning appointment for that day. The customer will further testify that Lora Riker didn't say anything about her son dying the previous day, but instead said she and Leroy had an appointment with a custom home builder. The customer will describe Lora's demeanor, tone, and tenor on the phone as excited and jovial. She learned about the death of the defendants' son from the newspaper later that same day."

The courthouse audience stirred again, with a warning from the judge to remain silent.

"You'll also hear from an expert forensic pathologist from Louisville, Kentucky, who'll testify concerning her review of the medical examiner's report and photographs, and her expert opinion as to the cause of Michael's death. The forensic pathologist was unable to examine Michael's body because the defendants had his remains cremated the same day his body was released by the medical examiner. However, the forensic examination by the pathologist and her expert opinion will establish Michael Riker's death was by homicidal means and methods."

Judd nudged me in my ribs and whispered, "I sure hope so."

Paula in her best prosecutorial tone, "Collectively, these witnesses will testify, and the state will introduce convincing evidence that will be overwhelming regarding the guilt of both defendants beyond a reasonable doubt for each and every charge. The evidence will demonstrate a clear, ongoing pattern of deception by the defendants stretching back many years. This case is part of that same pattern of conduct and has the same or similar intent, results, accomplices, principals, victims, or methods of commission, and is otherwise interrelated by distinguishing characteristics."

Paula went on to state: "The defense will attempt to distract and confuse you. They will argue that even if everything presented by the prosecution is true, it's all circumstantial evidence. They will argue that there is no direct evidence or witness testimony that the defendants conspired and planned to adopt Michael with the intent to collect on two life insurance policies totaling $650,000. Don't allow the defense to misdirect your attention away from the evidence. They'll also attempt to argue there is no direct evidence either defendant was involved in causing the death of Michael Riker. Lastly, the defendants' counsel will try to argue their clients are the real victims here because they were insurance novices when it came to life insurance, and they were sold two life insurance policies by unscrupulous insurance agents and a greedy insurance industry. Leroy Riker's attorney will likely argue Mr. Riker was unaware of the existence of the two policies because he wasn't involved in the family finances and his wife hadn't shared that fact with him, and therefore, he didn't knowingly have anything to gain from Michael's death."

"Plausible deniability," Judd whispered, just before Paula corroborated his thought and discussed what that meant.

"In legal terms," explained Paula, "this is referred to as plausible deniability. All these distractions and arguments will ring hollow based on the overwhelming circumstantial and direct evidence you'll see and hear. Fingerprints are not circumstantial evidence. DNA is not circumstantial evidence. An eyewitness, who also provides audio recordings, is not circumstantial evidence."

"Now she needs to wrap it up," I whispered back to Judd.

"When you retire to the jury room to begin your deliberations, I don't want you to forget who the real victim is. It's Michael, a little boy who deserved none of this. His dream was to grow up and become a test pilot or some other exciting and dangerous occupation. He wanted to stretch his wings and fly like an eagle. You'll hear testimony from Michael's friend, Danny Williams, who will recount such an occasion the day before his death. Leroy Riker suggested Michael do something very dangerous and potentially fatal by walking on a bridge railing, and at the same time telling him, 'Don't let me see you do it.' That mixed message was meant to tempt Michael into slipping and plunging into the fast-moving, swollen Yellowstone

River. When that didn't work, Michael suffered a depressed skull fracture by the hands of his adopted father who drug him into the water to drown."

Once again, the audience expressed shock and horror, with the judge admonishing them to remain quiet.

"You will hear from a cooperating co-conspirator," continued Paula, "who will testify he was hired by Leroy and Lora Riker to be, in effect, a back-up murderer, in the event Leroy Riker lost his nerve to kill his adopted son himself. This witness will testify and provide direct evidence in the form of tape recordings that document the conspiracy. Afterward, Leroy and his wife lured the witness back to the same campground under the pretense of paying him money, where Leroy Riker was lying in wait to ambush and murder this witness — the only witness to the boy's death."

The judge once again demanded silence in the courtroom as the audience erupted.

"Lastly, the state will introduce circumstantial evidence of Lora Riker's death at the hands of her husband, Leroy," concluded Paula.

Judd elbowed me in the ribs and exclaimed, "Damn. I think Paula's going to get a conviction."

51.

A TELEVISED DEBRIEF

December 3, 2001 6:00 p.m.

Rosemary Meadows, a popular television anchor for "Courthouse Live Coverage," was young, attractive, intelligent, and very well-informed. For her loyal followers, it didn't hurt that she was also an avid outdoors person. Almost everyone in Western Montana spent a great deal of their personal and recreational time participating in some form of outdoor activities.

Her program provided in-depth legal analysis and commentary on complex legal and criminal justice topics. One of her frequent guests was Barbara McQuinn, a former judge and federal prosecutor who presently had a criminal defense practice in Helena. Having been both a prosecutor and now defense attorney made Barbara eminently qualified to explain what was going on not just inside the courtroom, but also inside the heads of the prosecutor and the defense attorney.

Inside the news studio, TV anchor and the legal expert discussed the events that had just unfolded as the jury took a brief break.

"Barbara, I must say the prosecutor's opening statement sounded very compelling," Rosemary Meadows remarked.

"Opening statements are designed to sound compelling Rosemary. They are intended to give the jury a broad picture of the evidence they can expect to hear. However, you must keep in mind the state has the burden to prove each and every element of what is alleged and now that the state has outlined their case so specifically, the jury will know if the prosecutor fails to establish, with credible evidence, everything they have presented in this opening statement," explained former judge Barbara McQuinn.

"That's a good point Barbara. So, what do you think we can expect to hear from the defense?"

"Your listeners can expect to hear multiple defenses. The first one I always fall back to when I don't have a good defense is, "The best defense is a good offense." If you don't have favorable facts on your side, the job of a good defense attorney is to convince at least one member of the jury that your client is innocent and being prosecuted for no good reason. Another way to look at this is, if you can't win the jury with facts, you befuddle the jury with misleading and confusing information. Like I said, you only need to convince or confuse one juror and you have at least won a hung jury and sometimes that's enough."

"What else do you think we can anticipate from the defense?"

"There are two defense strategies that come to mind. The first one is called the "Mashed Potato Defense." This is where the defense attorneys throw everything against the wall to see what sticks."

"Barbara, does that tactic really work?" Rosemary asked.

"It seldom does, Rosemary, but it's sometimes worth a chance. If nothing else, the judge might make a mistake and open the door to an appeal or commit a reversible error."

"What's the other defense you mentioned?"

"I call it the Ostrich Defense," Barbara answered. "This is where the defense attorney puts his or her head in the sand and tries to ignore all the evidence. By doing so, they are hopeful one or more of the jurors will do likewise simply because the defense counsel is so confident about the evidence's lack of significance and the innocence of their client."

"Like the old saying, 'If you tell a lie often enough and to enough people, even the lie starts to sound like the truth,'" added Rosemary.

"Exactly," Barbara agreed.

"Do you think they'll cross-examine the witnesses?" Rosemary asked.

"No," answered Barbara. "They don't want the jury to hear the same damaging testimony multiple times. I also don't expect they'll put any witnesses of their own on the stand for the same reason."

"That all sounds counterintuitive. So, you don't think even Leroy Riker will testify in his own defense?" Rosemary asked.

"As a defense attorney, that would be the last thing I would advise him to do. He would be under oath and subject to cross-examination. Evidence not otherwise permissible would potentially be admitted into evidence for impeachment purposes. Leroy Riker already doesn't have a good reputation for honesty. Putting him on the witness stand would amount to legal malpractice," Barbara opined.

"Well, let's listen to defense counsel for Leroy Riker make his opening statement to the jury," Rosemary Meadows continued.

52.

MORE COURTROOM DRAMA

Notes

Detective Russ Wyatt on the Case

Park County District Court
December 3, 2001, earlier in the day

"Ladies and gentlemen of the jury, my name is Douglas Cannon, and I represent Leroy Riker. To save time and avoid redundancy, the defense and the state have agreed to allow the admission of documents maintained in the ordinary course of business."

Another jolt of electricity swept the silent courtroom, as people waited with bated breath. The notoriety of the case and copious media coverage had built up to this very moment.

"You've already heard the evidence the prosecutor intends to put forward," the defense attorney continued. "Let me just caution you, their evidence does not, and will not, prove Leroy Riker committed any crime. You'll hear a lot of speculation and conjecture. The state will attempt to convince you that one and one equals two, when in fact, their one and one equals a big zero. Both Leroy and Lora Riker were big believers in life insurance. They both had substantial amounts of life insurance for themselves, and they also had a substantial life insurance policy for their biological daughter, Susie. When Michael was adopted, they wanted to treat him equally and acquired the identical life insurance for him as they had for their daughter."

As we watched from the back, Judd and I could see his eyes dart up and down at the seated jury, surveilling whatever skepticism they might reveal.

"Susie's life insurance increased right along with Michael's policy amounts. Both policies were whole life policies that accumulated a cash reserve with each monthly payment, meant to fund both children's college education and guarantee the children's ability to obtain life insurance as adults. The Rikers were loving parents who wanted only the best for both children, even if that meant they had to go without some things for themselves."

After another stealthy assessment of the jury's reaction, he pushed on. "Yes, there were times when it was difficult to make the minimum premium payments, but they always found a way. As for the tragic death of Michael, for which Mr. and Mrs. Riker are heartbroken, there's no evidence linking either parent to his accidental death. Michael was an active ten-year-old boy who had a reputation for goofing around. The rocks near the water were wet and slippery. It would've been very easy for him to slip on those rocks, hit his head, and fall into the pool of water. Mr. Riker did everything he could to save his son, including CPR. Once others joined in to help, he sped down a forest service road, at great risk to himself, to seek help at the Wilsall Fire Station. He knew it was going to be an all-volunteer department, and he wasn't sure how he would contact anyone once he arrived. It was roughly thirty-six miles from the Shields River Campground in the Gallatin National Forest to the Wilsall Fire

District 3 station. The drive took almost an hour. Mr. Riker prayed throughout the entire ordeal."

Less than convincing, I thought, bracing for the defense attorney to place more halos on the monsters' heads. It was revolting.

"The fire department aid crew traveled back to the campground and transported Michael back the same 36 miles to the Wilsall High School football field for a helicopter transport to the Bozeman Health Deaconess Hospital. The original autopsy report was correct when it concluded Michael's cause of death was accidental drowning. Only after the sheriff's department persisted in harassing my clients, and only after the life insurance companies' bad faith determination to withhold payment, did the coroner change his cause of death. Mr. and Mrs. Riker would never have purchased the $400,000 policy from Northwest Insurance had it not been for the sales pressure from the agent to buy more insurance. The second policy from the Montana Life Insurance Company was for only $250,000 and was intended to replace the first, more expensive policy. The Rikers fell victim to the disinformation that was foisted on them to buy more insurance. It was merely a twist of fate both policies happened to be in force at the time of Michael's accidental drowning."

After listening to the opening argument by the defense attorney, the judge recessed the jury until the following morning. Rosemary and Barbara discussed what they heard with their TV audience.

"Barbara, what do you think of this opening statement by the defense? It sounds like some of the defenses you outlined earlier."

"The ostrich defense, to be specific. *Nothing to see here folks, so don't bother listening.* When the state starts their examination of witnesses, we'll start to see other strategies and legal techniques."

"What would you expect, being a defense attorney yourself?"

"Well Rosemary, I think you'll see defense counsel attempt to break the prosecutor's rhythm by making numerous objections, even though in most cases there'll be no basis for the objections. This confuses and throws off witnesses' testimony and their line of thought. For some witnesses, frequent objections are maddening, and border on harassment or badgering. If the defense counsel can get to the state's witness by employing this method, it might diminish the credibility of the witness, and the defense will score points without having to cross-examine the witness or put on their own witnesses," Barbara explained.

"Barbara, the trial ended today without any witnesses taking the stand. What should we expect in court tomorrow?" Rosemary asked.

"The state will start laying the foundation for their case with multiple witnesses. So, tomorrow is likely to start off slowly," Barbara replied.

"Okay then, that's all the time we have for today," Rosemary announced. "We'll be back tomorrow evening with our legal analyst, Barbara McQuinn, to talk again about what happened in court then. Until tomorrow, this is Rosemary Meadows, wishing you all a good night," she announced while standing in front of a TV camera.

53.

DAY TWO

December 4, 2001, 6:00 p.m.

The next evening, the TV production crew was once again standing in front of the courthouse as Rosemary Meadows started off her show, "Courthouse Live Coverage," inside the news studio.

"Good evening again, this is Rosemary Meadows, along with our legal analyst, Barbara McQuinn. Tonight, we are going to discuss what happened today in the insurance fraud and homicide trial of Leroy and Lora Riker. Lora Riker is not actually present in court because she is missing and presumed dead. Some evidence suggests she might have committed suicide, but other evidence suggests and points directly to Leroy Riker's involvement in his wife's disappearance and presumed death. Together, they are accused of adopting a ten-year-old boy, then purchasing $650,000 in life insurance for him, and finally attempting to collect on the life insurance following his suspicious death while on a fishing trip with his father. The prosecution is attempting to show both defendants acted together in an elaborate plan that resulted in the boy's death."

"Barbara, what happened in court today? Were there any surprises from witnesses?" Rosemary Meadows asked as the program started.

"As somewhat expected, the court started hearing from the state's first witness at 9:00 a.m. The first two witnesses were employed by the State Department of Child and Family Services and testified about the foster care system, the application process and the duties and responsibilities of child case workers. The only real surprises that came out, at least for anyone who has not been a foster parent, was how very little authority, by law, the agency has to fully vet foster parents before placing a child into a home," Barbara replied.

"Can you explain that further, Barbara? What do you mean when you say the state has little legal authority to vet a foster parent?"

"From what we heard from the first two witnesses; prospective foster parents complete an application to the state to become foster parents. Very little of the information, if any, on the application is ever verified and there are no requirements in the law for the applicants to submit any documentation in support of their application. The application is like a job application and asks questions like where you live, how long at the current address, and where did you previously live. How much do you make, and what are your current living expenses? Are you financially able to support your existing family with your income? There are no requirements the applicants submit any bank statements, proof of employment or proof of address. In addition, the legislature has not provided any monies that would allow Child and Family Health Services to perform any background checks. The other thing that came out in court today was how much the state was paying the Rikers for foster care. It was approximately $1,700 per month, all of which was intended to go towards the direct care and benefit of the foster child."

"Do we know, Barbara, if the money was spent for the purpose for which it was intended?" Rosemary asked.

"One of the identified problems is the state apparently has no way to track how the money is spent once it's in the hands of the foster parents," Barbara responded. "I believe we can expect an expert witness in the next day or two, who will be able to trace what became of the foster child support money."

"There was another interesting development today," Rosemary mentioned.

"Yes," said Barbara. "It came first from the caseworker who was assigned to Michael Riker, the now-deceased son of the defendants. The caseworker's testimony was supported by another foster child who had been in the Rikers' household for only a few months, placed there prior to Michael's placement. After only a few months, the young girl asked to be removed from their residence because she was fearful. Reportedly, she told the caseworker the Rikers were having sex parties in their residence and on at least one occasion they asked the young girl if she wanted to watch in order to advance her sex education."

"That sure riled up the defense," Rosemary noted.

"Yes, indeed. After heated objections, the judge allowed the evidence because it went directly to the issue of the Riker's qualifications and character as foster parents. When the prosecutor attempted to put the young girl on the witness stand, the defense fought tooth and nail to prohibit her testimony. However, after hearing all the defense arguments, the judge allowed the young girl to testify, and her sworn testimony corroborated that of the case worker's."

"The defense counsel did their best to try and rattle the young girl by making objections to every question asked of her," Rosemary observed.

"That was awful," Barbara said. "The judge at one point reprimanded the defense attorney for his frivolous objections during a side-bar conversation. That doesn't happen very often in a courtroom because attorneys are expected to heed certain norms and rules of decorum."

"Were there any other witnesses who testified today for the prosecution?" Rosemary asked.

"Yes. Kevin Ross, a private investigator for the two life insurance companies, testified regarding his sworn interview with Leroy and Lora Riker within days of when the insurance companies became aware of the boy's death," Barbara said.

"Barbara, why do you think they even consented to speak to the private investigator, especially if it was recorded and under oath? Why not just decline to make any statement?"

"The Rikers were between a rock and a hard spot, Rosemary. Under the contract terms of the life insurance policies, they were required to participate in any insurance company investigation, and to truthfully answer all questions in an examination under oath. A refusal would have automatically voided the life insurance policies. So, in answer to your question, apparently, they assumed they could mislead and confuse their way through the EUO," Barbara explained.

"One other thing, the private insurance investigator was the only person to interview the Rikers under oath, or for that matter, any interview at all, apart from the interview with the sheriff deputy the night of the drowning. After this mandatory EUO interview, they declined all requests from law enforcement for an interview," Barbara responded.

"Is that unusual? If this was truly an accidental drowning and the father could shed any light on what transpired that day, wouldn't he demand such an interview," Rosemary asked.

"It may seem unusual, but there are many reasons someone might decline to be interviewed. Some people refuse polygraph examinations or refuse breathalyzer tests just out of principal," Barbara replied.

"But still, this seems very different," responded Rosemary.

"Sounds exactly like someone with a guilty conscious to me," Judd said softly.

"Please tell our viewers, Barbara, what information the prosecutor elicited from the private investigator?" Rosemary asked.

"Mr. Ross testified that he interviewed both the Rikers in their home and they did not have an attorney present. They both appeared relaxed and open to answering questions," Barbara commented.

"That seems like a good start. What else?" Rosemary added.

"The Rikers told him Michael had a birthday coming up in three weeks and Lora had purchased some gifts and had them on layaway. Just a week prior to the fishing trip, she brought home two fishing poles, a tackle box and a bicycle. They hid the child's size fishing pole and the bicycle with the plan to surprise him at his birthday," Barbara explained.

"Did the Rikers say why they didn't leave everything on layaway until a day or two before Michael's actual birthday?" Rosemary asked.

"Apparently, that question wasn't asked," Barbara responded.

Judd whispered in my direction; "We know why."

"So, they brought the items home, hid most everything, but left one fishing pole standing in the corner of the living room. Why did they do that?" Rosemary asked.

"Mr. Ross was asked that question by Paula Jennings and he was unable to offer an opinion or an answer," Barbara replied before continuing to summarize Kevin Ross's testimony. "Lora told Kevin Ross she intended on letting the first insurance policy lapse for non-payment of premiums at the time she purchased the second policy. The second policy was intended to replace the first one. Lora said it was a coincidence and just fate that both policies were in effect at the same time when Michael drowned. Just three weeks later, the first policy would have automatically expired. Do you agree, Rosemary?"

"Absolutely."

"Leroy went on to tell Kevin Ross how he drove the four kids to the KPRK bridge on Thursday and to the campground the following day. Ross testified the Rikers told him how much of a daredevil and adventurous child Michael was, which is why Leroy cautioned Michael to not show off on the bridge," Barbara continued.

"So, if the Rikers knew that in advance, why wasn't Leroy paying more attention to Michael when he should have been able to anticipate something the boy might do?" Rosemary asked.

"According to Kevin Ross's testimony, Leroy said he was focused on fixing his flat tire," Barbara replied.

"The Friday of the drowning, Lora took Suzie and her friend shopping while the guys did their thing, according to what Lora told Kevin Ross. Leroy told Mr. Ross the only reason he separated Michael and Danny was because Michael wanted to fish and the two of them were throwing rocks and making too much noise," Barbara added.

"Did Paula ask Mr. Ross if Leroy had taken Danny downstream and told him to wait there and he would be right back?" Rosemary asked.

"Kevin Ross's response was 'yes,' that is what Leroy had told him during his interview," Barbara answered.

"What did Kevin Ross say about Leroy's explanation of his actions upon learning Michael was in the water?" Rosemary asked.

"Ross explained that Leroy told him that he had jumped into the water to save his son but was unable to do so. Leroy also told Ross, according to Ross's response to a question from Paula Jennings, that Leroy couldn't swim and was concerned about both Danny and Michael if he were to drown," Barbara said.

"How long did Leroy tell Kevin Ross he was gone from both boys and what he was doing?" Rosemary asked.

"Ross testified that Leroy told him he was only gone for a few minutes while he drove around the campground looking for a better fishing spot where both boys could fish together."

"Did Mr. Ross challenge Leroy during the EUO to explain what was wrong with the place Michael was fishing at?" Rosemary asked.

"No. But that wasn't Ross's job at that time," Barbara explained.

"Barbara, can you explain your last statement? Why wasn't it Ross's job to challenge statements made in an EUO?" Rosemary wondered.

"Because an examination under oath is intended to seek information from the insured. This is where the investigator wants to elicit statements in anticipation of an insurance claim. If the investigator starts challenging the insured, the interview might go sideways in a hurry," Barbara explained. "Mr. Ross knew it was better to collect as many facts from the insured and lock them into their version of events, be they truthful or otherwise, that could be later proven or disproven through an investigation."

"Additionally, Kevin Ross also testified that Leroy told him he frantically drove to the Wilsall Fire Station after several unsuccessful attempts to perform CPR on Michael," Barbara continued. "So, it sounds like all of Kevin Ross's testimony was hearsay. He could only testify to what the Rikers told him. Right?"

"That's true, Rosemary, but don't forget that Ross's interview with the Rikers was audiotaped and under oath," Barbara added.

"True. Did the defense cross-examine Mr. Ross or make any objections during his testimony?"

"It might seem odd to some, but they did not, Rosemary. Mr. Ross was one of those witnesses the defense knew could hurt their case, and they didn't want to draw more attention to his testimony by asking him questions. They also didn't want to alienate any member of the jury by making frivolous objections. So, the defense wanted Mr. Ross to get off the witness stand as soon as possible."

"Who else testified today, Barbara?"

"The state called the Deputy Director of the Montana State Office of Insurance Commissioner in the Life Insurance Program. He testified how, although not improper for life insurance agents to sell policies for minor children, it was highly uncommon and unusual for such a policy to exceed $50,000 and even that amount would only be seen in the more affluent households."

"So, Barbara, in the opinion of the insurance deputy director, a single policy of $400,000 would be highly unusual, but two overlapping policies valued at $650,000 would be totally out of the norm?"

"Extremely out of the norm, Rosemary."

"Were there any other surprises in court?" Rosemary asked.

"The state continued to call their foundational witnesses. One of the key witnesses was Dan Player, a Certified Fraud Examiner, someone akin to a forensic accountant. Player was hired as an independent forensic insurance investigator by the life insurance companies. Through his analysis of five years' worth of financial records, the state was able to introduce some very interesting and potentially damaging evidence against the defendants," Barbara answered.

"Can you summarize some of his testimony for us?" Rosemary inquired, looking directly in the camera and pointing at the audience.

"Mr. Player testified the defendants had not been financially solvent for years," Barbara explained. "Their bank accounts were often overdrawn; at least one bank closed all their accounts due to Lora's bad check writing activity. They had one home foreclosed on by the mortgage company. They had three prior bankruptcies and Lora Riker had been arrested twice for passing worthless checks. Their current residence is a rental, and they have difficulty making their rent payments. Regardless of the money they received as foster parents, it never made a difference. After Michael was adopted, they no longer received money from the state, but they did receive money from Social Security, which also didn't make a difference."

"Troubling," said Rosemary.

"And then some," Barbara agreed. "Mr. Player also testified he found a prior insurance claim for the theft of personal property which an arbitrator determined was fraudulent. He also testified the defendants had filed a fraudulent federal tax return where they listed a fictitious dependent. In addition, he testified about interviewing two potential business partners of Lora Riker whom she had convinced to purchase life insurance for $250,000 and list her as the insurance beneficiary. And Rosemary, the prosecutor asked Mr. Player to offer his expert opinion and Rosemary, I believe you have the transcript of his response."

"I do, indeed."

"Reading directly from the transcript, Mr. Player offered the following explanation. The professional ethics rules of the Association of Certified Fraud Examiners prohibit me from expressing an opinion as to the ultimate issue of guilt or innocence. That determination is up to the jury. However, in my expert opinion there is substantial evidence to support a finding of guilt. Based, in part, on the multiple inconsistent statements and actions of the defendants. One such action was both defendants' interest in having a custom home built the day before Michael died, for the same exact price of the intended life insurance windfall. Another is the statement Leroy Riker knew nothing about Michael's life insurance policies. I believe the evidence supports the conclusion he knew about the life insurance prior to Michael's death," Rosemary read.

"The evidence also supports the conclusion the Rikers created an alibi of his not knowing about it?" Barbara continued. "In addition, Leroy Riker gave multiple explanations to different individuals concerning how Michael had died.

"It is also totally unbelievable, under similar circumstances, there is not a father who would have jumped into the pool of water to save his son from drowning, regardless of a fear of water or an inability to swim. There is also the unexplained 15–20-minute time gap between the time Leroy Riker separated the two boys and before returning without a homemade fishing pole for Michael's friend. Two credible witnesses disprove his statements he drove around the campground looking for another place where both boys could stand together and fish. There are also inconsistencies concerning whose idea it was in the first place to separate the two boys and why. Michael's friend, Danny Williams, said it was Mr. Riker's idea. Leroy Riker alleges it was Michael's idea. These are just some of the reasons supporting my conclusion as it relates to the evidence," as Rosemary wrapped up reading Dan Player's testimony.

"Wow," Barbara continued. "If the prosecution has witnesses who will testify in support of the expert's statements, we have more interesting facts yet to come—"

"Indeed, we do, Rosemary," Barbara interjected. "The next two witnesses to testify provided some of the additional facts the state needed to show a pattern and practice of fraud. The first of those witnesses testified about being approached by Lora Riker to join her in a business venture and partnership. She told Mr. Roger Bennett they should each purchase life insurance policies for $250,000 and name each other as beneficiaries. Mr. Bennett said he purchased his life insurance policy and Lora did not."

"And the next witness?" Rosemary nudged.

"The next witness was a prison inmate who had worked with Lora Riker at the all-women prison in Billings," answered Barbara. "At the prison, Lora supervised a janitorial crew of 3 to 4 inmates. During the period of incarceration, the inmate testified Lora showed interest by questioning the cleaning crew women concerning how they would commit the perfect crime. Upon the release from prison, she testified Lora approached her about going into the house cleaning business as an equal partner. Once again, the topic of they both purchasing life insurance for $250,000, and naming each other as beneficiaries, came up. The witness said she purchased her policy and Lora did nothing."

"What about the next two witnesses who testified today on behalf of the government?" Rosemary asked.

"They were primarily credibility witnesses. One addressed the credibility of Lora Riker and the second addressed the credibility of Leroy Riker. The first witness testified she was a house cleaning client of Lora's and the day after Michael died, she had an appointment with Lora. She said Lora called to cancel the cleaning appointment and during her testimony described Lora's mood on the phone as excited and even jovial. Lora told the client she had an appointment with a building contractor on the same day and didn't want to miss the appointment. Oddly, Lora said nothing to the client about her son dying the previous day," Barbara explained.

"The second witness testified he was a neighbor of the Rikers, correct, Barbara?" Rosemary asked.

"Yes, he spoke with Leroy Riker a few weeks after Michael died. During that conversation, Leroy told his neighbor, Michael had fallen out of a boat while fishing with the Wilsall Fire Chief and drowned," said Barbara. "The next two witnesses called by the government were the life insurance agents involved in selling the two life insurance policies to Lora Riker. Their testimony was important for a couple of reasons. First, both agents testified Lora Riker was very familiar with life insurance policies in general, as well as the insurance industry, including insurance terminology. They also testified she knew exactly what she wanted in the way of a whole life, versus a term life, insurance policy. Second, the insurance agents testified

Lora Riker told them she wanted to keep the life insurance policies for Michael a secret from her husband."

"Barbara, that sounds exactly like what the defense is betting their entire case on. I mean, isn't it true that if the defense is able to show Leroy Riker knew nothing about the existence of either life insurance policy the state's case falls apart?"

"That's true, Rosemary. The entire premise of the state's conspiracy, insurance fraud and homicide case rests on Leroy Riker knowing about the insurance policies, thereby giving him and Lora a financial motive for their son's death. If the state is unable to prove Leroy's knowledge of the policies, they will fail to establish a motive. No motive means no conspiracy, no fraud and no homicide. That would be a double win for the defense and an almost guaranteed acquittal for both defendants," Barbara stated.

"Can you summarize for our audience what else we learned from the insurance agents' testimony?" Rosemary asked.

"Sure, Rosemary. The first agent to testify was the one who wrote the policy, which included the accidental death rider. The total value of that policy was $400,000. The agent said he was very impressed with Lora Riker's knowledge and sophistication regarding insurance policies. She knew what she wanted and the benefits of a whole life policy. Lora told the agent she wanted to keep the life insurance policy a secret from Leroy. The agent explained Lora wanted to surprise her husband later. The agent said Lora often had difficulty keeping Michael's policy payments current and he received numerous insufficient fund checks. Since a portion of each payment went into a cash reserve account, he often had to dip into that account in order to make the required policy payment. According to the agent's explanation, Lora told him she wanted the whole life policy because the cash reserve account benefits would enable money to grow in that account for the benefit of Michael later in life," Barbara explained.

"But if the cash reserve account was being used to make insurance payments, it doesn't sound like Lora or Michael was receiving the benefit for which the account was intended," Rosemary said. "Is that an accurate statement, Barbara?"

"That is an accurate statement, Rosemary. By continuing to draw money out of the cash reserve account and treating it as their piggy bank, they defeated the entire purpose for having it."

"So how did the second insurance policy come into play?" Rosemary asked.

"According to the second insurance agent, he thought he was writing an insurance policy to replace the first policy. At least that is what Lora told him was her intent," Barbara said. "That's why he sent a notice of insurance replacement to the first insurance company's agent."

"So, Barbara, did the first policy expire automatically as Lora stated?" Rosemary asked.

"No, it didn't. According to the first agent, Lora brought him a money order the very day the policy was set to expire and she wanted the money applied to Michael's policy to keep it in effect for one more month. Lora told the agent, only then did she want the first policy to lapse," Barbara explained.

"Let me get this clear in my head," Rosemary said. "By extending the first policy for another 30 days, both insurance policies remained in place that much longer? Is that correct?"

"That's correct," Barbara replied. "Don't ask me why she wanted to do that, given her explanation to the second insurance agent that it was just too expensive to maintain both policies."

"Did the second insurance agent also testify that Lora wanted to keep the insurance policy a secret from Leroy?" Rosemary asked.

"Yes, he did Rosemary. Lora provided him almost the exact same explanation as what she told the first agent," Barbara replied, and then summarized the agents' testimony. "Lora told both agents she wanted to show Leroy she could show initiative on her own and she was going to surprise Leroy later with the fact she'd purchased Michael's insurance without his help. She wanted the agents to send all correspondence to their house addressed only to her."

"I see. So Barbara, how soon after Michael was adopted did Lora purchase insurance for Michael?"

"According to the testimony of the first agent, Michael's adoption was final in early October and Lora brought Michael in the following week, something like six days later," Barbara said.

"Did the Rikers' daughter, Susie, also have life insurance, according to either insurance agent?" Rosemary asked.

"According to the testimony of both agents, Susie had the identical coverage as Michael," Barbara responded. "Before Michael was adopted, her policy was only for $100,000, with no accidental life rider."

"Did that amount change over time?" Rosemary asked.

"Yes. According to the testimony of the first insurance agent, about two and a half years after Susie's first policy was written, the Rikers wanted to change her policy to $250,000, plus an additional $150,000 accidental death rider," Barbara responded.

"When did Michael obtain his life insurance policy as it relates to when Susie's policy was changed?" Rosemary asked.

"The first insurance agent said Michael's policy was issued within days after Susie's second policy. His policy was identical to Susie's," Barbara explained.

"Barbara, did either insurance agent know how long Michael was living in the Rikers' residence as a foster child before he was adopted?" Rosemary asked.

"Michael lived with them for 10 months before he was adopted."

"Did both agents testify about having the same difficulty with worthless checks?" Rosemary asked.

"Yes. Those same problems existed even when the only policy was for Susie," Barbara explained.

"Barbara, did either insurance agent explain what they would do when the insurance payments for the children were late or NSF?"

"Rosemary, the agents testified the procedure changed over time. When there was only Susie's policy, the first agent would call their house or send a written letter, addressed to both. After Michael's policy was in force, both agents were instructed by Lora to only call when Leroy was working or he'd be sleeping," Barbara said.

"Both agents testified that there was typically insufficient money in the cash reserve account to make a premium payment for either child. There were numerous times one or both policies were about to lapse for non-payment," Barbara said.

"Did we learn from the insurance agents how much Michael's and Susie's insurance premiums were per month?" Rosemary asked.

"Yes. According to the first agent, their premium payments were $75 per child, per month."

"And how much were the payments with the addition of the second policy?" Rosemary asked.

"Again, according to the testimony of the second agent, the cost was $90 per month per child and that was for only $250,000 of life insurance," Barbara replied.

"So, the Rikers couldn't afford to pay $75 per month, per child, or the equivalence of $150 total, yet Lora went out and acquired a second policy that cost a total of $180, while at the same time still paying on the first policy. Do I have that right Barbara?" Rosemary stated.

"That's what both agents testified to Rosemary."

"There was one final point of interest the prosecutor elicited from the first insurance agent," Barbara said.

"What was that?" Rosemary replied.

"The prosecutor asked the agent if he knew of any reason Leroy Riker might have insisted Michael's sports physical results be placed into his school record just days before his death?"

"And what did he say?" Rosemary asked.

"The agent said the only plausible explanation he could think of was if either life insurance company were to make inquiries regarding recent medical tests, the test results would be readily available. The agent went on to say this is more likely to take place when a death follows soon after a policy is issued, especially if the policy was issued without the need of any medical examination, as was the case concerning Michael's insurance policies," Barbara stated.

"What would be the reason for the insurance companies caring about any recent medical tests after a death?" Rosemary asked.

"It would be to look for any unreported pre-existing conditions of the insured. If such pre-existing conditions were found to exist and not divulged on the insurance application, that might form the basis for denial of an insurance claim. A failure to report pre-existing conditions would amount to fraud on the application for insurance. If the defendants were aware of this, they might want to be proactive by having a recent medical exam available someplace," Barbara explained.

"Was there any cross examination by the defense," Rosemary asked.

"No," Barbara responded. "Both these insurance witnesses all but destroyed Lora's explanation why she wanted the whole life policies. The defense didn't want the jury to hear this information a second time."

"Barbara, what was the prosecutor hoping to establish through the two life insurance agents' testimony?"

"Rosemary, the prosecutor had at least two goals. One is to establish Lora Riker's knowledge of life insurance. This will counter the defense narrative that the insurance agents took advantage of someone and up-sold a needless policy. The second is to show the extent of the planning that went into the conspiracy. The prosecution is attempting to demonstrate that the defendants started planning their crimes long before they adopted Michael. The state wants to show the first step in their plan was when the parents first purchased life insurance for their biological daughter. Subsequently, after Michael was adopted, the parents were able to point to their daughter's life insurance when they purchased an identical policy for him. Then, after Lora Riker purchased a second policy for Michael, they also had to purchase a second policy for their daughter. Remember the ostrich defense. *Nothing to see here members of the jury, all just part of our normal practices so just put your heads in the sand and ignore the obvious,*" Barbara McQuinn responded.

"Explain to me, Barbara, how this argument by the defense does not help them and how the prosecution hopes to overcome that defense?" Rosemary asked.

"The prosecution still needs to demonstrate, at least circumstantially, either how illogical it is to believe Leroy Riker was unaware of what his wife was doing behind his back, or have other evidence in their back pocket they plan to spring on the jury through their last one or two witnesses," Barbara replied.

"Playing devil's advocate, why is it so hard to believe Lora's version of events that she was acting alone and without the knowledge of her husband and that she really was planning on surprising him later with the fruits of her good judgment and initiative?" Rosemary asked.

"You need to keep in mind when Susie's life insurance policy was first purchased, both Leroy and Lora were actively involved in that process. You also need to remember all the financial difficulties they had over several years that resulted in major marital disruption. If you consider how Leroy changed his normal and established pattern of writing checks prior to Michael's adoption, and then abruptly ended that practice after Michael was adopted, you must ask yourself why he did that? On top of that, Leroy resorted back to his old practice immediately after Michael's death. All that suggests Michael's adoption was the motivating factor for this change of practice, and the big question is why," Barbara said.

"All very good points Barbara. It remains to be seen if the jury must grapple with that issue or not. Maybe the prosecutor has the answer to these and other questions," Rosemary replied.

"We have not yet heard from any sheriff department witnesses or other experts. When do you expect they will testify?"

"They'll have to testify tomorrow, Rosemary, because there was no time left today when they finished up with these witnesses."

"That's all the time we have for tonight's show. We'll see our viewers and our expert, Barbara McQuinn, back here tomorrow," as Rosemary signed off.

54.

DAY THREE

December 5, 2001, 6:00 p.m.

"Welcome back, Barbara, and good evening to our viewers. We are live from the studios of Courthouse Live Coverage. What surprises did Paula Jennings have in-store today?"

"Rosemary, Paula started the day with multiple law enforcement witnesses, who continued to paint the picture of what happened. Then they followed up with primary fact witnesses who were present the day Michael died at the Shields River Campground. The fact witnesses included a young friend of Michael's who had been invited to come along on the fishing trip, and on another trip the day before. Then there was another couple who were camping directly across from where the defendant parked, and they too presented some interesting testimony. Paula completed her case with the Park County Medical Examiner, a forensic pathologist, a custom home building contractor, and lastly with two surprise witnesses. These last five witnesses were a perfect way for Paula to conclude her case. Collectively they established a very high bar for the defense to overcome," Barbara explained.

"With that introduction, let's get into the first two sheriff department employees. What did we learn from them today, Barbara?" Rosemary asked.

"Park County Deputy John Peet testified he and his partner were dispatched to the scene of a reported drowning last October. Apparently, it was the fire chief who was already on the scene and had requested their presence. When Deputy Peet and his partner Deputy Morris arrived at the Shields River Campground, they met the fire department aid vehicle departing the scene. The deputies spoke briefly with the fire chief and then proceeded to conduct a preliminary investigation by interviewing Leroy Riker, Mr. and Mrs. Sterling, a couple who were camping nearby, and the young friend of the deceased, Danny Williams. Afterwards, when the two deputies had an opportunity to compare notes from their respective interviews, they concluded there were way too many inconsistencies between what Leroy Riker said and what the other witnesses said. At that time, they both expressed concerns Michael's drowning might not have been accidental at all."

"Barbara, can you give us some examples of those inconsistencies?"

"Sure, Rosemary. Riker said he had separated his son and Danny Williams, at the request of Michael, because Michael wanted to fish alone. Danny Williams told the deputy it was Leroy's idea to separate both boys. Riker said when Danny told him that Michael's body was submerged, he ran as fast as he could and jumped into the water to rescue Michael. Danny told the deputy that Leroy Riker did not jump into the water or even wade into the water. It was Danny who pulled Michael from the water after Leroy tied a rope to Danny's hand. Leroy Riker said after he had taken Danny downstream, he drove around the campground to find a better place where both boys could fish together. Yet Mr. and Mrs. Sterling said they were watching Leroy Riker's truck the entire time, and it never moved."

"Apart from the interviews that both deputies conducted, did they describe anything else they did at the campground?"

"As the first responding officers to any potential crime scene, they took photographs with two cameras. They captured images of the pool where Michael drowned and the surrounding area. They also took photographs of the area downstream where Danny had been left alone, as well as documenting the campground in general, the view between the Sterling's campsite, and the location where Leroy's truck was parked, just to name a few. They also took GPS readings in the area to make sure the campground was located within Park County."

"Barbara, did they testify about taking photographs of the fire pit?"

"Deputy Peet said he was later asked to return to the campground and take specific photos of the fire pit and the rocks surrounding it."

"Did he say why and by whom the request was made to specifically photograph the fire pit and surrounding rocks?"

"That request came from a forensic pathologist, by way of the medical examiner. The pathologist was working from a theory the rock that caused the skull fracture might have been from the fire pit because the boy's head injury was not consistent with a round river rock," Barbara said.

"If evidence supports the pathologist's theory, it will certainly put Michael's death in a whole new light, wouldn't it, Barbara?"

"Indeed, it would."

"Barbara, you mentioned there were other sheriff department employees who testified. Who else spoke today?"

"Detective Russ Wyatt was the lead detective and the next witness. The detective said he, along with his partner Detective Steven Judd, initiated a criminal investigation of the drowning death after several anomalies became evident," Barbara responded.

"What kind of anomalies did he testify about?"

"He said Leroy Riker made several inconsistent statements regarding the events of that day. He told the 911 operator his son had jumped into a pool of water. However, there was no place near the water from which his son could've jumped."

"Riker told others that his son must have slipped on rocks; hit the back of his head and then somehow fell into the water. Leroy conveyed to others that he had jumped into the five-foot-deep pool of water to rescue his son. However, his clothing wasn't wet, other than the front of his shirt and his pant legs up to his knees. He told other witnesses he was afraid of the water and for that reason he asked eleven-year-old Danny Williams to wade into the water to rescue Michael. Leroy said it was Michael's idea to separate him and Danny Williams, even though Danny had been invited as a guest of Michael's. Danny said it was Mr. Riker's idea to separate the boys. Leroy said after he separated Danny and Michael, he drove around the campground to find a better fishing spot where both boys could be together. Leroy didn't have any explanation why the spot Michael was fishing at was not okay for both boys. Also, Roger and Judy Sterling said they were watching Riker's truck the entire time from their campsite, and his truck never moved. We also learned that the day before Michael died; Leroy said he drove Michael, Danny, his daughter Susie, and a friend of hers to look at the Yellowstone River at the old KPRK Bridge. Leroy said that was Michael's idea, but Danny said it was Leroy's idea," Barbara explained.

"Was there any one fact they discovered as part of their criminal investigation which led them to believe Michael's death was not accidental?" Rosemary asked.

"Yes, indeed, Rosemary. Detective Wyatt identified more than one thing that suggested Michael's death was highly suspicious and potentially criminal. He testified about learning, in the event of accidental death, Michael Riker had not one but two life insurance policies totaling $650,000, naming his parents as beneficiaries. He also testified the Rikers were financially strapped and had been for several years," Barbara said.

"Did he say anything about whether Leroy was aware of the two life insurance policies purchased by his wife?" Rosemary asked.

"Yes, he did, Rosemary. From their criminal investigation, they established Leroy and Lora had always been involved in making important decisions together, including purchasing life insurance for their daughter, Susie. Leroy had also been actively involved in the household's financial matters, including paying bills and writing checks. However, that changed the day before Michael's adoption was final. Leroy abruptly stopped that practice and didn't resume writing checks until the day after Michael's death," Barbara responded.

"Was there any evidence introduced today from any search warrants?" Rosemary asked.

"Yes. The sheriff detectives served search warrants on multiple financial institutions and both life insurance companies. They also executed a search warrant on the residence of Leroy and Lora and on the pickup truck owned by the Rikers. At the residence, they found several years of federal income tax returns, including the tax return that listed a fictitious dependent. In the defendant's computer search history, they discovered Google searches using the keywords: fraud, insurance fraud, life insurance, alibis, perfect crime, drowning, skull fracture, sex, and porn. In the bedroom were books and articles relating to insurance fraud, as well as a videotape that was taken the day after Michael Riker died which depicted the campground, the river, and specifically of the pool where Michael drowned. The video showed a laughing Lora and Leroy Riker, and Leroy casually walking into the pool, up to his shoulders, and joking about how cold the water was on his genitals. He then proceeded to put his head entirely underwater, and he came up holding the fishing pole Michael had been using the previous day."

"How utterly sick and morbid," Rosemary responded.

"I agree," said Barbara. "Both defendants then laughed about returning the fishing pole for a cash refund."

"My God. It keeps getting worse, doesn't it."

"It doesn't stop there, Rosemary. They also discovered other videotapes in the bedroom depicting adult sexual activity inside their residence between both defendants and unknown adult individuals. In the pickup truck, they located a grey wool boot sock that matched identically the murder weapon that was found at the campground with the help of the victim's cocker spaniel, Max."

"Was the sex video admitted into evidence?"

"No. The defense strongly objected, and the judge sustained their objection. However, the other video of Leroy wading into the water was admitted," Barbara said.

"That had to be damaging evidence, right?" Meadows responded.

"Yes, it was Rosemary, because Leroy had told Danny Williams he was afraid of the water and that was his reason for asking Danny to retrieve Michael's body in the first place. This video showed just the opposite," Barbara said.

"Barbara, who testified next?"

"Danny Williams was up next. I think rather than me summarize his testimony, it would be best if we play it in its entirety. You will be able to hear how much the defense really didn't want this witness to testify and the extent to which the defense tried to rattle and harass the young witness," Barbara commented.

"It's really a shame this poor boy had to be subjected to this courtroom experience. I'm sure he was still traumatized by the events of that horrible day," Rosemary said.

"I think you will be surprised how well young Danny Williams held up under the badgering from the defense attorney. He never deviated from any of his prior statements, and his memory appeared very consistent," Barbara commented.

"Let's roll that tape," said Rosemary.

55.

DANNY TESTIFIES

Notes

Detective Russ Wyatt on the Case

"The prosecution now calls Danny Williams."

"Objection! The defense objects to this witness for relevancy, lack of credibility, and being prejudicial," Douglas Cannon said.

"Overruled! The state may continue with this witness," the judge ruled.

"This is starting off just like I expected. He's trying to badger and intimidate the boy," I said to Judd in a whisper.

"Please state your full name and your age."

"Daniel Williams. I'm now twelve years old."

"Do you prefer being called Danny or Daniel?"

"I prefer Danny."

"Okay Danny. Do you understand what it means when you swear to tell the truth, the whole truth and nothing but the truth?" Prosecutor Paula Jennings asked.

"Yes. It means I must tell the truth and only the truth. That I should not leave anything out that is the truth, and that I don't add anything that is not true."

"Danny, do you know why you are here today and what this trial is about?"

"Objection! Calls for speculation. Vague. Witness not qualified," defense counsel Douglas Cannon argued.

"Overruled!"

"Careful counselor," the judge warned. "The witness may answer."

"Yes. It's about whether Mr. and Mrs. Riker are guilty of a crime."

"Exactly," Judd murmured quietly.

"How well did you know Michael Riker and his parents?"

"Not well. We attended the same school after he moved here, and we rode the same school bus together on some days. We also hung out with each other some weekends, and after school, but not very often," Danny Williams said.

"Did you ever go on road trips or outings with Michael and Mr. Riker?"

"Yes. I went with them and Michael's sister and her friend to the KPRK Bridge over the Yellowstone River the day before Michael died, and from there I went with them to the Shields River Campground because Mr. Riker wanted to look around. The very next day is when I went fishing with only Michael and Mr. Riker at the campground."

"When you went to the KPRK Bridge over the Yellowstone River, do you know why and whose idea it was to go there? What did you do there?" Paula asked.

"I don't know why we went there, and Michael told me he didn't know why either. I think it must have been Mr. Riker's idea. When we got there, Mr. Riker said he had to fix a flat tire or something like that, and we kids ran out onto the bridge to look at the river."

"Flat tire, my ass," I whispered to Judd.

"Did Michael get in trouble for anything while you were there?"

"Kinda. Mr. Riker had told Michael, 'Don't be a show-off' and 'I don't want to see you trying to walk on that bridge railing.' When Michael attempted to climb onto the railing, Susie screamed, and Mr. Riker looked up and yelled at Michael. Michael told me he thought his father had dared him to do that and since his father had his back to us, Michael said his father wouldn't see him do it. Therefore, Michael thought it was okay if he did it," Danny replied.

"Danny, what do you think would have happened to Michael if he had fallen into the Yellowstone River that day?"

"Objection! Calls for speculation," Douglas Cannon interrupted.

That's not speculation. That's common sense, I thought.

"Overruled! The witness may answer," the judge ruled.

"There is no doubt in my mind he would've drowned. The river was moving really fast," Danny replied.

"So, from the bridge, you said you all went to the Shields River Campground. What happened there?" Prosecutor Jennings asked.

"Mr. Riker parked his truck in a campsite next to the river and told us kids to remain in the truck, and he'd be right back. He walked down to the river, looked around a few minutes, and came back to the truck, and we all left," Danny said.

"Do you know what Mr. Riker was looking for or why he did what he did?"

"Objection! Calls for speculation," Douglas Cannon argued.

"Overruled! Go ahead and answer, Danny," the judge said.

"Both counsels will approach the bench," the judge directed. "Whispering, you know better than to make frivolous objections. I'll not have it in my courtroom! If you have a legitimate objection,

I'll hear it. So, tread carefully counselor. You both may step back now."

"All Mr. Riker said was he was looking for a fishing spot for tomorrow so the two of us could fish," Danny replied.

"Okay Danny. I want to ask you some questions now about the next day when you, Michael, and Mr. Riker drove up to the Shields River Campground. Do you know what time you all arrived at the campground?" Prosecutor Jennings asked.

"It was about noon. I remember because Michael and I were hungry and Mr. Riker brought some snacks to eat, which we did."

"Did you eat the snacks when you first arrived, or did you go down to the river first?"

"When we first got there, Michael and I ran down to the river and started throwing rocks into the water. Mr. Riker joined us after a few minutes and we all just messed around and were throwing rocks. After a few minutes, Mr. Riker asked us if we were hungry, which we were, so we walked back up the hill to the truck and had our snack," Danny replied.

"What happened after you all ate?"

"Mr. Riker told us we could go back down the hill to the river, while he prepared a fishing pole for Michael."

"Did Mr. Riker have more than one fishing pole?"

"When Mr. Riker came down to the river, he only had one fishing pole for Michael. There was a hook on the fishing line, but he didn't have any bait on the hook. Michael asked his father if he had any fish eggs or worms for bait. Mr. Riker told him no, but then Michael spotted some bushes with white berries, so he tried to use the berries as bait," Danny said.

"Danny, were you upset there wasn't a fishing pole for you to use?"

"A little. I thought I was going fishing with Michael and not just stand there watching Michael fish."

"Is that what you did, just stand there and watch Michael fish?"

"Mr. Riker and me watched Michael for a few minutes, but we were also joking around and throwing rocks."

"Did that seem to bother Michael, that you and his father were joking around and throwing rocks while he was trying to fish?"

"Not really. Michael knew he wasn't going to catch any fish anyway without any real bait."

"What happened next?"

"Mr. Riker said me and him were going to leave Michael alone and he was going to find me another place where I could fish using a homemade fishing pole he'd make just for me from a tree branch. Me and him walked down the river a short distance and around a bend. He told me to wait there, and he'd return with a homemade fishing pole in a few minutes. I couldn't see Michael from the place he took me," Danny said.

How convenient, I thought, nudging Judd's side.

"Danny, did Mr. Riker return in a few minutes with a homemade fishing pole?"

"No. Like, he was gone at least 15, maybe 20 minutes and when he did return, he didn't have a fishing pole or even a tree branch with him."

"Did Mr. Riker say anything to you?"

"It was kinda odd, because the first thing he asked me was, if I'd seen or heard anything? I must've had a strange look on my face because he quickly changed his question to, had I seen or heard anything from Michael?"

"Had you seen or heard anything?"

"I saw Mr. Riker squatting in the woods, and he appeared to be watching me. I didn't tell him that, and he really didn't give me a chance anyway before he changed his question," Danny said.

"He was also stalling and killing time, as well as Michael," Judd whispered. I nodded in agreement.

"Danny, had you seen or heard anything from Michael?"

"No."

"Danny, when Mr. Riker returned to the place he told you to stay at, did you notice anything unusual about him?" Prosecutor Jennings asked.

"I noticed his pant legs were wet up to his knees. He told me he fell into a mud puddle. That surprised me because I hadn't seen any mud puddles anyplace."

"Then what happened or what did Mr. Riker say?"

"He said we should go find Michael. He told me to look down by the small pond where Michael had been fishing and Mr. Riker said he would walk up to the bathrooms to see if Michael was up there. When I got to the top of the small hill that went down towards the river, I could see Michael underwater in the small pond. I looked around for Mr. Riker and he was still walking towards the bathrooms, so I yelled at him to come quick," Danny emotionally said.

"And did he come quick?"

"No. He just walked slow. I yelled again that Michael was underwater in the small pond, and he started walking a little faster," Danny said while obviously reliving the events of that day in his head.

"No child this age should ever have to experience seeing a dead body," I said softly to Judd.

"Danny, then what happened?"

"We walked down to the edge of the pond. We could see Michael floating face down close to the bottom and the current was kinda moving him around, like, slowly," Danny said.

"Did Mr. Riker make any attempt to go into the water to rescue Michael?"

"No. He told me he couldn't swim and was afraid of the water. He asked me if I could swim, and if he tied a rope around my wrist would I go into the water. I told him I could, so he went back to his truck and returned with a rope. He then tied the rope around my wrist, and I waded into the pond," Danny replied.

"What father or parent wouldn't have jumped into the water?" Judd whispered.

"Danny, how tall are you. Was the water over your head?" Jennings asked.

"I'm almost five feet tall. The water wasn't over my head, but I needed to put my head under the water to see Michael well enough to reach him. Michael was moving around and each time I reached for him, my arm would get pulled backwards by the rope around my wrist. After I asked Mr. Riker a couple times if he was pulling on the rope, I was finally able to reach Michael's hand and pull him towards me and Mr. Riker."

"Did Mr. Riker say anything to you when you asked him if he was pulling on the rope?"

"No. He just ignored me."

"How long did it take you to get Michael out of the water?"

"Maybe five minutes."

"Then what happened?"

"Mr. Riker carried Michael part way up the hill towards the truck and laid him down to do CPR."

"Do you know what CPR is and how do you know about it?"

"I don't remember what the letters stand for, but we learned about it in school. I know it is something you do for people who aren't breathing."

"How long did Mr. Riker perform CPR on Michael?"

"Just a couple minutes at the first location. He picked Michael up again and carried him further up the hill and put him down behind where his truck was parked and started CPR again."

"Danny, let's change topic momentarily. When you first arrived at the campground the day Michael died, did you see any other campers or vehicles there?" Paula asked.

"There was a small tent in the campsite next to where we were parked, but there was no one around it and there was no vehicle there either. While we were eating our snack, another man and woman drove into the campground and started setting up their tent in a campsite close to the bathrooms, which were on the other side of the campground," Danny responded.

"Okay. So, you were saying Mr. Riker carried Michael up the bank and started CPR a second time. How long did he do that, and did he have help from anyone else?" Paula continued.

"Mr. Riker did CPR about another five minutes and the man and woman saw what was going on and they came over to see if they could help."

"Did anyone, that you know of, try to call for help on a phone?"

"I remember Mr. Riker, like, checking his cell phone the day before and he said there was no phone service at the campground. The man and woman also tried to use their phones, but that didn't work either," Danny said.

"Did anyone drive for help?"

"Yes. After maybe fifteen or twenty minutes of Mr. Riker and the other man taking turns giving Michael CPR, Mr. Riker said he would drive down the mountain and try to get help at the Wilsall Fire Station. I stayed at the campground and the man and woman took turns giving Michael CPR. The man and woman knew how to do CPR better than Mr. Riker," Danny replied.

"What do you mean the man and woman knew how to perform CPR better than Mr. Riker?" Paula Jennings asked.

"Leroy is a trained correctional officer, and he didn't know how to properly perform CPR? Bull," I quietly said to Judd.

"When the man and woman were breathing into Michael, I could see Michael's chest move up and down, just like I learned in school. When Mr. Riker tried breathing into Michael, I never saw anything happening to Michael's chest."

"Was it dark when Mr. Riker left to drive towards Wilsall?"

"Yeah, it was really dark."

"How long was Mr. Riker gone?"

"About two hours. When he returned, you know, he was riding in the fire chief's car and there were two medics in an ambulance."

"Did you hear Mr. Riker tell the fire chief or the two medics he had jumped into the water to save his son?"

"Yeah. He said that to the two medics and to the other man and his wife."

"Was that a true statement by Mr. Riker in your opinion?" Paula asked.

"No. That was a lie. I'm the only one who went into the water," Danny said.

"Did you hear Mr. Riker say anything else to the fire chief or either medic?"

"I heard him tell the medics Michael must've hit his head after slipping on the rocks along the river and then Michael must've fallen into the water."

"Was that also a lie?"

"Yes."

"Did the rocks seem slippery to you when you, Michael and Mr. Riker were down by the fishing-hole?"

"No. The area was flat next to the river and next to the fishing-hole and I don't remember anything being slippery. I also don't remember any rocks you had to stand or walk on near the fishing hole," Danny said.

"Danny, at any time did you hear Mr. Riker tell anyone that Michael must have jumped into the water and hit his head?"

"No, I didn't hear him say that. There was no place Michael could've jumped from and hit his head."

"Do you know if Michael could swim?"

"Michael told me he never learned to swim, and that he was afraid of water," Danny replied.

"Did Michael tell you why he was afraid of water?"

"He told me when he lived in Texas, an older boy once tried to drown him by holding Michael's head under water. Ever since then, Michael said he had nightmares about drowning. That's why I know he wouldn't have jumped into the water," Danny said.

"Do you know if Michael was still alive when the medics got there?" Paula asked.

"The man and woman who were doing the CPR when the medics arrived said they believed Michael was still alive and the medics said Michael still had a pulse when they first checked him."

"What happened next?"

"The medics said Michael needed to get to the hospital right away and they put him into the fire department ambulance. They said they had a helicopter waiting for them at the Wilsall High School and it would fly Michael to a hospital in Bozeman."

"Did you see anyone else at the campground the night Michael died?" Paula asked.

"Yeah. While the man and his wife were giving Michael CPR, there was a strange man, dressed in all black clothing, who stood next to me for a very short time," Danny replied.

"Danny, do you know where this man came from or remember anything about him?"

"I don't know where he came from, and I don't know where he went. He was just there one minute and gone the next. The only thing I remember about the man is he had pictures drawn on the backs of both hands."

"Did you describe the pictures to the police?"

"I forgot about the man that night when I spoke to the police, but remembered him later when I spoke to the police again. The police showed me some pictures at the police station, and I found some very similar pictures. I was also able to describe the man in more detail, except I never saw his face," Danny said.

Good job, Danny. You did it, I thought.

"The government has no further questions of this witness," Paula Jennings stated.

"Any cross examination by the defense," the judge asked.

"No, Your Honor," defense attorney Cannon responded.

56

BACK TO
"COURTHOUSE LIVE COVERAGE"

Barbara McQuinn and Rosemary Meadows continued their analysis of the courtroom saga.

"You're right Barbara. That was powerful testimony, and the young witness never lost his composure. Are we nearing the end of the prosecution's witnesses?" Rosemary asked.

"We are, Rosemary. The next witness was Roger Sterling. He and his wife were camping across from Riker's truck and they wanted to relocate their campsite to his, as soon as Riker left. They planned on camping for several days, and they could tell he was there for only the day. Roger Sterling said Leroy Riker never moved his truck the entire time they were there, which was in direct contradiction of what Riker had told the private investigator."

"What else did the Sterlings testify to? Did they observe any unusual behavior by Leroy?"

"Roger said they watched Leroy take Danny downstream and then return to his own pickup. Roger testified that Leroy seemed to be pacing back and forth, sometimes in the downstream direction and then back towards his pickup. At other times, he walked upstream and appeared to be talking to himself near a tent at that location. Sometimes he would walk downstream and then he'd disappear into the woods along the riverbank for several minutes and then he would walk back in the direction of his pickup again," said Barbara.

"Did they say anything about seeing Danny Williams?"

"Roger Sterling testified that it wasn't until they observed a very excited Danny Williams and saw Riker carrying Michael's limp body up from the river, they knew something was amiss. Roger said Danny was running towards their campsite and he and his wife met him in the center of the campground. Danny told them Mr. Riker needed their help and Michael had drowned."

"What happened after they arrived at Leroy's campsite?"

"During his testimony, Roger said he offered to help Leroy perform CPR and Leroy rejected his offer. Roger said he didn't think Leroy was performing CPR correctly," Barbara said.

"Did the prosecutor ask Roger why he thought that? I would assume as a state correctional officer that Leroy would have been fully trained on performing CPR," Rosemary said.

"She did, Rosemary. Roger said Michael's chest was not rising with each lifesaving breath. He said a rising chest is a sure indicator that air is getting into someone's lungs. After several minutes of CPR, Leroy said he would leave and try to find a cell phone signal to call for help, or he would drive to the Wilsall Fire Station and summon help there," Barbara said.

"What else did we learn today from Roger Sterling's testimony?"

"Paula Jennings asked Roger if it appeared to him whether or not Leroy had jumped into the water. Roger responded by saying Riker's clothes were mostly dry, except for his pant legs and the front of his shirt," said Barbara.

"Barbara, it sounds like Roger Sterling's testimony pretty much supported Danny Williams's testimony," Rosemary said.

"That's true, Rosemary. The last four witnesses for the government are key to the prosecution," Barbara announced.

"Okay then. Let's get right into the testimony of Dr. Edwards, the Medical Examiner for Park County, followed by Dr. Kay Burkett, an expert forensic pathologist, then Mr. Don Jackson, owner of D.J. Custom Homes, and almost lastly, the prosecution's cooperating witness," Rosemary said.

"Sounds good. I think we should save the biggest star witness for last," Barbara added.

"That sounds really interesting," Rosemary said with a smile. "Please tell us what each of these witnesses had to say today?"

"I think the easiest way to do that, Rosemary, is to discuss both the testimony of Dr. Gary Edwards, with the Park County Medical Examiner Office, and Dr. Kay Burkett, an independent forensic pathologist. Their testimony dovetails into one uniform story," Barbara said.

"What did they say?"

"Dr. Edwards said he performed the autopsy on Michael Riker and issued his findings as to his cause of death," Barbara said.

"What were his findings, Barbara?"

"He stated his initial finding relating to Michael's cause of death was accidental drowning."

"How did Dr. Edwards arrive at that determination?" Rosemary asked.

"He testified that someone told him that the young boy likely hit his head on some rocks and then fell into the water. His autopsy showed a lethal amount of water in his lungs, sufficient to deprive him of oxygen for a significant time period. The doctor also said the deceased had a skull fracture that was consistent with his head encountering a rock or other hard object," Barbara summarized.

"Did Paula Jennings learn from Dr. Edwards who told him this information?" Rosemary asked.

"Not exactly. The doctor said he had a recollection of the defendant contacting him about his son," Barbara said.

"Did he offer anything more substantive?"

"Somewhat. The doctor testified Leroy was very anxious for him to finish the autopsy so he could release the boy's body. Leroy told him that he didn't understand why an autopsy was necessary for what was obviously an accidental drowning. During that conversation, Leroy might've said something about his son hitting his head on rocks. According to the M.E., he was also receiving pressure from both of Michael's parents so they could bury their son as soon as possible," Barbara responded.

"Did Prosecutor Paula Jennings ask the doctor to what extent he had examined the skull fracture?" Rosemary asked.

"Yes, she did. His answer was initially he didn't have a reason to examine the skull fracture in any detail. It was his conclusion the death was caused by drowning. The skull fracture contributed to, but was not the primary cause of death," replied Barbara. "Paula Jennings then followed up by asking if there was a time or event that caused him to examine the skull fracture in greater detail and if so, whether his conclusion regarding the significance of the skull fracture change?"

"And what did he say to that?" Rosemary asked.

"His answer was yes. He then went on to describe the involvement of Dr. Kay Burkett. The M.E. said Dr. Burkett was a nationally renowned forensic pathologist, and she asked that he provide her with his autopsy report and all photographs he'd taken of the deceased, which he did. Dr. Edwards went on to describe how Dr. Burkett later called him to discuss her observations and conclusions," Barbara explained.

"Did Dr. Edwards say if he was influenced by his interactions with the pathologist?"

"He said he was ashamed to admit her observations were spot on and there were things he had missed. He said even though Dr. Burkett didn't have the benefit of a body to examine, she was able to conclude the skull fracture was not consistent with someone falling backwards and hitting their head. The location of the skull fracture was on the top of the head and not the back, and the direction of impact with a hard object was downward and not from the back towards the front," said Barbara.

"Dr. Burkett sounds very thorough."

"This is why she is nationally renowned," Barbara said. "Dr. Edwards went on to describe how Dr. Burkett concluded, and he concurred, that the shape of the object was irregular, something akin to a rock with broken edges, and not smooth or rounded like a river rock. In addition, the amount of damage caused to the skull was greater than what would be experienced by a person less than five feet tall falling backward," Barbara summarized. "Dr. Edwards testified that, based on the conclusions of Dr. Burkett, he amended his autopsy report."

"In what way did Dr. Edwards amend his report, Barbara?"

"Dr. Edwards said he amended the report to say: manner of death was undetermined," she replied.

"Did he explain why he amended the manner of death from accidental drowning to undetermined?"

"Dr. Edwards was asked that very question, and he said because there were significant issues that brought into question what caused the blunt force trauma to the top of the victim's head. Was it an accident or was it inflicted by someone yet unknown? The job of a medical examiner isn't to investigate a cause of death. He said that is left to law enforcement. The death certificate could be amended again if new information became available," Barbara explained.

"Are medical examiners limited by what causes of death they are allowed to reference?"

"Yes. He testified that their options are limited to either: Natural, Accidental, Suicide, Homicide or Undetermined. In this case, he was able to rule out Natural and Suicide. By listing the manner of death as Undetermined, the death certificate might change later to either Accidental or Homicide once further investigation was done," Barbara said.

"What did Dr. Burkett have to say?"

"Dr. Burkett was hired by the insurance companies as their expert, and was tasked with reviewing the autopsy report, notes and photographs taken by the Park County Medical Examiner, Dr. Edwards. As part of her analysis into the cause and manner of death, her role was to look for any evidence of criminality that might have contributed to the drowning death of the victim."

"Did Dr. Burkett agree or disagree with Dr. Edwards initial conclusions?"

"She said she concurred with most of his finding, including the conclusion drowning was the direct cause of death. However, she did not concur the manner of death was accidental. From the photographs she examined, there was no evidence of bruising, the absence of which was inconsistent with someone falling on rocks. The most suspicious and troubling observation she made was the size and depth of the deceased's head injury. Dr. Burkett testified that she determined whatever object the boy's head encountered was approximately 8cm by 10cm, or about the size of an adult's hand. The object was also irregular in shape because the skull fracture clearly showed a deeper depression in the center, than around the edges, and the object wasn't round but rather asymmetrical with sharp sides and edges."

"What about the object's trajectory?" Rosemary asked.

"She noted the direction was downward on the uppermost portion of the skull, and that too was inconsistent with a reported backward fall and hitting one's head on smooth river rocks. Dr. Burkett asked Park County detectives if any of the rocks near the river and those specifically near the place the deceased was fishing had any of these specific characteristics. She went on to testify the detectives told her all the rocks near the river and specifically near the fishing hole were typical round river rocks. They also told her, and the photographs she reviewed confirmed, there were very few rocks in the immediate vicinity of the fishing hole. However, she testified the rocks around the fire pit contained smaller, broken pieces of basalt and broken granite rock, all about hand size and irregular in shape."

"Did either Dr. Edwards or Dr. Burkett address whether or not any trace elements were discovered in Michael's skull fracture?"

"Dr. Burkett testified the medical examiner's notes and his final report didn't have any reference whether he performed any examination for trace elements in the head injury. Finding such material would've been very unlikely considering the victim had been floating in a moving pool of water for an unknown time period, but it would've been potentially helpful to know whether such an examination had been performed. Since there no longer is a body, such an examination is now impossible," Barbara replied.

"What type of trace material might have been present in the head wound and what might those trace elements prove?" Rosemary asked.

"Dr. Burkett testified the depression in the skull was significant. Not only did the victim suffer significant blood loss, but also the loss of cranial fluids. It is possible there might have been organic material left in the skull, such as rock fragments or carbon, which could have been used to determine the type of rock and its composition; for example, whether the composition of the rock was basalt or granite. If basalt rock fragments and traces of carbon were present and there were no basalt rocks near the river, it would've been possible to match the type of fragment to those basalt rocks found near the fire pit. If traces of carbon were present, it might've been possible to match that carbon to the carbon found around the fire pit," Barbara summarized. "It was also possible that fiber, from what now is presumed to be the murder weapon, might have been present," Barbara said.

"Did either doctor rule out any man-made objects that might have caused the skull fracture?"

"Both doctors agreed that the shape of the skull fracture did not compare to any man-made tool, such as a hammer or tire iron. Any such tool would have left a very distinctive impression," Barbara replied.

"So Barbara, what was Dr. Burkett's ultimate determination?"

"She testified that her expert medical opinion as to the cause and manner of death was from a powerful blunt force trauma exerted to the top portion of victim's head by an irregular shaped rock from behind and in a downward motion, resulting in a depressed skull fracture, compression of the spine and subsequent drowning. She said it was not possible to conclude from which injury Michael ultimately died because both the skull fracture and the drowning would have been fatal. Therefore, her ultimate conclusion was that Michael Riker died by homicidal violence."

"That testimony must have had an impact both to the jury and the audience."

"Absolutely. The members of the jury were all leaning forward in the jury box and there was an audible gasp in the courtroom when Dr. Burkett delivered her ultimate findings," Barbara said.

"Let's take a short break, Barbara, after that compelling testimony, and allow everyone watching to catch their breath," Rosemary said.

"That is a good idea, Rosemary. When we return, there is more breath-taking testimony to come," Barbara said.

After a brief commercial break, Rosemary announced, "We're back. Who's the next witness you alluded to before the break?"

"The prosecutor called Don Jackson, a custom homebuilder, who owns his own business."

"Will you please summarize for our listeners what Don Jackson said?"

"Sure. He said, Lora Riker called him and wanted to discuss building them a custom home in Livingston. The following day,

Leroy Riker called and wanted to set up an appointment to meet and go over floor plans, costs and possible locations for the home they had in mind."

"Did he provide a date when this occurred?"

"He said they met in his home office on the 8th of October. The first phone contact with Lora Riker was on the 7th. They brought several magazines and other books that contained model floor plans and elevations of homes. Mr. Jackson said what they wanted built wasn't possible within the budget they had set. He told them they needed to lower their 'want list' or modify their maximum budget. It was obvious to him they'd already done a great deal of research on floor plans and amenities," Barbara said.

"What did Mr. Jackson say was the Rikers maximum budget?"

"They initially wanted a four bedroom, four bath, two story log home constructed on five acres with a view of the mountains and the Yellowstone River. Their maximum budget was $650,000," Barbara said.

"That's an interesting and familiar number," Rosemary commented. "Did Paula Jennings ask Mr. Jackson if he knew when, in relationship to Michael's death, he met with both defendants?"

"He said the meeting took place the day before their son died," Barbara replied.

"Wow. That is significant," Rosemary commented. "How was Mr. Jackson able to be so specific on that date?"

"Mr. Jackson testified that he maintained a file for every client. In the Rikers' file, he had notes of their meeting, a copy of the original signed contract, a copy of the $1,000 post-dated check written by Leroy Riker, and copies of newspaper articles regarding the boy's death," Barbara replied.

"Did he say why they wrote him a post-dated check? How far into the future did they date it?" Rosemary asked.

"Mr. Jackson, said they told him their checking account didn't have sufficient funds to cover the check at that time, but they were confident in one month's time the funds would be on deposit to cover the check, and they'd then proceed with additional funds as the acquisition of real property and construction moved forward," Barbara said.

"Did Mr. Jackson know how the Rikers arrived at their maximum budget?"

"He testified that he asked them how they arrived at their budget and whether it was a firm number. He said they didn't tell him how they'd arrived at $650,000, but said that was their maximum," Barbara explained.

"Did he discuss alternatives with the Rikers?" Rosemary asked.

"He did. He suggested they change the lot size from five acres to one acre or smaller. The Rikers told him they could get by with two bedrooms and two baths, but for resale value, they preferred to have at least three bedrooms and at least two baths. The Rikers were also not firm on having a log home. Mr. Jackson told them he would work up some plans and options for both two and three bedrooms, with just two baths," said Barbara.

"Interesting they would consider only a two-bedroom home," Rosemary commented.

"Did Mr. Jackson know how big their family was?" Rosemary asked.

"Mr. Jackson said the Rikers didn't specifically say, but he assumed since a two-bedroom home would be big enough, there likely were not more than three people in the home. That would include the parents' master bedroom, with an en-suite bath and a child's bedroom. The only reason they wanted more bedrooms was for resale value," Barbara replied.

"Do we know why the building contract wasn't going to be honored?" Rosemary asked.

"Mr. Jackson testified that Leroy called him a few weeks later and asked that he return the security deposit check, and Leroy told him they weren't going to go through with their plans," Barbara said.

"And did he return the check to them?" Rosemary asked.

"Yes, he did. He testified the Rikers called him before the date on the postdated check was valid. By that time, he was aware their adopted son had died. He also learned the Rikers had one daughter who was about a year older than their adopted son, Michael. He said that got him thinking, that if they had two kids, why was a two-bedroom home going to be sufficient for the four of them? Mr. Jackson testified he made up his mind at that time that he didn't want to have any business with them," Barbara responded.

"What reason did he offer for that decision?"

"He said he learned through the newspapers that there was a life insurance policy on the boy. The papers never said how big the policy was, but his conscience would not allow him to take any money from the Rikers because it would feel like taking 'blood money,' and he wanted no part of that. He said he had an uneasy feeling about the entire arrangement and was glad to return their security deposit and be done with them," Barbara responded.

"Did Mr. Jackson actually use the term 'blood money?'"

"Yes, he did Rosemary. You can imagine how that went over in the courtroom," Barbara said. "In fact, the judge once again had to admonish the spectators, because there was an audible expression of shock."

"I can well imagine. That is a very loaded phrase," Rosemary replied.

"Indeed it is. Normally the defense would object and move to strike such a statement, and a judge typically would sustain such an objection. However, the defense did not make a motion, and now it is in the court record," Barbara explained.

"Was Mr. Jackson ever asked if he knew where the Rikers were getting the money for the house?"

"He was asked, and he said no. He got the impression it was going to be an all-cash transaction, with no loans or mortgage involved."

"Well Barbara, you promised another bombshell witness and you certainly delivered," Rosemary announced.

On camera, Barbara McQuinn and Rosemary Meadows continue their analysis of the live courtroom drama.

"Was that the last witness for the prosecution Barbara?" Rosemary asked.

"Actually no. They saved their surprise bombshell witness until the very end. Of course, he was not a surprise to the defense, but he certainly had the jury and the entire courtroom on the edge of their seats."

"Let's not waste any time then. Tell us who this witness was and summarize his testimony for our viewers."

"The witness was a man named Donald S. Petrolli. He was a former prison inmate who was serving a thirty-year sentence for homicide in the same prison where Leroy Riker worked as a correctional officer. Mr. Petrolli was paroled only recently after serving twenty years. He testified that Leroy and Lora Riker approached him with a proposition."

"What was this proposition, Barbara?"

"Petrolli said he was part of the criminal conspiracy to murder young Michael Riker. His role was more like a backup murderer in the event Leroy Riker lost his nerve to complete the task."

"How did that bombshell land in the courtroom?"

"With shock and horror. Here's a man, testifying under oath, that the Rikers hired him to kill their son, Michael. Felons rarely make for convincing witnesses, but if he is able to present corroborating evidence, independent from his testimony alone, it could be very convincing to a jury," Barbara added.

"Please continue Barbara."

"Petrolli testified he watched from a concealed location, known only to Leroy. He testified Leroy put a rock from the campground fire pit into a large sock and then walked up behind Michael while he was fishing and hit Michael over the head. He said Michael collapsed immediately, partly in and partly out of the water. According to his testimony, Leroy then stepped into the water and pulled Michael in further. Leroy then picked up Michael's fishing pole and threw it into the same pool," Barbara summarized.

"Was that the extent of his testimony, Barbara?"

"No. Petrolli said the following week, Leroy wanted to meet him at the campground in order to pay him $500, the agreed-upon price for Petrolli just being present. Petrolli said the agreed-upon price was $1,000 if Petrolli had to kill the boy for Leroy."

"That sounds pretty dramatic. What happened at the campground the following week?" Rosemary asked.

"Apparently, Leroy and Lora started having concerns that Petrolli might turn against them. That following week, Leroy laid in ambush for Petrolli and shot him. Leroy left the campground believing Petrolli was dead. However, Petrolli was only hit with a glancing shot off his ribs, and a bullet fragment penetrated into the bicep of Petrolli's left arm. Petrolli produced two tape recordings that were played in court today, over the strenuous objections of the defense. One recording took place at a bar in Wilsall where all three of them discussed the conspiracy and the other recording was of a phone call between all three of them where the plot was discussed and what role Petrolli would have. There were also security cameras at the bar that captured the three of them talking."

"It would seem the case is getting insurmountably difficult for Leroy Riker to overcome," Rosemary surmised.

"With all of the cumulative evidence of an eyewitness, audio recordings, DNA from the murder weapon, and then you add in all the substantial circumstantial evidence, I don't see an acquittal happening," Barbara opined.

57.

MAX, THE SURPRISE WITNESS

"It appears that prosecutor Paula Jennings is hoping to introduce one last witness. This should be interesting," Rosemary said.

Barbara said, "So true, Rosemary. Paula asked for the court's indulgence regarding a very interesting eyewitness to the murder."

"Did the defense have any objections?"

"Absolutely. Mr. Cannon argued they were not provided with the names of other witnesses."

"Paula Jennings replied that the prosecution only recently became aware of this witness and had insufficient time to make the defense aware," Barbara responded.

"The judge directed both counsels to approach the bench," Barbara said, "where, in a whisper, the judge asked for the identity of the last eyewitness. Then Paula introduced her proposed witness as Max. The judge asked if Max had a last name or if that was his last name."

Barbara continued to explain the sidebar dialogue between the judge and the prosecutor. "Your Honor," Paula began seriously, "Max is the deceased victim's beloved cocker spaniel who was present when the boy was struck from behind. The dog witnessed everything. Max is also responsible for hiding the murder weapon, and then directing detectives Wyatt and Judd to its location."

Both Barbara and Rosemary grinned at the camera at this refreshing turn of events.

"Upon hearing this introduction, Mr. Cannon angrily objected and said he was opposed to turning this trial into an animal sideshow," Barbara continued.

"Who would have ever thought a dog would be the prosecutor's surprise witness!" Rosemary exclaimed.

"It is unusual, but the judge could allow the dog to be a witness under limited circumstances," Barbara said.

"What kind of limited circumstances?"

"There needs to be a proper foundation laid by Paula Jennings and the judge would need to provide additional jury instructions at the end of the trial regarding what weight, if any, the jury should give Max as a witness," Barbara replied.

"So, what did the judge do?"

"The judge said the prosecutor's request was highly unorthodox and questioned exactly what the prosecutor expected the dog to do."

"How did the prosecutor respond?"

"She said that she expects Max will positively identify the defendant as the assailant."

"How did the courtroom audience respond to that statement?"

"Actually, the entire conversation took place quietly during the sidebar, so the audience wasn't able to hear anything. However, after the judge directed counsel to return to their tables, her next statement obtained a murmured chuckle," Barbara said with a smile.

"How so?"

Barbara continued, "The judge ruled she would allow Max to identify the person who killed Michael, but she added that Max and Paula Jennings were on a short leash, so she cautioned Paula to tread carefully."

"I can understand why that might draw a chuckle," Rosemary said.

"Paula then called Max Maddox as a witness, and as expected, Mr. Cannon renewed his earlier objection, and the judge denied his motion for the record," Barbara said.

Barbara continued, "Detective Wyatt made a gesture with his hand to detective Judd, standing to the rear of the courtroom. Judd stepped into the hallway and returned with Max, who proudly entered the courtroom on a leash with his head lifted skyward. It was almost like the cocker spaniel knew his role as he proudly made his grand entrance and appeared excited to do his part," Barbara commented. "Judd then passed the leash off to detective Wyatt."

"Detective Wyatt," said Paula Jennings "would you please tell the jury what you know about Max?" Barbara paraphrased.

Barbara continued without a pause, reciting the testimony of detective Wyatt. "Max was the companion and close friend of Michael Riker, as well as of Michael Maddox, before his adoption and name change. They were inseparable. It's like when someone said one name, it was always quickly followed by the other. Max was with Michael on the day he died. We know that because of testimony from other witnesses. At the approximate moment Michael was struck, three witnesses said Max was seen emerging from behind Riker's pickup on a dead run, carrying something in this mouth. Max ran into the woods and did not reappear until after the medics and the sheriff's deputies departed the campground. At that time, he showed up at the campsite of Mr. and Mrs. Sterling. Max knows at least three words, but no one has tested the full extent of his understanding. We know Max understands, 'yes,' 'no' and 'search.' He'll respond appropriately with one bark for 'yes' and two barks for 'no.' Upon the command of 'search,' Max led detective Judd and me to the sock he had taken from the riverbank and hid under a log in the forest," Barbara summarized.

Barbara led the jury through the steps as the prosecutor asked, "Max, can you identify the person or persons who hit Michael?"

"BARK!"

"The prosecutor then asked Detective Wyatt to lead Max through the courtroom, starting in the back," said Barbara.

Barbara continued to explain, "As Max zigzagged his way through the attendees in the courtroom, with no reaction, he eventually approached the prosecution and defense tables. Detective Wyatt kept a tight hold of the leash and didn't allow it to reach too far. When Max was alongside Leroy Riker, he sat, growled loudly, and bared his canines. The jury members were all leaning forward in their seats closely watching Max's reaction."

"I bet that got everyone's attention," Rosemary said.

"It did, but what surprised everyone was the reaction of Leroy Riker, who abruptly exclaimed with fear in his eye, 'Get that damn beast away from me. He's a damn biter.'"

"Max, is that the person you saw strike Michael over the head?" Barbara again paraphrased the prosecutor.

"BARK!"

"Thank you, Max. You are excused," the judge said, as Max continued to growl at Leroy Riker. The state then rested their case," Barbara said.

"Barbara, I'm sure it was not lost on the jury that the amount of money the Rikers were expecting to receive from Michael's life insurance and the maximum budget that they were willing to spend on a new house was the same. The forensic pathologist's testimony was also exceptionally damaging to the defense. How did the defense hope to overcome this evidence?" Rosemary asked.

"You're right, Rosemary. These last four human witnesses were extremely damaging. As to how the defense responded, you'd be surprised."

"In what way?"

"The defense offered no witnesses at all. I believe their defense, on appeal, is going to be ineffective assistance of counsel," Barbara answered.

"How does that work?" Rosemary asked. "Isn't that like the defense counsel admitting to an incompetent job?"

"The proper term is ineffective, rather than incompetent, but in the event Riker obtains new attorneys to represent him on appeal, the grounds for the appeal would be ineffective assistance of counsel. Under US law, ineffective assistance of counsel is a claim raised by a convicted defendant asserting that the defendant's legal counsel performed so ineffectively that it deprived the defendant of the constitutional right guaranteed by the Assistance of Counsel Clause of the Sixth Amendment to the United States Constitution," Barbara explained.

58.

CLOSING ARGUMENTS

Notes

Detective Russ Wyatt on the Case

December 6, 2001, 9:00 a.m.

"Ladies and gentlemen of the jury, the prosecution rested their case yesterday. As it appears the defense has no witnesses, we will move to closing arguments by the state," the judge announced.

"Thank you, Your Honor," prosecutor Paula Jennings began. "Ladies and gentlemen of the jury, when we started this trial the state provided you with an overview of the charges against both defendants and summarized the evidence you would hear. The state remains confident the evidence presented at trial substantiated all the allegations as we had previously outlined them. At the beginning of the trial, the judge gave you instructions on how to consider both direct and circumstantial evidence and instructed you to ignore the ages of witnesses when considering their credibility."

Every person on the jury sat forward just a bit to carefully absorb her words.

"Throughout this trial, you've heard testimony from multiple witnesses, some of whom are considered experts in their field. You have also examined documentary evidence supporting the testimony of the witnesses. Allow me to summarize what you've heard and seen. I ask you to use your common sense during your deliberations. As jurors, you can't get into the mind of the defendants, but your common sense will dictate the logical conclusions you must reach."

"Hey Wyatt, I hope and pray the jury has common sense," Judd muttered under his breath, on pins and needles.

"Leroy and Lora Riker are each charged with two counts of conspiracy to commit insurance fraud and two counts of conspiracy to commit deliberate homicide," she continued. "Leroy Riker was also charged with one count of attempted deliberate homicide and two counts of actual deliberate homicide, with extenuating circumstances. When the state first prepared for this trial, it was with the expectation both Leroy and Lora Riker would be on trial together. I'm sure you have observed for yourselves, Lora Riker's chair is empty. Currently, Lora Riker is missing and presumed dead at the hands of her husband, Leroy Riker. Regardless, the state proceeded with the facts of this case against Lora Riker, in absentia, as if Lora Riker is alive and well, albeit missing and not present."

A quiet but distinguishable buzz filled the courtroom as the anticipation built.

"It is the state's position the evidence demonstrates the first conspiracy started around the time the defendants purchased life insurance for their daughter, Susie Riker. Within days after Michael's adoption was final, they purchased identical life insurance for him. Had they just purchased the life insurance for only Michael, it would have been more suspicious. Therefore, it was necessary as part of the conspiracy for both children to have identical policies. Both policies were called whole life policies, versus term policies. Whole life policies accrue a cash value over time but are more expensive. They do, however, make the most sense as a life insurance policy for a child because the cash value will accumulate over time. That is, assuming the cash reserve account is left untouched. However, any competent financial advisor would say there are other better investment vehicles for a child. In Michael's and Susie's case, the Rikers often were unable to make the minimum premium payment of $75 for each child and therefore dipped into the cash reserve account in order to make these payments; Thereby negating the benefit and their stated purpose of the whole life policies."

Those two dirtbags killed Michael for the money. It's so obvious. C'mon, let's get a conviction, I said to myself, impatient at the seemingly unending nature of these types of arguments.

"Counsel for the defense also wants you to believe the only reason Lora Riker went shopping for a second insurance policy was to save money. However, that isn't true either. The defense wants you to believe the second policy was intended to replace the first policy, which had a face value of $400,000 in the event of accidental death. The second policy cost $90 per month, per child, and only had a face value of $250,000. Remember, it was important that each child had identical coverage to dissuade any suspicion of ulterior motives."

"If the spectators were allowed to boo, they would," I told Judd as a negative undercurrent flowed every time one of the Rikers was mentioned.

"Defense counsel also wants you to believe Leroy Riker was clueless about any of the life insurance policies for Michael, even though he'd been actively involved in the first life insurance policy purchased for their daughter. So, why is this important? If they are convincing, it would be difficult to prove a conspiracy and there could be no financial motive for murder if Leroy Riker was truly unaware of the life insurance," Jennings continued. "You heard testimony from Certified Fraud Examiner, Dan Player. Mr. Player testified he performed an analysis of all checks written from the Rikers' bank accounts. Mr. Player also testified that up to the day Michael Riker was formally adopted, Leroy Riker actively participated in check writing, along with Lora Riker. Starting the day of Michael's adoption and lasting until one day after Michael's death, Leroy Riker didn't write any checks. Why the sudden change?"

"Because they're frauds and murderers." Judd's whispered opinion was surely shared by nearly everyone watching, including the televised audience at home.

"The simple and logical answer is because he needed to distance himself from the checkbook and the checking account in order to maintain his 'I know nothing' defense. This, then, is one of two smoking guns showing his knowledge of Michael's insurance policy. There is no other explanation."

Prosecutor Jennings took a breath while her condemning argument struck home, and then continued, "The second smoking gun, which demonstrates clearly both defendants' knowledge of the life insurance policy, is the testimony from the owner of D.J. Custom Homes. Remember how Don Jackson testified he was contacted a couple of days prior to Michael's death by both defendants. He also testified the defendants clearly had been researching and designing their dream home for some time. Mr. Jackson also testified the defendants told him they could get by with only a two-bedroom home, thereby suggesting to Mr. Jackson there was only one child in the home. Your common sense will tell you both defendants had already written Michael off as a member of their family before Michael died. Did they have a premonition of his impending death?"

"I almost admire the days of Judge Roy Bean, the hanging judge," I remarked quietly, nearly spitting in contempt.

"Remember also the testimony you heard from the two life insurance brokers. They were told it was Lora Riker's intention to let the first insurance policy, valued at $400,000, lapse for nonpayment, once the cash reserve account was empty. At that time, they'd be left with only the $250,000 policy for Michael. But that wasn't what happened, was it? Lora Riker extended the first policy for another month by making an additional premium payment. That extended the overlapping coverage of both policies, now having a combined value of $650,000. However, it would be too suspicious if both policies remained in effect for much longer. That meant time was running short to carry out their plan if they were going to maximize the benefit from both policies."

A hum of agreement wafted through the air once again, and a sense of impatience. It seemed apparent this was a slam-dunk case, and yet Prosecutor Paula Jennings was leaving no stone unturned.

"If Michael were to have fallen off the bridge over the Yellowstone River while three witnesses were present, that would have taken care of multiple problems. Fortunately for Michael and unfortunately for the defendants, that didn't happen, and plan B was now necessary. Plan B was the fishing trip and the requisite drowning. It was a now-or-never situation, and Lora Riker was no longer going to be patient with her husband dragging his feet. She had put too much work and planning into their conspiracy to allow any further delays."

"She's really pouring it on thick and covering every base," Judd said in a hushed tone. I nodded, silently cheering on Paula and her prosecutorial skills.

"So, what do we know about the fishing trip? The first thing you learned during the trial was the defendant went to the campground the previous day with four children. His purpose was just to look around, and he was there for only a matter of minutes. The following day, he returned to the campground, even though he now knew how primitive it was and how far it was from any services. He also now knew the campground had no cellular service. You heard from several witnesses when the defendant arrived at the campground, he only had one fishing pole, even though Lora Riker had purchased two poles. Shortly after arriving, the defendant separated the two friends and took young Danny Williams downstream and out of view of Michael Riker. He then instructed Danny to remain there and promised to return shortly with a fishing pole fashioned out of a tree branch. Danny Williams testified Mr. Riker was gone between fifteen and twenty minutes. On one occasion, Danny saw the defendant watching him. The defendant told the insurance investigator when he left Danny, he drove around the campground to find a better place where both boys could be together and fish."

"Yeah, that whole trip was calculated for a kill. No doubt," I said, careful to be heard by Judd only and not the audience behind us.

"You heard testimony from Roger Sterling that he and his wife were watching the defendant's pickup and it never moved. Danny Williams also testified when Mr. Riker returned, his pant legs were wet, and Mr. Riker quickly offered an explanation about falling in a mud puddle as the reason his pants were wet. However, Danny Williams and Roger Sterling testified they didn't see any mud puddles or other standing water anyplace in the campground, except for the water at the river's edge. Danny Williams also testified that Mr. Riker instructed him to go look for Michael down by the river and around the small pond created by stacked rocks, while the defendant walked slowly towards the bathrooms to look for Michael. If you find this behavior odd for a father, it is. Once again, your common sense should tell you a father would go to the last place he knew his son to be and the place where the most hazards were located. Was it because he knew what he would find at the river and didn't want to be the one to make the discovery? Or was it because the longer his son was underwater, the greater the likelihood the drowning would be successful?"

"Exactly," whispered Judd amid copious whispering by everyone in attendance.

"I really like Paula's continuing theme to the jury about using common sense," I whispered back.

"The defense will argue that Michael slipped on river rocks while fishing, fell backward, was knocked unconscious when he hit his head, and then somehow fell forward and into the pond of water. Again, I ask you to use your God-given common sense and ask your-selves exactly how that is even possible. The next thing you should be asking is how Michael's fishing pole ended up in the water along with his body.

"There is no way on God's green earth that they won't convict," I whispered and both Judd and I studied the jury.

"You've heard testimony from the medical examiner and the forensic pathologist who confirmed Michael's skull fracture was on the top of his head and in a downward direction. They also testified there was no expected bruising on his back, shoulders, arms, buttocks or anyplace else that would support the hypothesis Michael fell backwards. The skull fracture was also inconsistent with hitting his head on round river rocks, but instead was consistent with being hit in the head with a fist-size irregular shaped rock. Now, I want you to consider all these facts as we know them. The obvious conclusion is someone hit Michael with a rock from behind, causing him to fall forward with his fishing pole and into the water, where he drowned. In addition, the defendant showed very little concern or urgency when Danny Williams informed him that he had found Michael in the water. Using your common sense, now ask yourselves what you or any parent would've done under similar circumstances. Would you have run to the river? Would you have jumped into the water without a second thought? Would you, based on your training on how to correctly perform CPR, have performed CPR to the very best of your training and ability? Remember, Danny Williams and Mr. Roger Sterling testified the defendant, Leroy Riker, wasn't doing CPR the same way Danny had learned it in elementary school, or in the manner that would provide any benefit to Michael. Yet, Leroy told Roger Sterling, that as a correctional officer, he was fully trained on how to properly perform CPR. Was this just one more attempt to delay giving lifesaving aid to his son?"

At this point, Paula Jennings placed her hand on the jury box, drew a breath, dramatically paused, and looked each jury member directly in the eye.

"Remember also the testimony from the fire chief about the defendant's under-the-breath comment to the effect, "What have I done?" Was this a statement regarding how guilty he felt about bringing two young boys to the river miles away from any emergency care, or was this a statement of remorse, fear and guilt concerning his own actions?

The courtroom erupted, causing the judge to pound the gavel.

"Importantly," Paula Jennings continued, "we have the various statements made by the defendant concerning his son's cause of death. Did Michael jump from some fictitious height into the water, as first reported by Leroy Riker to Sharon Mills, the 911 dispatcher, thereby explaining the location of the head injury? Or did Michael fall out of a boat, as told by Leroy to his neighbor and then reportedly to the neighbor's pastor? Lastly, you'll remember the testimony from young Danny Williams, that the defendant told him about being afraid of water and that he couldn't swim. That was the explanation the defendant offered for not going into the water himself to save his son. Was this another delay action?"

"Hell, yeah," hissed Judd, quietly vocalizing the majority opinion of everyone in the chamber.

"Then we have Danny's testimony, the defendant tied a rope around his wrist and asked the young friend to go into the water. Remember Danny's testimony that as he was reaching out to Michael's floating body near the bottom of the pool, his arm would be gently pulled backward by the rope? Was this yet another delay intentionally done by the defendant?"

Again, Paula Jennings paused for dramatic effect.

"Now compare all of that to the video the following day when both defendants and their daughter returned to the river's edge.

Lora Riker videoed her husband while he laughingly waded into the same pool of water to retrieve Michael's fishing pole. Where was the fear and apprehension then? You'll remember the testimony from multiple witnesses saying the defendant had reported jumping into the water to save his son, yet all these witnesses said the defendant's clothes were not wet, other than his pant legs and the front of his shirt from carrying Michael's limp body out of the water. How can both versions be correct?"

"They can't," came a few voices behind us, causing the judge to caution the room yet again.

"The state's last human witness, who you just heard from, was at the campground and saw everything. He was also part of the conspiracy right up until the very moment Leroy Riker delivered the fatal blow to the top of his adopted son's head. Mr. Petrolli is certainly no saint or an ideal witness. However, murder conspiracy cases are seldom neat and clean and do not involve the nicest people. If that were the case, there would not be as many murder conspiracies. Believe what you may from Mr. Petrolli's testimony, but remember his testimony was supported not by just one, but by two audio tapes and furthermore by the physical evidence. In addition, Mr. Petrolli accurately described the murder weapon and described watching Max, the dog, grab the sock and run away with it. Both the sock and the rock had DNA evidence, as well as fingerprints, of the defendant."

"That's one fine cocker spaniel," said Judd with a smile and a wink.

"Ladies and gentlemen of the jury, after you hear from defense counsel and receive further instructions from the court, you'll be excused to begin your deliberations. I fully expect, based on the totality of the evidence, circumstantial and direct, you'll return a unanimous verdict against both defendants of guilty of all charges so Michael's young, innocent soul can finally be at rest. To use an old metaphor, 'If the pieces of the puzzle fit, you must vote to convict.' Thank you. The prosecution rests," Paula Jennings concluded.

59.

THE DEFENSE CLOSES

December 6, 2001, 10:00 a.m.

"Is the defense ready for closing argument?" The judge asked.

"Yes, Your Honor. The defense will be brief," answered Douglas Cannon. "The burden of proof for a criminal conviction is beyond a reasonable doubt." The state has failed to meet that burden. All they have is speculation and theories. The only so-called evidence they have provided is all circumstantial, at best. Where are the state's credible eyewitnesses who can testify Mr. Riker is responsible for delivering the fatal blow? The word of an ex-convict does not qualify as a credible witness, nor does the bark of a dog. Ask yourselves, ladies and gentlemen, isn't it plausible a clumsy, energetic, young boy could stumble forward and hit the top of his head on an irregularly shaped rock, rather than fall backward, and while dazed, then fall into the water and drown? There is absolutely no way of knowing whether he fell forward or backward into the water. No one was there to prove one way or the other what happened. Where are the state's witnesses that the life insurance policy was for anything other than what the defendants said it was? A way to save for their children's future. And where are the state's witnesses to prove our clients conspired together to purchase the life insurance for their son for a nefarious purpose? Lastly, where are the state's credible witnesses that prove Leroy Riker knew anything about Michael's life insurance policy until after his death when Lora Riker told her husband about it?"

"In our opening comments to the jury, we told you the state's evidence of one plus one would not equal two, but instead would equal a big zero. That was true then, and it remains true now. You must acquit the only defendant who is on trial today of all charges, not just because he is innocent, but also because the state failed to meet their burden of proof. Therefore, the defense respectfully asks that you return a verdict of not guilty on all counts. Thank you for your attention and service. The defense rests," Douglas Cannon said.

60.

JURY DELIBERATIONS

December 6, 2001, 10:30 a.m.

"The time has come ladies and gentlemen of the jury for you to retire to the jury room and begin your deliberations," the judge began. "But first, I'm going to give you further jury instructions that will outline the necessary legal elements of each crime as charged. Your job will be to consider all the evidence and decide if the required elements for each offense have been established, beyond a reasonable doubt. Only then can you return a unanimous verdict of guilty or not guilty. You'll be allowed to take the instructions into the jury room with you and use the instructions as a guide during your deliberations. You are to consider each charge, against the defendants, separately. Any testimony you heard during the trial that was related to any uncharged offense you will ignore. I encourage you to respectfully discuss, debate and attempt to reach a unanimous consensus. If you have questions, you are to write down those questions and deliver them to the bailiff. The bailiff will deliver your questions to me, and I'll respond to your questions in writing. Do not rush in your deliberations. The charges you are considering are serious, and

353

you should devote a sufficient length of time and energy to reach a decision. If you feel you're unable to reach a unanimous verdict, after all reasonable effort, you are to notify the bailiff."

61.

THE VERDICT

December 6, 2001, 3:45 p.m.

"I have been informed by the bailiff that the jury has reached a unanimous verdict on all, but one count," the judge announced. "Will the foreperson of the jury please read the verdict for each count."

The foreperson spoke: "As to count one against Leroy Riker, for the crime of conspiracy to commit insurance fraud against Montana State Life Insurance Company, the jury finds the defendant GUILTY."

A small rumble swept across the courtroom.

"As to count two against Leroy Riker, for the crime of conspiracy to commit insurance fraud against Northwest Life Insurance Company, the jury finds the defendant GUILTY."

A smattering of applause came from the spectators, which caused the judge to admonish them. "Silence, please, as the foreperson speaks."

"As to count three against Leroy Riker, for the crime of conspiracy to commit deliberate homicide of Michael Riker, the jury finds the defendant GUILTY."

Despite the judge's warning, shouts and applause ensued.

"As to count four against Leroy Riker, for the crime of deliberate homicide of Michael Riker, the jury finds the defendant GUILTY."

The courtroom erupted with dozens shouting "Justice for Michael!" The judge slammed her gavel and responded with "Order in the court! I will clear all spectators from the courtroom, if necessary."

"As to count five, against Leroy Riker, for the crime of conspiracy to commit deliberate homicide of Donald Petrolli, the jury finds the defendant GUILTY."

More murmurings of approval.

"As to count six, against Leroy Riker, for the crime of attempted homicide of Donald Petrolli, the jury finds the defendant GUILTY"

More smatterings of applause.

"As to count seven, against Leroy Riker, for the crime of deliberate homicide of Lora Riker, the jury was unable to reach a unanimous verdict."

With a backdrop of a few moans and groans, the judge said, "Ladies and gentlemen of the Jury, once again I want to thank you for your time, attention, and for your willingness to serve on this jury. Some cases are more emotionally draining than others, and if any of you feel the need or desire for professional counseling as a result of what you've been exposed to during this trial, I strongly recommend you privately and confidentially speak to the bailiff. I know I speak for all of us, the death of a child can be difficult to cope with, and the evidence and testimony the jury was exposed to during this trial you may find exhausting. There is no shame to ask for and receive counseling.

"At this time, the defendant will be held in custody pending his sentencing two weeks from today," the judge ruled.

"I'd say that went about as expected, wouldn't you?" I asked Judd.

"Yep. What do you think his sentence is going to be? Any wagers?" Judd replied.

"Whatever it is, it's not going to be long enough, now that the death penalty is off the table," I replied.

"I sure hope the judge does not make the sentence concurrent for each count, but rather makes them each consecutive. If she does that, he will never see the light of day as a free man again," said Judd.

"Are you going to be in attendance for his sentencing?" I asked.

"Wild horse couldn't keep me away. You?"

"Same here."

62.

SENTENCING

Notes

Detective Russ Wyatt on the Case
December 20, 2001, 9:00 a.m.

The sentencing of Leroy Riker commenced two weeks after the trial.

"The court is now in session for the sentencing of Leroy Riker," the judge declared.

"Would the defendant please rise? Never in my career on the bench have I encountered a sadder, more disgusting and more disturbing case as this one. You and your wife had a complete family, but you chose to adopt Michael Maddox. Why? Was it for the extra $1,700 you received each month from his father's social security? Even with that amount of extra income, you were still unable to make financial ends meet. The evidence presented in court made it clear your only objective and motive was greed. You decided between you and your wife that rather than make just an extra $1,700 per month, you would come up with a scheme to enrich yourselves with as much money as you thought you could get away with. You were careful, or so you thought, to not appear too greedy and insured

Michael for $650,000, thinking that any higher amount might attract too much scrutiny."

Sounds like the judge is upset, I thought.

"You were also very deliberate in your planning to have a ready-made alibi so that the person who carried out the ultimate plan wouldn't appear culpable. Your wife had the responsibility of obtaining both life insurance policies, and you had the responsibility of planning and carrying out a cold, premeditated murder. Your ultimate plan involved conspiring together to cash in on Michael's life insurance policies and the only way for you to do that was to have Michael die. If Michael had fallen off the KPRK Bridge over the Yellowstone River, there would have been no need to kill him. It obviously would have been a tragic accident, with credible witnesses. Since that didn't happen you had to have a backup plan, and the fishing trip was that plan. Everything you both learned while working for the Montana State Department of Corrections you used for evil and to satisfy your own greed. What you obviously didn't learn was that crime doesn't pay and there is always evidence of a crime regardless of how careful or smart you might think you are."

You got that right, the voice inside my head agreed.

"Obviously, your greed was your undoing. When you finally decided the date Michael would die and you both would become rich, you just couldn't wait a few more days before engaging a custom home builder. You also thought you were being careful to avoid writing any checks after Michael was adopted. What you didn't plan on, and what the Certified Fraud Examiner discovered, was the evidence you left behind when you changed your well-established pattern of writing checks. The other problem you had, which is one many people have, is that lies are much harder to remember than the truth. The inconsistencies in your stories were just too obvious and left an easy trail of circumstantial evidence demanding to be followed."

"The absence of evidence is sometimes evidence itself," I whispered to Judd.

Judd nodded in agreement.

"The amount of premeditation that is evident in this case is beyond what I have ever seen before. You obviously started planning long before Michael was ever adopted. You purchased identical life insurance for your biological daughter to mirror what you intended to purchase for Michael. You couldn't afford either policy, but you obviously made a conscious decision that most of the premium payments would come from each child's cash reserve accounts and not directly from your bank account. Personally, as a mother and grandmother, I'm beyond disgusted with you both."

All eyes were on Leroy as the judge lambasted him. People held their collective breath to learn of the murderer's fate.

Throughout this time, Leroy Riker sat stoic, with his eyes focused on some imaginary spot on the table in front of him, while his attorney's hand rested on Riker's shoulder. He was no longer smug about all his careful planning and execution. His time as a free man was about to end, and he knew full well what fate awaited him in prison. He had no place to run and no one to blame but himself.

"Therefore, it is the sentence of this court, as it relates to Leroy Riker, for the crime of insurance fraud; you are sentenced to a term not more than ten years for each count, as provided for by law. For the crime of conspiracy to commit insurance fraud, you are sentenced to a term not to exceed ten years for each count. For the crime of conspiracy to commit two counts of deliberate homicide, you are sentenced to a term of not less than ten years and not more than one hundred years for each count. For the crime of attempted deliberate homicide, you are sentenced to a term of not less than ten years and not more than one hundred years. For the crime of deliberate homicide, you are hereby sentenced to a term not less than sixty years and not more than one hundred years. Furthermore, it is the decision of this court that your sentences will run consecutively for a period not less than one hundred years. The deliberate homicide statute allows me to impose a death penalty, and notwithstanding the recommendation of the county prosecutor for the death penalty, I've declined to do so. That would only result in unending appeals.

The defendant is remanded to the custody of the Department of Corrections to begin his sentence. Leroy Riker shall receive credit for time served. This court is now adjourned."

"Wow, high five. Three consecutive 100-year sentences. That should be the last we hear or see of Leroy Riker," I told Judd.

"Unless he appeals," Judd replied.

"Don't even think that. Even with the ineffective assistance of counsel argument, I don't think there is any attorney out there who would represent him on that basis. I sure didn't hear anything else that would be a reason for an appeal," I said.

December 20, 2001, 10:00 a.m.

Riker was transported to the Deer Lodge State Prison, where he had previously worked, pending a review by the Department of

Corrections to determine where he should be permanently incarcerated. He was placed in an isolation cell with two guards located directly outside his cell. Twenty-four hours later, prison staff found Leroy Riker dead in his cell from a 'broken neck.' The prison doctor ruled Riker's death to be self-inflicted. There were no witnesses, evidence of foul play, no autopsy, and no death investigation ever initiated. Both guards swore they never left their posts and did not see or hear anything suspicious. Even though the prison had lost one of its own, which under normal circumstances, would have caused heaven and earth to be moved in an investigation, the prison system just wanted to move on. Riker was an embarrassment to the entire Montana State Department of Corrections. Not surprisingly, there was no publicity of his death, and no one outside the prison system ever became aware of what became of the correctional officer with badge No. 40.

63.

FINAL JUDGMENT

Notes

Detective Russ Wyatt on the Case

The Prison Brotherhood successfully avenged the attempted murder of Donald Petrolli, a founding member of the informal prison organization, and successfully obtained justice for the murder of an innocent ten-year-old boy, whose birth name was Michael Maddox, son of Martha and Cecil Maddox and brother of Eric Maddox.

Eric Maddox, after aging out of the foster care system, eventually settled into a new life. He got married, had a family of his own, and was successful in business. Now, as an adult and father himself, Eric was watching a TV exposé about the tragic death of a young boy who had died in Montana several years earlier. Eric had a sickening premonition in his gut that the TV program was about his younger brother, Michael.

However, the boy featured in the exposé had an unfamiliar last name at the time of his death. At the very end of the program, the producers mentioned the full names of Michael and Martha Maddox, and at that very moment, Eric knew Michael was gone forever.

Eric fought for justice to assure Michael's death was not in vain. To that end, he pursued changes not only to state laws, but also to policy changes by agencies whose responsibility it was, and should be, to protect foster children from harm. Many of the changes Eric sought were opposed by lobbyists and partisan politics. Detractors argued that imposing more rules on foster parents would only discourage people from applying in the first place. However, the hue and cry over Michael's tragic death did bring about some positive policy and legislative improvements.

State agencies received legislative funding to investigate the financial stability of foster families to make sure the child being fostered was not for profit and that there was a caring and able family to nurture the foster child.

State insurance laws were changed to provide for greater oversight by insurance commissions when it came to insurance companies and insurance agents selling life insurance for a minor child.

Martha Maddox finished her prison sentence and remained drug-free. While in prison, she learned the necessary skills to earn a living wage.

Susie Riker lived with her grandmother until she was eighteen and graduated high school.

Lora Riker's body was never found.

As for Max, well, he became a badge-wearing Park County Sheriff's Department canine deputy. And as expected, Max and I were inseparable.

Rest in peace, Michael.

Gone, but not forgotten.

ABOUT THE AUTHOR

Ken Wilson worked 27 years as a state investigator. Upon his retirement from public service, he formed a consulting business for law firms, prosecutors, and law enforcement agencies, specifically in the area of white-collar and organized criminal activities. In total, Ken's investigative career spanned 45 years before retiring permanently in 2000. During his career, he investigated the Executive, Legislative and Judicial branches of state government, and was a recognized expert witness in state and federal courts.

Ken began his writing career by composing case reports. From there, he wrote articles for professional periodicals. *Guilty as Sin* is his first full-length novel.

He grew up spending much of his time traveling between the Pacific Northwest and Montana. His wife of 44 years grew up in Texas. He has a daughter, a son, and three grandchildren, and hopes this book makes the world a better place for future generations.